I bought this book for myself. I enjoyed it so much I've bought all of Rusty Bradshaw's books and haven't been disappointed yet! They are well-written, and most of them have a surprise ending. Death in Hazard is one of those books! You won't be sorry about getting this book. Yes, I recommend it.

See more reviews at www.rustythewriter.org

This book is dedicated to my brothers and sisters -- Linda, Michelle, Bobby, Donny and Steve -- who shared with me the experience of living in Dubois, Wyoming.

What readers are saying about Rusty Bradshaw's books.

The Rehabilitation of Miss Little

Captivating!!

This story is very well written! Rusty does such a great job describing the scenario; he doesn't suck you in - he absorbs you! You feel like you are among the characters. And you have to keep reading to find out what drives people to do what they are doing. I hope Rusty keeps writing! I look forward to reading another book by him!

Awesome book!

This book was highly recommended to me, so I bought it. I'm so glad I did! I'm not much of a reader, but this book was hard to put down. It kept my attention from start to finish. It's a great story. Kind of sad about what she went through, but a good ending. I can hopefully look forward to more books from this author!

Moist on the Mountain

Awesome!

Another good book from the author! Love his writing. I got the book for me and finished it in a couple of days. I was so interested in the story it was hard to put down.

Fun book to read

Keeps you interested, and didn't want to put the book down until finished.

Gorge Justice

The Best 1 Yet

As I've said before, I'm not a reader, but after reading the first two books from Rusty Bradshaw, I thought I'd read the third. This book is his best yet. I finished it in three days! It made me cry, made me sad, angry and happy. It's worth reading!!

Excellent reading

I couldn't put this book down once I started reading it. I was with the character the whole way and hoped that she would finally get justice. Rusty did an excellent job in writing this because you could feel yourself in the surroundings that he described and picture the beautiful scenery. You will not be disappointed in purchasing this book. It is unthinkable what the main character went through and it will keep you on the edge of your seat!

Battle for Stephanie

Kept my interest

Very interesting story that kept me interested 'til the end! I have read all of Rusty's books, and I have enjoyed every one of them. I can't wait 'til the next one. Keep 'em coming!

A Real Page Turner

Fast-paced action, family dynamics and a story that involves issues that our nation is dealing with right now. Like many novels, it comes down to good vs. Evil, and the Granny is evil indeed! You will love the action as the kidnapping and search for Stephanie unfolds and culminates in unexpected twists and turns and and ending that will leave you wanting a sequel. Rusty Bradshaw is and author on the rise; catch him now and enjoy the ride. PS: The book would make a great movie!

Death in Hazard

Unputdownable

Don't start this book unless you have time to read it cover to cover because you won't want to put it down once you start! Rusty is so good at taking a very real subject and writing a story, placing you right in it. He makes you feel like you are there amongst the characters. I so look forward to his next book!

Murderous Reunion

Rusty Bradshaw

Chapter 1

It did not turn out to be exactly the kind of family trip Neil Ren had hoped for when he dreamed up the idea of taking his family to explore the history of the "Old West."

Born and raised in Oakland, California, Neil developed a passion for history. He was most interested in the history of the United States -- how it was formed and how it grew to be the world power that it had been. Because it had been so sensationalized in movies and books through the years, he was most interested in the westward expansion of the country in the 1800s.

In his youth and as he grew older, he wanted to visit the places he had read about and seen in movies and television shows. But such trips, as numerous and spread out as they would be, would cost money.

So, he worked hard to get to those places he longed to visit. Coming from a poor family, Neil had to do it himself if he wanted to get a college education. No scholarships came his way, so federal financial aid and his own elbow grease in a variety of jobs were the paths he had to take.

Once the degree in business administration was received, it took a year to find a job. He threw himself into his work at a company in the Oakland area that manufactured and distributed copy machines. But after the turn of the 21st century, the explosion of digital technology and the trend of businesses going paperless, the demand for such equipment diminished.

Neil followed the digital trend and found his way into the world of cellular telephones, first as a franchise store owner and eventually in a middle management role with the cell company for which he had owned a franchise.

Along the way he met and married Cristy Wilkes, who made a career for herself in real estate. They were the parents of two children: son Tim, now twelve, and daughter Jeri, fourteen.

They still lived in the Oakland area, having moved from the middle-class suburb of Walnut Creek to the Woodminster neighborhood.

While Cristy was luke warm to Neil's idea of visiting Old West sites, the children were much less excited. As 21st-century kids, they were more interested in their digital devices and gaining status. Trapsing around dusty little towns looking at things from the past did not appeal to them at all.

Tim and Jeri were sullen and withdrawn during the buildup to the trip and during the flight from San Francisco to Jackson Hole, Wyoming, for Neil's first trip to discover the Old West. Because he had read that Butch Cassidy, the famous outlaw who teamed with the Sundance Kid and others for a series of train and bank robberies in the region, once owned a ranch near a small town about eighty miles southeast of there, he and the family were headed for Dubois.

Even the majestic beauty of the Teton mountain range that met them as they stepped off the airliner and during the early part of the drive in the rented minivan did not get more than a perfunctory glance from Tim and Jeri.

"After we go to Dubois, we'll come back and go through Yellowstone Park," Neil said.

"Oh boy, we can't wait," Jeri said, the sarcasm dripping from her lips.

A trip that usually took travelers ninety minutes was two-and-a-half hours for the Rens. Neil and Cristy stopped several times to marvel at some of the sites -- the expansive vista of the Grand Tetons just outside Jackson Hole, the small sign on Togwotee Pass marking the Continental Divide; the Pinnacle peaks with a light covering of snow, even though it was late-summer; Books Lake Falls; and the Tie Hack Memorial, all along Highway 26.

They stopped at each one to take photos. The children reluctantly -- and not without protest -- gave up their tablets to half-heartedly participate. At two of the stops, they had little choice as there was no Internet connection to keep their eyes glued to the glowing screens.

As they drew closer to Dubois, the terrain changed a little. They had passed between dense, tall pine trees on both sides of the highway much of the way since Togwotee Pass. But shortly after Brooks Lake Falls, they were in a small valley with a lush, green meadow stretching out to the right before jutting up to form the mountains, with the highway skirting the mountains to the left.

Several miles later, the mountains on either side were further back, and cultivated fields and scattered structures took the place of the meadows. To their left, beyond the fields, were dusty brown foothills, some tinted a dull red.

Then, more buildings began to appear on either side of the highway. That change in scenery was enough to tear the kids' attention from their electronic distractions.

"Are we there yet?" Jeri asked, for what seemed to her parents like the hundredth time, in the irritated teenage tone that had become her trademark.

"The motel should be just ahead on the left," Cristy said after consulting her printed directions.

Tim looked around while his sister bent her head down to her tablet again. Most of the homes and businesses sprinkled on both sides of the highway looked modern like they had been built in the past ten years or so.

"This doesn't look like an Old West town," he said. "This is just the outskirts of town," his father said patiently as he pulled into the motel parking lot. "It will look different when we get into the heart of it."

The motel certainly fit Tim's impression of a more modern structure. Painted a deep red, the two-story, box-shaped building looked very much like so many other motel chains throughout the country.

Neil parked the van under the overhang in front of the office and went inside to see if their rooms were ready. He was back out quickly.

"We can't check in until about two, so we're going into town and check things out and get some lunch," he told his family.

"How far is town?" Jeri asked in a huff.

"Just around the bend in the road," Cristy informed her.

That got the children's interest, if for nothing else to satisfy their skepticism about their father's enthusiasm about this town being an example of the Old West. They were not disappointed as they went through the first mile of the town proper.

To the right of the highway was a scattering of homes and what looked like commercial buildings. A line of thick trees marked a river passing through town. Past the waterway, the land jutted up to form a bench that gradually turned into taller mountains. On the left, the highway was lined with businesses in some modern-looking buildings and some that had obviously been in place for years, while homes were spread along a gradually sloping hillside before it jutted almost straight up to a plateau.

But when the highway made a slight curve to the left, the character began to change. While the children were only slightly impressed, what their father saw brought all the research he had done about this small town and Butch Cassidy's connections to it rushing back into his mind. By the time they got to the downtown portion of the main street he was more enthralled than even he expected to be.

The area that is now Dubois, Wyoming, was originally the winter home of the Mountain Shoshone natives, also called the Sheepeaters. During the summers, they lived in villages in the surrounding mountains. The first Europeans came into what is known as the Wind River Valley in the early 1800s, and the first homesteaders began to arrive in the 1870s. The first homestead claim was filed in 1889, a year before Wyoming became a state.

A community formed in the area and businesses began to pop up to provide for the early residents. Ranching became the dominant occupation in the region, but it wouldn't be long before another industry supported residents.

In his research of the area, Neil had read that the well-known outlaw Butch Cassidy owned and managed a ranch north of what would become Dubois. He also reportedly walked the streets of the community, buying cigars and groceries in a general store on the main street and doing business at a red stone bank nearby -- an institution he never robbed.

Guides in the area many years later would identify structures in the woods surrounding the town as hideouts of Cassidy's gang of robbers, most often called the Wild Bunch but also known in the Bighorn Mountains area as the Hole in the Wall Gang.

Some old-timers claim to have seen him in town after his supposed death in a gunfight in Bolivia, South America.

Local legend has it the community was called Never Sweat because of the relatively mild summers and the cold winters. When the town was incorporated in 1914, residents wanted to take the name of Tibo, the Shoshone language word for stranger or white man. Another version claims the name was chosen because it was the nickname residents of the Indian reservation southeast of the town gave to the Episcopal missionary who served them.

In any case, the United States Postal Service rejected both Never Sweat and Tido as unsuitable. The town was actually named for Idaho Senator Fred Dubois. That name was chosen by Wyoming Governor Joseph M. Carey, who was a friend of the senator. The Idaho statesman was also on the postal committee that rejected the other two suggested names.

The same year the town was incorporated, the Wyoming Tie and Timber Company began operations in and near the town. The company cut the timber in the mountains west of town and sent it down a series of wooden water flumes to the Wind River, then floated them to Riverton, seventy-five miles southeast of Dubois, for distribution. The company became the nation's largest supplier of railroad ties.

The "tie hack" days ended in 1949, after which Louisiana-Pacific operated a large sawmill in the town. It was the community's largest employer until it was shut down in 1988. Smaller lumber operations continued, but thereafter, the town's economy became based on tourism.

⚬—⚬

The Rens stood on the sidewalk on the south side of Ramshorn Street, which was part of Highway 26 and scanned the three blocks that made up the central downtown area. All the buildings had an Old West look to them, with wooden facades. On the north side, every building had an overhang in front and the sidewalks on both sides of the street were not standard concrete. They were made up of two-by-six wood planks about six feet in length. Each plank, including the ones that made up the sidewalks on the south side, had names cut into them with a router. Just names, no dates or other details.

"Who are these people?" Tim asked.

"Probably those who first settled here," her father answered. "That would be my guess."

Neil had seen photos of the Dubois downtown, but it was a little different seeing it in person.

"This is awesome," he said out loud. The children rolled their eyes.

Stepping to the edge of the boardwalk, Neil checked both ways for traffic. There was only one car several hundred yards away traveling east. He motioned for the rest of the family to follow, and they crossed the street.

One of the first buildings was a pizza parlor, and they went inside to have lunch.

With an hour left before they could check in at the motel, they walked along the boardwalk toward the town's main street intersection where Highway 26 came north, then made a ninety-degree turn west. The northern stretch was 1st Street, and the western stretch through town was Ramshorn Street.

They saw several shops, including a souvenir store, a couple of art galleries, an old-time photo studio and gift shop, and a clothing store. They crossed the street and walked by a honey store, a steakhouse, a bar, a cafe and another gift shop. That little walk took less than thirty minutes. But Neil was eager to get in one quick look at one of the area's historical sites before they called it a day, so they headed back to the motel.

Even though it was not quite two o'clock in the afternoon, their rooms were ready, and the clerk allowed them to check-in. They quickly got their overnight belongings into the rooms, and while the family got back in the van, Neil checked in with the clerk about the best place to go.

"We're going out to a place where Butch Cassidy hid out," he said as he got into the driver's seat and began driving back through town.

The clerk, who was new to the community, had actually told Neil about an old homestead north of town that she believed was near the ranch that Cassidy had apparently owned.

"But is it some place he could have hidden out?" Neil asked.

"I suppose it's possible," the clerk answered.

Following the clerk's directions, Neil drove through town, continuing east past where Highway 26 curved ninety degrees to became Ramshorn Street, through a series of right-angles to a road up the side of a bench that ran the length of the town, then turning one-hundred-eighty degrees. The road ran along the top of the bench and provided a stark contrast in the landscape.

On their left was the town, with trees and lawns in various states of care. A stream ran north and south through the middle of town, connecting with another, running east and west on the southern side. To their right was a barren sandstone landscape with a number of ravines, gullies, buttes and hoodoos, nearly all tinted in red hues along with the sandy tan base color. It looked very much like the terrain in the opening scenes of the original movie "Planet of the Apes."

After a couple of miles, the terrain became flatlands with dry wild grass and a few sagebrush plants scattered around. A few more miles later, they came to a ravine and stopped the van at the top, where the road dipped down into it.

The clerk had instructed them not to try to drive the van down into the ravine. As they walked down, they saw why. The road was barely wide enough for one vehicle and was mostly bare rocks of various sizes until they were nearly at the bottom.

In contrast to the flatland above, the ravine, about forty feet below the rim, had tall prairie grass covering the land amid pine and spruce trees. Running through the ravine was a swift-moving stream about thirty yards across. On the far side, the terrain was similar to the badlands they had passed on the bench, but the buttes and such were taller.

To their left, as they faced the stream, was a cabin. It had clearly seen better days. Looking like it was made of Lincoln Logs. It was well-weathered. On closer inspection, they found wood flooring inside that had rotted away in most places.

Next to the cabin was a fire pit made from stones, which appeared to have been taken from the upper roadway. This was obviously not a feature of the original cabin, and Neil could see it had been used recently. Black ash covered the ground inside the stones, and there were small pieces of blackened wood.

While their parents continued to look over the cabin, the children walked in the opposite direction, following the stream, until they found a second cabin. It looked much like the first.

When they looked inside, they saw something just inside the front opening. At first, it appeared to be a mound of dirt. But as their eyes became accustomed to the darkness inside the windowless structure, they noticed the mound was smoother than one would expect from a pile of loose dirt. As they stood and stared and their eyes became more accustomed to the dim light inside, the mound took on a familiar shape.

Tim gingerly stepped inside and bent over the mound. It appeared very smooth and had a dark tan color. He reached out and touched the color. It felt a bit cold. He reached to the far side of the mound and gently pulled toward himself. Instead of plowing a row in what he thought was a pile of dirt, the mound slowly rolled over. Staring up at him was a dirt-caked face, the eyes and mouth wide open. He panned his head to the right and saw a woman's breasts, a belly and a pair of bare legs. All were covered in a thin layer of dirt.

"Holy crap," he muttered.

At the same time, his sister, just outside the cabin's entrance, let loose a sustained scream that bounced off the ravine walls. Hearing their daughter's screech, their parents headed toward the noise at a dead run.

Chapter 2

About the time the Rens were driving through Dubois headed for the homestead cabins, Craig Reilly was driving past Burris, Wyoming, in his copper-colored 2017 Dodge Ram single-cab pickup truck. He had put eight hundred twenty-four miles behind him since he left his home in Salina, Kansas, very early that same Saturday morning.

He was headed for Dubois to attend a week-long celebration of his high school class. It had been fifty years since the group took that short walk in the school gym to get what they had all worked so hard to receive -- their diplomas.

Part of the largest class to have ever passed through the small-town school, Reilly had never attended any of the group's reunions in the past. In fact, he had not returned to his hometown for the past twenty-three years. His last trip back had been to bury his mother, Rose, who had died of a heart attack while tending bar in one of the two such establishments on the town's main street.

Rose and her husband, Chester, had been life-long residents of Dubois, having descended from two families that moved there in the first years of the 20th century. Chester died in a logging accident when Craig was four years old; his younger sister, Kathleen, was one, and his brother, Daniel, was seven. All three children had been born in Lander, a city seventy-five miles from Dubois.

While Daniel and Kathleen had remained in Dubois following their high school graduations, Craig had loftier ambitions. He wanted out of Dubois as quickly as possible. Not that he hated the town. He, in fact, enjoyed growing up there. But he knew there was more to see and do in the wider world than his hometown had to offer.

He had been back prior to his mother's death. A few visits here and there. A couple of returns for special events. He was there for both his siblings' marriages and had returned to help his sister move to a new home and adjust after her divorce.

Reilly had been active in high school. He had been an athlete, his favorite sport being football. A three-year letterman, he had not been a star, but he also wasn't a benchwarmer. A 'tweener, as he came to think of it later in life. He was also on the Rams' basketball and track teams. A little less than a 'tweener in both.

His drive back now for the reunion took him through the Wind River Indian Reservation. Lander was just outside the reservation's southern boundary. He went through the small town of Fort Washakie and the Burris area, where there used to be a post office and small store. But as he drove past, looking to his left, he saw neither was still in operation. A little further on was the turnoff to the Dinwoody Valley, a place his family had visited on occasion for camping. As he drove past the Red Rocks, a formation of deep red-colored hills where Highway 26 makes a sweeping turn from due west to due north along the banks of the Wind River, he remembered so many trips by there getting to road athletic events. The small population of the state meant towns and high schools were widespread, and they were all long trips. The shortest were to Wind River, Shoshoni and Ethete, with the rest -- to Meeteetse, Basin, Byron, Deaver and others farther north -- at least three hours one-way. The Rams spent a lot of time on buses.

He was also a member of several clubs and acted in plays, mostly old-time melodramas.

Several miles along, he saw a massive building to the left of the highway with the river behind it. It was a military vehicle museum that had been built during his 23-year absence. He knew about it, of course. Daniel had bragged about it, said it would put Dubois on the map as a destination center. He was curious to check it out but knew that would be one of the activities on the reunion schedule.

Craig had not intended to attend this reunion, despite the urgings from several of his classmates who had maintained contact with him over the years. It was not that he did not want to see and interact with his classmates. He had been friends with nearly everyone in the class.

But he was not excited about sitting around rehashing old stories from fifty years ago. In his mind, once they all grabbed those diplomas, they had turned a corner in their lives. Whether they stayed in Dubois or ventured near or far, those high school days were history and -- good or bad -- should stay there.

Most important he was not eager to relive his most recent past with his classmates.

⭕⭐⭕

After receiving a degree in criminal justice at the University of Wyoming, Craig Reilly went looking for a job. The most logical route was police work. But he had his sights set on something else. Craig's goal was to be a Secret Service agent.

Having failed to get signed on right out of college, he settled for work as a campus policeman at the University of Colorado in Boulder. His ultimate goal never changed, however.

Five years in Boulder gave him enough experience to secure a job as a patrolman in the Denver Police Department, where he served for ten years. During that span he made two more attempts to join the Secret Service, but failed each time. After the second rejection, he spotted an opening in the Salina, Kansas Police Department. It was for a patrolman, a lateral move, but his time in Denver showed him it would be nearly impossible for him to advance into a squad room as a detective.

As a patrolman, he had assisted in several murder cases in which he was the first officer on the scene. He had a keen insight into detail, but the information he passed on to detectives, while instrumental in solving each case, was not credited to him. Trying to hold on to their jobs, the detectives did not want a lowly patrol officer moving up the ladder.

Salina was an attractive possibility because it was a smaller department than Denver but still large enough to provide advancement opportunities. Craig's decision paid dividends shortly after getting the job. He again assisted in a couple of murder cases. But this time, his talent for noticing important details and his deductive reasoning were not usurped by detectives. Just the opposite. Within two years, he was promoted to detective in the department's robbery and homicide squad.

In his first few years in Salina most of his work was on robberies. There were a few murders, but he was not assigned to any of them. He was beginning to think he had moved to a dead-end job. However, murders exploded to more than twenty in 2003, and the homicide detectives were overloaded, so Craig handled nearly a third of those cases. His success rate was phenomenal, and it got him noticed.

Offers from other departments came his way. He declined each one, however, hoping that the one he had always hoped for would come through. But he heard not a peep from the Secret Service.

Three of those 2003 murders he handled appeared to be the beginning of a series of related crimes. The modus operandi was so eerily similar in each case. But Craig's sharp eyes spotted inconsistencies that other detectives had missed. Because of that, he was able to close each case, which turned out to be unrelated to each other, himself quickly.

Several years later, there was a series of killings in Kansas City, Missouri, with identical MOs that had police there baffled. There were five victims in the Missouri city, but when a sixth occurred across the state line in Kansas City, Kansas, police recalled Craig's work on the three Salina murders that at first were thought to be serial killings. They asked him to consult.

All of the female victims had been strangled after they were sexually assaulted in their homes. The Missouri murders had yielded tiny thread patterns on the victims' necks that came from a specific type of scarf. Craig studied closeup autopsy photos of the Missouri victims but was called in soon enough that he could examine the sixth victim's body personally.

Using a powerful magnifying scope, he checked the thread patterns and found them to be slightly different. Further, he was able to identify the scarf used, which led to a suspect. The man was quickly brought in and questioned. Under intense interrogation, he confessed to the crime. He claimed to have read all the media reports of the Missouri murders and wanted to see what it felt like to kill someone in that way.

Following the admission, the Kansas City, Missouri police assigned their murders to the same suspect and considered their case closed, despite Craig's vehement arguments to the contrary. Two days after the case was closed, another victim, killed under the same MO with the same Missouri thread pattern, was discovered in the Missouri city. An autopsy revealed the woman was killed one day after the confession in the Kansas slaying.

In their official report, Missouri detectives attributed their decision to close the case to Craig's identification of the thread pattern on the Kansas victim as the same -- not slightly different -- as those in the Missouri deaths. Craig's report was quickly dismissed as a "defective detective's" way of covering his ass.

So once again, Craig was betrayed by a metro city police department, whose public relations machine pounded their version of events into the public, eager to have a killer in their midst now behind bars. Craig's insistence that the Kansas murder was not connected to the Missouri slayings was ignored, or in cases where it could not be, it was downplayed and sometimes criticized as someone trying to grab the spotlight.

Most of his colleagues in Salina failed to believe the muck coming out of the Kansas City department. They knew Craig to be truthful and accurate to a fault and certainly not someone who craved attention for himself. He was always quick to give credit to those around him and minimize his own involvement.

But the damage was done, and his career, as far as other police departments were concerned, was muddied.

About seven miles from Dubois was another road heading south to the three lakes -- Ring, Trail and Torrey -- another area familiar to him from family and Boy Scout camping trips. As he drove down the hill five miles from the center of town, Craig began to replay old memories of his time in Dubois. Memories that had long been pushed to the back of his mind. Some pleasurable, some not so much.

He tried to concentrate on the pleasurable ones.

When the road leveled out, Craig glanced to his right and saw the trees lining the Wind River. He recalled several float trips he and his classmates had taken on the waterway from one end of town to the other. He remembered one specific trip with one of his football teammates, who was a year older. On a single semi truck tire inner tube, they began on Horse Creek and got caught for a few minutes in the whirlpool, where the creek emptied into the Wind River. That trip ended right about where he had looked over from his truck at the river.

Further on, near where the highway curved from west to north and became 1st Street, to the left was the spot where the large mill had been. Now an empty piece of ground, it reminded him of the times as a teenager when he stood on the platform next to the conveyor that took scrap wood into the burner, which looked like a badminton birdie stood on its wide end. It was his task to grab chucks of wood and fill a truck below for winter firewood at home.

Just up the road past the welcome sign proclaiming Dubois as a winter wonderland, the road curved north, and to the right, up the hill, was the cemetery where his mother and father were buried. Not such pleasant memories.

Then he went past the Episcopal church before making the ninety-degree left turn onto Ramshorn Street. While growing up in the town, this main street through the community had been two lanes, with cars parked diagonally in front of the businesses. But the state had widened the road to four lanes and now parallel parking was required.

The width from boardwalk to boardwalk had not changed, but looking back on it, Craig remembered the street as more narrow. It also reminded him of the time a large grizzly bear had walked, in the middle of a warm summer day, down Horse Creek Road, making a left turn, then leisurely sauntering along Ramshorn Street's center stripe right through downtown and on up to Dump Hill and the badlands beyond.

If the sound had been able to carry the several miles to town as he passed over the Horse Creek bridge, he would have heard Jeri Ren's scream of terror out at the homestead cabin.

Blissfully ignorant of that event and what it would lead to, he drove on about one hundred more yards and parked in front of one of the eight motels in the town proper.

It featured a main building that looked like an old two-story log cabin with a steeply sloped roof. Two dormers stuck out on the street side, part of the upstairs rooms. The main building had always reminded Craig of the chateaus in Austria and Bavaria he had seen photos of. Behind the main lodge were individual cabins, also reminiscent of small log cabins. In the back was a small grassy park with a couple of picnic tables and square steel barbecue grills staked into the ground. He knew that from cutting through the motel property on his way to the single-building school a block away, which had been torn down several years earlier.

The motel and school properties were in the shadow of an elongated hill that extended from the plateau that used to house the town's small airstrip to Ramshorn Street. It was about sixty feet high at its peak and sixty yards wide at the base. On the east side was Horse Creek Road.

At the peak of this elongated hill, there used to be a water tank, long since out of use, where he used to go to play submarine commander, climbing down into the tank from the round opening at the top with a rusted steel ladder below. Later, when he was in high school, the football coaches had sent team members up the hill and around the tank as part of their conditioning regimen, sometimes in shorts and T-shirts but most times in full pads and practice uniforms.

Craig sat in the truck for a few minutes, savoring the good memories. He had not expected to feel nostalgic. But the feeling just washed over him as he drove through town. It was a strange feeling. It had been so long since he had been back to his hometown that he anticipated none of this. After twenty-three years, he figured there would be so many changes that the place would not look the same.

That was true to a certain extent. The school he had attended had been demolished and a new one built in the northeast part of town. Several years ago, the entire north side block of downtown had been destroyed by fire but had since been rebuilt. The character had been preserved, but all the businesses there were different.

Despite that, certain things always stayed the same.

He was startled out of his thoughts by a light tapping on the window right next to him. He turned his head quickly and had to catch his breath. He was staring into the beautiful face of Anna Welch.

"You going to come in, or do you need to continue playing with yourself for a while?" she asked. Even through the closed window, that soft, silky voice made him shiver with delight.

Chapter 3

They had waited a little extra to get to the back corner booth in hopes of having a little privacy. But, the cafe in the middle of the block on the south side of Ramshorn Street was not large. It was a popular place for the locals and tourists alike. There were few times, even in the winter but especially in the summer, when it was not packed.

In business since before World War II, the cafe operated under a number of names until shortly before Craig entered school. It had seen a number of competitors come and go through the years, but it had always been the most popular eatery in the community. That was due to its friendly atmosphere and the fact that every dish was prepared from scratch. Excellent customer service was also a priority throughout its history.

Throughout his school days, Craig had never seen outdoor dining at the cafe. That had appeared one year during one of his infrequent visits and had been the norm ever since. It was the only way the owners could increase capacity.

"Haven't seen you in a long time," Anna said, raising her voice several octaves to be heard over the buzz of conversation in the enclosed area. "What brings you back?"

When she raised the volume of her voice, there was a huskiness to it that made it sound even sexier than it was normally. Craig shivered in his seat at the sound of it, as if he felt a winter chill on this mid-August evening.

"The reunion," was all he said.

After Anna had earlier escorted him inside the motel lobby of the motel, he was surprised as he watched her open the half door to the motel office and step inside. She called up his reservation list and checked him in. She then guided him to his room on the second floor.

The motel's interior was very much like the exterior, with polished log walls, stairs, railings and furniture. While the exterior logs were a dark brown, almost black, the interior was of a lighter shade, almost desert tan. The rooms were the same. His was one in a dormer that overlooked Ramshorn Street and with a view of the Wind River Mountain Range beyond the town to the south.

Aside from questions and answers about his accommodations, there was no conversation except an agreement to meet later for dinner together.

Two years younger than Craig's sixty-seven years, Anna had not changed much at all since he had last seen her twenty-three years ago at his mother's funeral. And that wasn't his old crush rising to the surface.

Sure, her lightly curled hair streaming past her shoulders was showing some gray within the auburn color he remembered. But her piercing brown eyes still looked right through to his soul, and her light olive skin was as smooth as a baby's bottom. Only the hint of crow's feet were at the corners of her eyes.

As he sat looking across at her at the cafe, he recalled snatching a few sideways glances at her as they walked along the sidewalk together on the way to dinner. She wore a powder blue tank top that was a half size too small, showing off the cantaloupe-sized breasts. She also had on a pair of cutoff jean shorts that were high enough to show every inch of her legs. They made her look taller than her five-foot-three-inch frame.

"Just the reunion?" she asked, snapping him out of his remembrance.

"I hadn't planned on it," he said. "But I heard from enough people who said everyone would be here for this one that I felt a little guilty about not coming. So here I am."

"Why wait so long to come back?" she asked.

He was glad the waitress came right then to take their order. Her question was not one he was ready to answer, especially to her. But she wasn't put off so easily.

"So why so long?" she asked again when the waitress took their orders to the kitchen.

Craig looked around the room, hoping to find a distraction to help him dodge the question. But the other diners were not anyone he knew, and they were too engrossed in their own conversations.

Anna cleared her throat, clearly trying to bring his attention back to her.

"I've just been busy with things," he said. "Like my job, for one."

"Too busy to come see old friends?" she asked. "People missed you, you know."

"I doubt that," he said.

"Plenty of people miss you," she said with a little edge to her voice.

"Like who?" he shot back.

"Like me, you dipshit!"

She was a little louder with the last remark and it drew some stares from the others in the cafe. Some were a little embarrassed, while others anticipated a public squabble, something to put some excitement into their evening.

They sat silently for a few moments while Craig digested her words. He had taken her on a couple of dates in high school, but there had not been a romantic relationship. Not that he didn't want one. Anna was so popular with the boys that she dated a lot of them. He was a bit shy in high school and not as assertive as he became after getting involved in law enforcement. So when she was dating someone else, he didn't make any effort to change the situation.

He had no idea how she felt about him. His thinking at the time was that if Anna, or any other girl for that matter, were interested in him, they would say so or give some subtle signs. None had, so he believed none were. With hindsight, he had come to recognize that some, including Anna, had sent signals, and he simply missed them.

They said very little during their meal, just small chit-chat about the upcoming reunion events. He paid for dinner, over her objection, and began their walk back to the motel by crossing Ramshorn and heading west. Again, they were silent until they were crossing Horse Creek Bridge.

"I had a huge crush on you in high school," Anna blurted out.

Craig was only slightly surprised. Over the years, he had thought about it, and his law enforcement training helped him see things in a different way than he had way back then. He saw the signs that he did not see then.

"I didn't know that then, but I think I figured it out over time," he said.

Anna slipped her arm into his as they stepped off the bridge walkway. In his short-sleeved button-up shirt, he felt her skin against his, and he felt that chill again.

"Why didn't you ever say anything to me when you realized it?" she asked.

"Life had gone on for both of us. I moved away, you got married," he said. "I didn't see the point."

"But I didn't stay married," she said as if that were the only reason he had given.

They were silent again as they crossed Horse Creek Road.

"Did you ever get married?" she asked, although she knew the answer.

"No. I just never found the right woman for me," he said.

There was silence between them again until they were standing in front of the motel. They turned to face each other and he took her hands in his. They were small, dainty hands with well-manicured fingernails. Seven inches taller than her, he looked down into her radiant face. He leaned down and prepared to kiss her.

A siren in the distance stopped him an inch from her lips. They both looked to the west and saw a Fremont County Sheriff's Office SUV screaming east on the main street. They watched it roar by, a few vehicles moving to the right side of the road on both sides to let it pass. They continued watching as the SUV, lightbar flashing and sirens wailing, continued on Ramshorn through the main intersection, wound through several right-angle turns and up the road on Dump Hill. It made the left turn at the top and continued its speedy run north.

⊙═⊙

Small towns are notorious for the fast spread of gossip. In Dubois, a town whose population never topped one thousand people, gossip traveled faster than a Japanese bullet train. Apparently, that was something that had not changed about his hometown.

As he descended the stairs, freshly showered and shaved, from his room the next morning at six o'clock, he heard Anna. She must have been on the telephone because he only heard her side of the conversation.

"Who was it?" he heard her ask, followed by a short silence. He was at the bottom of the stairs when she spoke again.

"Holy shit!" she said. "How did you find out?"

Another short silence as Craig rounded the stair railing and looked toward the fully open half door leading to the the motel office. She shot a brief smile his way. But Craig's cop spidey sense kicked in. Though he had retired nearly a year ago, that sense of something amiss never left a law enforcement officer. At least not the best ones.

"Did they take the body to Lander already?" Anna asked her caller.

That ramped up Craig's level of interest. During the summer, the town's ambulance was busier than in the winter as tourists got lost in the woods and fell into ravines and sustained injuries or were hurt when they tried to pet or feed the fuzzy animals up there or wandering into town. But the tone of Anna's voice and the look of concern on her face told him this did not fit into those categories.

"OK, I gotta go," Anna said. "We'll talk later."

She hit the "end call" button on her cell phone and laid it on the desk inside the office. She took the few steps that got her next to Craig, and she guided him into one of the chairs and she sat on the log-framed sofa with the stuffed cloth covering.

Most of the boarders at the motel were not early risers, so they were alone in the lobby and probably would be for at least another hour.

"They found a dead body up at the homestead cabins last night," she told him. "That was what the deputy that we saw speed through town was heading to."

The last part, he guessed, but he let her continue providing the information she had.

"That was a friend who works at the clinic," Anna said, gesturing toward her phone. "They took the body there, and they will transport it to the medical examiner's office in Lander in a few hours."

"Was it some tourist who got bear smacked?" he asked.

"My friend said from what she overheard it might not have been an accident," Anna said. She paused a moment before continuing.

"Craig, it's someone you know. She was in your class," she said.

Craig and Anna sat on a bench outside the Dubois Medical Clinic. The facility, on a piece of land adjacent to the old mill property, was new to him. When he lived in town, the only medical operation had been a small building with three rooms -- a lobby, office and exam room. It was staffed by a receptionist and a medic, not a doctor.

He remembered getting rudimentary physical exams there before each football season. The only thing he remembered about those exams was the so-called test for hernias. It consisted of the medic placing his finger up under the patients' balls and telling them to turn their heads and cough.

The joke among the athletes was the medic just liked to feel up young boys' nuts. Later, when he began seeing regular primary doctors, he learned that was the actual exam for hernias.

Now, the town had an actual medical facility that was staffed by two doctors and two nurses. In actuality, it doubled as a primary physician's office and an urgent care clinic. Anything more was handled by the hospitals in Lander or Riverton, seventy-five miles southeast, or Jackson Hole, eighty miles roughly northwest.

Since it was Sunday, the clinic was closed. But during weekends, the two doctors rotated being on call. This weekend it was Terrance Hall who was on call. He also happened to be Anna's primary care doctor. She called him right after giving Craig the news of the death. She talked him into letting them into the clinic. When the doctor arrived, he unlocked the door and led them into the lobby.

"So what was so important that you had to see me right away? Are you sick or injured?" Hall asked Anna.

She felt a little guilty for having led him to believe she needed to be there for medical reasons. But it was the only thing she could think of that he would agree to meet her at the clinic.

"It's not really me," she answered. The doctor looked toward Craig, who raised his hands in front of him, palms out, and shook his head. Hall looked back at Anna. She could see a bit of anger building on his face.

"It's about the body that was brought in last night," she stammered. "The word around town is that it is someone we both know. We wanted to see if that was true."

Hall's anger diminished a bit, and he breathed a little easier.

"Her next of kin was notified a couple of hours ago, so I guess it won't hurt to tell you," he said. "Her name was Jane Diaz."

"We did know her," Anna said. "She was Jane Lane in high school," she added when she saw Craig's puzzled look.

He nodded in recognition. While he knew her, they were not close friends. More like bodies passing in the hallways with a brief hi and wave. She was an average-looking girl then, a few pounds overweight, but she carried it well.

"Can we see her?" Craig asked.

"I'm not sure that would be appropriate," Hall said.

"She was my friend, my best friend," Craig lied. "I'd like to say goodbye."

Hall hesitated. He was struggling with his professional responsibility and ethics against his compassion for people's feelings. It was Anna who tipped the scales in Craig's favor.

Although happily married, Hall couldn't help but feel an attraction toward her, a woman thirty years his senior. It was more of a physical attraction. She was, after all, a beautiful woman. But her personality also pulled at his attraction strings.

"We both just want to see her one last time," Anna said.

"But she is not in the best of shape," Hall said. "She was attacked by something."

"It's okay," Anna said a little seductively.

That snapped the doctor's resolve and he led them back to an examining room where Jane was laid out flat on her back on an exam bed covered head to toe in a white sheet. There was some light pink coloration in the area where her head was. The doctor pulled the sheet back to expose her head and the shoulders, which had been cleaned of the light dirt covering the Rens had seen when they discovered the body. Craig noticed a two-inch cut on her left forehead near the hairline. It had been cleaned of blood, but he could tell it was very recent. It was what had left the light coloration on the sheet covering her.

Hall then stepped back and sat on a rolling stool next to the small desk built into the wall. Craig knew from having done this more than a few times in his career that she was naked under the sheet. He appreciated the doctor's discretion but was curious about one thing.

"Were there any signs of trauma to the body?" he asked before looking at what was exposed.

Hall was a little surprised at the question and Craig's professional tone. Craig took note of that and filed it away.

"No, nothing below the shoulders," Hall said.

With a quick glance from her chest to her toes and back again, Craig noticed by the shape of the sheet covering her that Jane had thinned out a little. He then turned his attention to her head and neck. He stood on the right side of the exam bed and stared intently for a moment or two. He then moved around to the other side, where Anna was standing. She had tears in her eyes, and Craig took her hand in his, as much to conceal from the doctor his more than grieving interest as to comfort her. He stared for another long moment, working hard to restrain himself from leaning in for closer looks or touching the body. That would contradict their professed personal interest in saying a final goodbye to a friend.

Without another word, Craig led Anna out of the exam room and back to the lobby, with Hall following close behind after closing and locking the exam room. He thanked the doctor, and they walked out to Anna's Jeep Wrangler and got in. They drove away without speaking. But Anna knew the wheels were turning in his head.

Chapter 4

Craig found himself back at the town's most popular cafe an hour after viewing Jane Diaz at the clinic. Anna had dropped him off. She had to go work the front desk at the motel so her housekeeper, who had been filling in while she and Craig were at the clinic, could begin cleaning rooms.

He sat at one of the tables outside the building. Three empty chairs were around the table. Tourists in a small line waiting to be seated eyed the empty seats, wondering why they were in line while this man had a table all to himself. Never mind that he had no food in front of him. They wanted to sample the fare at this cafe that so many people bragged to them about, and they wanted to do it quickly because there were other things they had on their agenda.

Craig was beginning to feel small pangs of guilt as the tourists' stares moved from the empty chairs to him when a man and a woman approached from behind him. Daniel and Kathleen looked much the same as they had the last time he had seen them a few years ago when they traveled to Salina to visit for several days.

He stood and gave each a long, warm hug. Though they did not see each other much, they were close in a way that was hard to explain. They each knew that they could count on each other no matter what the circumstances.

The tension in the line of tourists waiting to be seated eased a bit as the three siblings sat down.

"I'm so glad you came," Kathleen said. "It's been too long since you've been back."

The youngest of the siblings, Kathleen had always looked more like their mother than their father. But as the years went by, the similarity only grew more pronounced. Rose had been a petite woman with a nice figure and an attractive face. Kathleen was also petite, two inches taller than Anna, with a trim but athletic body. Her shoulder-length raven hair was cut in the same style their mother had worn for many years. She worked for the town as finance director, having been hired as a secretary out of high school then worked her way up the ladder. Being as it was Sunday, she was dressed casually in a short-sleeved button-up plaid shirt and khaki shorts.

"It's great to see you both," Craig said. "It will be fun to see some friends," he added.

Daniel, who recognized his younger brother's half-heartedness in the second statement, clapped his big, calloused hand on Craig's shoulder.

"You'll have a good time, you'll see," Daniel said.

The eldest sibling, two inches taller than his brother, got their father's height. He owned and operated the largest of the small lumber facilities in the community. In comparison to the large mill that used to be the town's largest employer, Daniel's could be considered a penny-ante operation. But he made a good living suppling lumber to local residents doing renovations and large developers who built more homes at the edges of the town. The museum east of the community had been a big boost for his business, and it would be again when the planned expansion got underway.

While Daniel's small mill drew most of the customers, he gladly referred people to the other operations when he had more work than he could handle. He even made occasional referrals when he could have taken the job himself. He was not out to put anyone out of business. Craig could see by the typical mill worker's clothing he wore that Daniel planned to be at the mill for at least a few hours that day.

"Did you just get into town this morning?" Kathleen asked. "Why didn't you tell us you were coming?"

"I got in yesterday afternoon. I made the decision to come at the last minute," Craig said.

"You can stay with me," his sister offered.

But Craig was more interested in staying where he was. Being able to see Anna daily was more to his liking. He also knew Daniel didn't have room for him comfortably. He, his wife, and their four children lived in a two-bedroom house.

"That's okay. I'm in the motel down by where the school used to be," he said.

Kathleen's look of disappointment almost had him changing accommodation arrangements -- almost.

"Anna," is all Daniel said. Craig gave his brother a questioning look, to which Daniel just offered a knowing grin.

Craig did not offer a response to his brother's implication that he wanted to stay at the motel to be close to Anna. Daniel had always guessed that his brother had a thing for her, but he had no idea how close his guesses had been.

After they ordered breakfast, they settled into a conversation that covered sharing stories from when they were young and catching up on each other's lives. Nearly ninety minutes later, under frequent disapproving stares from the cafe's wait staff as the line of hungry customers grew longer, they said their goodbyes, promising to get together later.

O◦◦O

Craig stopped by the motel after breakfast. He justified it in his mind that he needed a little rest, but that wasn't it. He hoped to see Anna, if only briefly, as he expected to be busy most of the day. The reunion activities were scheduled to begin with a reception at the community building followed by a late morning golf tournament.

Craig did not play golf, but he knew a little about the game. He planned to tag along with some of his classmates while they played.

When he got to the door of his room, he found an index card propped on the knob with one end inserted between the door and the jam. The card was blank on the side facing him. He took it and turned it over. On the opposite side was the block numeral "6." The number was one of those found in a sheet of numerals with one sticky side. The number, about two inches tall, was blue. He put it in the chest pocket of his short-sleeved button-up shirt.

He inserted his key into the lock on the door. Despite being in the 21st century, the motel owners had not upgraded the door locks to the electronic kind that used a card, the same size and shape as a credit card, to unlock the doors.

Craig smiled at that. It added to the old fashioned charm of the place, much like the Old West theme of the downtown blocks added to the charm of the town itself.

He entered the room and sat down on the bed, which had not yet been made up. He sat thinking for a few minutes but could not come up with any explanation for the index card. He stood, put his dirty clothes from the previous day into a plastic trash bag he had brought for that purpose and set it next to the duffle bag that served as his luggage. He then went downstairs, making sure the door to his room was locked.

Anna was at the half door that was the motel's front desk. She was checking in a customer, clearly a tourist and not one of his classmates in town for the reunion. He sat patiently on one of the lobby chairs until the man walked out the front door with his room key and headed for one of the smaller cabins.

"So, how was breakfast?" Anna asked as she left the office and sat in a chair across from him. She was dressed in shorts -- not quite as short as the day before -- and a polo shirt with the name of the motel embroidered on the left chest.

"It was good to see them," he said. "It's been a while."

"I'm surprised you didn't stay with one of them instead of in a motel," she said, then quickly added, "Surprised but not sorry."

"Neither of them really have room for me at their homes," he answered, fibbing a little bit about his sister. "I know Kathleen was disappointed."

"My gain, I guess," Anna said. She knew Kathleen and had been to her home a few times. She knew there was plenty of room there for Craig.

"Are any of my classmates from out of town staying here?" he asked.

"None of them made reservations, and now it's too late because we're full through the month," she explained.

"Really?" he said, surprised. "How did I get a room?"

"Just lucky, I guess," she said playfully.

When he had called three days ago to see if there were vacancies she had told him there was one room left. In fact, the room had been booked several months previously, but Anna had called that customer and told him the room was not available because of some damage done by a previous boarder and was under repair. Whether that customer found other lodgings, she did not know, nor did she care.

"Did someone come by and leave me a message?" he asked. She answered in the negative. He pulled the card out of his pocket and handed it to her.

"I found this on my door," he said.

Anna looked at the card, turned it over, and then over again. She handed it back with a puzzled look.

"Does anyone else know you are staying here?" she asked.

"I didn't tell anyone until Kathleen and Daniel about a half hour ago," he said. "It couldn't have been either of them because I came straight here after breakfast."

They were both silent for a few moments.

"Did you see anyone come in, go upstairs, then leave?" he asked.

"No, but I've been busy all morning, and I could have missed someone if they did come in," she said.

"Do you have any cameras covering the lobby?" he asked, looking around and seeing none -- at least none that were obvious.

"We're not quite that sophisticated," she said with a little giggle.

After a moment, he stood. She did the same and took his hands and looked deeply into his eyes.

"You have reunion stuff to do, and I'm busy here all day," she said. "Maybe we'll see each other later at the bar?"

There was no real reason to ask which of the two main street bars she was talking about. The most popular was in the middle of one of the downtown blocks, across an alley from the popular cafe.

"No doubt," he said, giving her hands a squeeze. She pulled him close and put her arms around his waist.

"I'll hold you to that, mister," she said, looking deeply into his eyes.

⊙━⊙

Craig drove to the community center located adjacent to the town park. It was a facility that did not exist when he went to school in the town. As the town evolved over the years to become an art enclave, the center was constructed and doubled as an arts and convention center. It was rented for special events, such as the reunion reception.

The opening reception was designed for class members to register and mingle for the first time in the week-long reunion.

Craig's original graduating class included 30 students, the largest class to receive their diplomas in the school's history. The group was proud of that fact and proud that it had the largest contingent of attendees at all-school reunions conducted from time to time. However, this was not one of those years for an all-school reunion.

Because it was the fifty-year anniversary, several members of the class decided they wanted an event all to themselves. And because it was such a large class, they wanted more than a weekend of events. They worked hard to ensure all class members attended this event.

Through the years the class number had diminished. Six members had died -- four from illness or natural causes, one from a fatal car accident and another who was rumored to have committed suicide but was officially listed as natural causes. The graduates included seventeen boys and thirteen girls. All the deaths were males.

But that changed yesterday with Jane's death. No official word had been released on the cause of death, but after he was able to examine the body, Craig had already made up his mind. But he kept that to himself. Her death was already a cloud over what had been planned as a festive week.

"Oh my God! He is here!"

A chubby woman at a registration table jumped up and advanced on Craig as he walked through the center's front door a quarter-hour after the registration was scheduled to begin. She gave him a warm hug and then stepped back to look him over.

She was just a few inches shorter than he. She had put on more than twenty pounds since he saw her last, and it was all concentrated at her hips and waist. Her face, surrounded by carefully curled brown hair, was still cute, just a little puffy.

"How are you, Diana?" he asked.

"Just fine. How about you?" she answered, then slipped her arm in his and escorted him to the table. "We didn't make you a name tag because we didn't think you were coming. You never answered our invitations."

"That's okay. I don't need a name tag," he laughed. "I don't think any of us do."

"You'd be surprised," she said as she handed him a registration book and a pen. He wrote in his name and email address, leaving other items blank.

"Now we should have a perfect attendance," Diana said. She noticed he made a quick count of the names in the book already. "They're not all here yet, but they're in town and should be around for the activities," she added.

"All except Jane," Craig thought to himself.

Diana led him into the main hall, where, for about thirty minutes, he was the center of attention since they had not expected to see him. That made him a bit uncomfortable.

But he chatted politely with everyone, including his athletic teammates, friends and some who had been in the class but did not graduate because their families had moved from Dubois before they finished high school. By his count, seventeen of the graduates were present when he arrived, and three of the remaining seven came within the next hour.

One of those was Tom Kincade, one of his sports teammates, who was serving as the town mayor.

"Hey, Craig, how are you doing?" Tom asked when they had a moment alone. "Are you still in Kansas?"

"Yep," Craig answered.

"Still working?" the mayor asked.

"Nope. Retired," he said.

"Well, from what I hear, you did a bang-up job there in Salina," Tom said. "If we had the budget for our own police department, I sure would have given you a call to try and twist your arm to help us out."

"You would have had to twist pretty hard. I was happy at the Salina department," Craig said diplomatically. While he was proud to tell people he grew up in Dubois, his plan had always been to experience more than the town -- and the state of Wyoming, for that matter -- had to offer him. He wouldn't judge those who chose to stay in the small town or the state, as nearly half his class had done, but he just wanted more out of life.

"I get it," Tom said. "You always did have your eye on the outside world. Nothing wrong with that."

Tom led Craig over to one wall of the main hall where, on the wall and tables there, displays of photos, yearbooks and other items provided a walk down memory lane. Tom patted him on the back and moved to another small group not far away. Craig chatted with other classmates as they, too, perused the displays.

Later, most of the men and some of the women adjourned to the golf course west of town. This was another amenity that was not present when Craig went to school in Dubois. It was added several years ago as the celebrities and upper crust from Jackson Hole filtered down to Dubois.

Craig was not a golfer, although he had played from time to time with officers in the Salina department. He was a lousy player, which was the main reason he shunned the game. But he wanted to hang out with some of his classmates. So he tagged along for the first few holes with a foursome that walked rather than used a cart. Then, he stayed put until another walking group came along.

This group had played two holes and were getting ready to move on when they heard a siren sounding from the direction of town. They stopped and looked toward the highway. A sheriff's office SUV was speeding westward. It then made a left turn onto Airport Road.

Chapter 5

Most commonly called "the tavern," the most popular bar in Dubois was generally always busy, even on Sunday evenings. This Sunday, while the place was crowded with tourists and Craig's classmates for the reunion, the mood was somewhat subdued. The word of Jane Diaz's death had spread like wildfire throughout the town. The reunion attendees were mourning in their own ways, and the tourists could feel the sorrow hanging in the air like a heavy winter snowfall.

Craig was sitting in one of the curved booths in the main bar area with six other people. The building's exterior consists of peeled logs over a wooden structure. The interior decor was made of diseased wood installed to enhance the western atmosphere when the building, originally built in 1919, was converted in 1935 from a pool hall to a bar. The stuffed heads of various wildlife lined the walls, including the canopy over the bar area. Booths lined the wall opposite the bar the backrests of which are also made of logs.

In the back was a room large enough for three pool tables and several dart boards along one wall. Next to the elongated bar area was a banquet room, added about the same time as the conversion from a pool hall, with a commercial kitchen that also served a steakhouse that fronted Ramshorn Street. The bar, banquet room and steakhouse are contained in the same building.

Craig sat in the middle of the booth with classmates to either side of him. Anna had come after they had gathered, and she squeezed onto one end of the booth seating. The classmates had been swapping stories from their school days. But the merriment was dimmed each time Jane's name came up. So they tried to avoid mention of her, which they found easier said than done.

They were into their second hour of conversation. They were all drinking. But Craig had only his second drink, a whiskey highball, in front of him. While he did his share of drinking while in high school and college, he found he didn't really enjoy beer or wine. So, in social settings, he ordered low-alcohol concoctions and nursed them over a longer period than most people.

During a particularly humorous story told by one of his former football teammates, Craig noticed two Fremont County Sheriff's deputies walk shoulder-to-shoulder by the booth. Each was scanning the crowd. The nearer one turned his head toward Craig and his friends just as he was about to pass by the booth. He stopped, nudged his partner and walked up to the table.

"You're Craig Reilly, right?" the deputy asked a little loudly to be heard over the din in the room.

"That's right," Craig answered.

"We'd like to talk to you," the deputy said, very business-like. "Privately."

All heads in the booth turned to stare at Craig.

"Privately might be a little difficult in here," Craig said, only half-jokingly. "Or even in this town."

"We have that covered," the deputy said, still stone-faced.

Craig nodded, and the three friends to his left slid out of the booth to allow him to exit. He followed the deputies out the front door and into the still warm air of the August evening, his boothmates and most of the rest of the bar's patrons curiously watching.

Once in the SUV cruiser parked just around the corner from the tavern, they headed east toward the edge of town. Craig was surprised and a little apprehensive when they pulled into the clinic parking lot. At nearly nine o'clock, it was surprising to see the lights on in the building.

⊙—⊙

The small meeting in the clinic lobby as midnight approached was a somber one. The Venetian blinds in the windows were drawn down and rolled closed, but from the outside, anyone driving by on the highway

37

or who ventured into the parking lot could tell there were lights on in the building.

It couldn't be helped. The only room in the clinic suitable for a meeting of five people was the lobby. Up the hallway was the examining room where the body lay covered on an exam bed.

"Are you sure of the identity?" one of the two deputies asked Dr. Hall.

"Very certain," he answered, a little emotion choking his voice. "Janine Brown was one of my regular patients."

"And you're sure the cause of death was strangulation?" the other deputy asked. They both had their notepads open in front of them.

"There is no doubt," the doctor said, some professionalism returning to his manner.

There was silence in the room for a few moments. It was the same conclusion the doctor had reached for the first victim, Jane Diaz.

"This in not good," Tom Kincade said. He had been summoned to the clinic before Craig.

"No, it's not good," Hall said angrily. "Not for Janine or Jane. Or their families."

"That's what I meant," Kincade said, a little embarrassed.

"No. You meant it's not good for the town," Hall said. "I know what your first priorities are."

Both deputies started to interject simultaneously, but Tom stood and pointed his finger at the doctor.

"Yes, as this town's mayor, I am concerned about the impact this will have," he shouted. "But both these women were my friends. I've known them much longer than you."

Hall stood and faced the mayor, ready to go at it with him. They had faced off before. Craig stood and got in between the two before the deputies could.

"This is not going to help the situation," he said, urging them both to sit back down. They complied but continued to eye each other with simmering irritation.

"We need to calm down and figure out just what this 'situation' is," Deputy Fred Maple said. A resident of Riverton, a larger town southeast of Dubois and twenty miles north of Lander, Maple was assigned to the area that included the smaller town.

In the hours since Craig was taken to the clinic, he was allowed to examine Janine's body in detail, much more detail than he was able to look over Jane's. Her body had been taken to Lander earlier in the day, where a full autopsy would be conducted by the county medical examiner.

On the exam bed, Craig saw a woman in her mid-sixties, but he knew she was nearly a year older than himself. She was a pretty, petite, brown-haired girl when they were in high school together. He noticed the years had been fairly good to her. Though her hair was nearly all gray now, she had retained her good figure, and she was almost as pretty as she had been. The hard-living of an Idaho farmer's wife had only slightly put a little more weight on her, and there were a few wrinkles on her sun-dried skin.

There was some bruising on her arms, indicating she may have been struck several times and her right eye socket was swollen and bruised. There was evidence of forced sexual activity. Though Craig had not examined Jane's body below the neck and upper chest, Hall admitted to him that she had marks on her arms that indicated she had been manually restrained and that she had been raped.

But the item of most interest to Craig was both women's necks. His visual examination of Jane showed him she had been strangled, the same as Janine. More importantly, his up close and personal study of Janine's neck convinced him both women were strangled with some type of cloth.

He had asked Hall if there had been any cloth recovered from the neck wounds of either woman. He had discovered some fibers in both wounds. Under a microscope, Hall said the fibers from both wounds appeared to have brown pigments.

"So what is this situation?" Tom asked, looking from the deputies to Craig.

"For the moment, we have two deaths that have some connections," Maple said.

"Okay, does that mean we can expect more murders?" Tom asked, a little testiness creeping into his voice. "Do we evacuate the town? What's the protocol here?"

"The protocol is to continue investigating and find the person or persons who did this and get them behind bars," Maple said calmly, hoping his demeanor would sooth the mayor. It did not. The deputy could tell by his body language. But Tom said nothing more.

"You need to go on with life in town and let us do our work," Maple said. "But we will keep you posted on any new developments."

Tom could recognize that he was being dismissed. He didn't like it but knew any protests would be in vain. He stepped toward the main entrance door, and the doctor moved with him to unlock it, relocking it after the mayor had left. As he walked out, Tom glanced at Craig, who had come to the entrance door but did not exit the lobby.

"Why are you staying and I'm not?" he thought to himself. He knew of Craig's history with the Kansas City serial killer case. The knowledge gave him chills.

⊙╍╍⊙

Maple and the other deputy, Travis Martin, flipped through their notebooks, reviewing the notes they had taken so far concerning the two deaths. Martin was normally assigned to assist tribal police on the Indian reservation southeast of Dubois, so he was not involved in the initial investigation of Jane's death. But now he was helping Maple.

He filled Martin in on his notes from Jane's death, and they talked about the similarities. During that discussion, Craig sat across the lobby, which was small enough that he overheard the deputies' conversation.

It was clear to him the two deaths were no accident. The MOs were also so similar that the two cases were at least related. But there were also signs that pointed to a more chilling conclusion, one the deputies could not make because they did not know what Craig knew.

He wondered why they had brought him to the clinic and asked him to remain after the mayor left. He got his answer quickly. Both deputies came over to where he sat.

"The sheriff asked us to talk to you about these cases because he knows you have been involved in multiple murder investigations before," Maple said.

So there it was, the first official acknowledgment of what Craig had suspected since giving Jane's body a cursory examination -- Jane's and Janine's deaths were considered by county sheriff officials as connected murders.

"How does he know that?" Craig asked.

"Because the mayor told him," Maple said. "The mayor also requested that you be consulted."

Craig had been in law enforcement long enough to recognize the resentment on the two deputies' faces. No police department leader or field officer believes they need help in solving crimes, even ones as drastic as murder. Craig understood their feelings. But if his suspicions turned out to be fact, they were going to need his help because he had knowledge and information they did not.

"What is your take on these deaths?" Maple asked.

Craig stood while he gathered his thoughts. He did not want to share with the deputies his suspicions until he was certain of the connection.

"First, I believe both women were killed by the same person," he began. "Second, I believe the same cloth item was used in the strangulations. Third, I believe both women were alive when the sexual assault started but died sometime during the act of penetration. Fourth, I believe no semen or other DNA evidence will be found in or on the victims."

"What leads you to those beliefs?" Martin asked.

"The doctor found brown and gold cloth fibers on the neck wound, embedded there because of the force used," Craig said. "They most likely came from a scarf or shawl."

"That could have been something they were wearing," Maple said. "But it's odd they would be wearing something with the same colors."

"Why do you think we won't find any DNA?" Martin asked.

"Remember that both bodies were found completely nude," Craig said. "When that family found Jane they said she seemed oddly clean for being in the old homestead cabin. She was found laying on her stomach, and only her front was covered with dirt, until the boy turned her over while she only had a very thin layer of dust on her back, butt and the back of her legs, according to the boy's recollection. The doctor found evidence of soap behind one ear."

"But you think there was penetration during a rape," Maple said. "Why would they find no semen?"

"The doctor found no evidence of sperm in her vagina and no smell of it," Craig explained. "But he did detect a faint smell of latex. That indicates a condom was used."

He let the deputies catch up, adding his information to their notes.

"I think the killer was squeezing the scarf, or whatever it was, around her neck while he was raping her and when he climaxed, the rush of adrenaline made him squeeze it so tight it left the fibers in the wounds," Craig said when the deputies had finished.

They stared at him for a few moments. He could tell Martin was a little nauseated, and Maple was angry.

"That's pretty sick," Maple said.

"Yes. Yes, it is," Craig replied.

It was just after one o'clock in the morning when Craig got back to the motel. He wanted to see Anna but knew she was most likely at her house and in bed by then. He resisted the urge to call her to talk, not about the meeting at the clinic. He wanted to talk about anything else in hopes he could get it off his mind.

Because he could not distract himself from other thoughts, he kept rolling all the facts over and over in his mind. He tried to sleep, but it was elusive. Every time he started to drop off, his suspicions came screaming back into his mind.

By the time the dim light of Monday started peeking through the small slits on either side of the dark curtains on the single window in the room, he had slept a grand total of twenty minutes since dragging himself into the room in the wee hours of the morning.

He needed coffee to help kick start his mind back to functionality. He took a quick shower, shaved, brushed his teeth and dressed in jeans and a royal blue T-shirt with a gold ram's head on the front he had ordered over the Internet several weeks ago. He slipped on a pair of white gym socks and his white athletic shoes.

Craig opened his room door and stepped out into the open hallway that looked down on the motel lobby. He was about to take his first steps away from the room when something on the floor caught his eye.

He stooped and picked up a white three-inch by five-inch index card. It was blank on the side that was facing up. He turned it over, and on the other side was the numeral "7" in the same block style as the first card.

Chapter 6

Sitting at the table on the small deck in the rear of the modest two-bedroom house on the corner of Mercantile and Watson streets, Craig let himself be hypnotized by the rhythmic flow of Horse Creek just a few yards away. It was quiet in the neighborhood, with few vehicles stirring up noise and dust on the nearby streets that were still graded dirt, just like when he went to school in town. Besides Ramshorn, which was a state highway, the only other paved street in town was First Street two blocks east of where he sat.

He was alone on the deck for the moment. Anna was inside her house putting the finishing touches on breakfast. When he found her in the motel office he had offered to buy her breakfast.

"I have a better idea," she had replied. "I'll buy you breakfast."

She then arranged for someone to come tend to the motel for a couple of hours and drove him to her house. She lived alone, having no children despite being married twice. Both her former husbands were controlling, which did not sit well with her independent personality. When they each turned to physical abuse to try and bring her into line, she promptly divorced them. Neither marriage lasted more than three years.

Craig was snapped out of his babbling creek trance by a plate being set in front of him. It was filled with eggs benedict, sausage patties and toast. Anna sat down across from him with her own plate. She had changed her polo shirt with the motel name and logo embroidered on the chest for a tight-fitting tank top.

"So, where did you run off to last night?" she asked before taking a bite of sausage.

He had mentally debated whether to discuss his visit to the clinic and his suspicions about the two deaths. He did not want to start a panic in his hometown. But more importantly, as a former law enforcement officer, he knew the tendency of all police agencies to avoid sharing information about an ongoing investigation unless it was essential to solving the case.

But at the same time, he felt he needed to share his thoughts with someone. If for nothing else to verbalize those thoughts. When he was on the job, it always helped him to talk to other officers and detectives, not just because hearing himself say it helped him visualize the evidence but because others often times provided additional ideas and theories.

He trusted Anna's discretion. He also knew she would be blunt with her own thoughts. There was also the possibility that because she had lived in town all her life she might have some insight, whether she realized it or not. On a deeper emotional level, he wanted her to be aware of what was going on in the event she, too, became a target of the killer. In addition, he wanted to let her know he trusted her.

"The mayor convinced the county sheriff that I might be helpful in solving these deaths," he said, being careful not to call them murders.

"So these weren't accidents," she said between bites.

Craig slowly chewed and swallowed his first bite of English muffin, ham, egg and hollandaise sauce. He savored the aftertaste on his tongue. It was the best he had ever tasted.

"It looks like that's a possibility," he said. "If this is any indication, you are a freakin' great cook," he added, pointing his fork at his breakfast.

"Barefoot and in the kitchen, just where every man wants me," she joked.

"Kitchen, bedroom, deck. Anywhere you'd like," he thought, smiling.

She smiled back knowingly.

"So what does it look like to you?" she asked.

For an instant, he tried to picture her without the tank top.

"The deaths, horn dog, I meant the deaths," she said with a smile that was almost an invitation to show what he wanted to see. He blushed a little, then stuffed a large bite of sausage into his mouth as a distraction.

"Well, they seem to be related," he explained as he chewed the sausage. "And from what I saw, they were no accidents."

They both ate a few bites, she letting that sink in and he trying to organize what he was willing to share.

"The way they were killed is familiar to me," he said slowly. "There was a case in Missouri that I was asked to consult on. It was multiple killings, and all the victims were strangled. So were Jane and Janine."

"How did that case turn out," Anna asked.

"It was the same person who killed them all. But the suspect was never caught," Craig said. "At least not to my way of thinking."

"What do you mean?" she asked.

"There was a similar case in Kansas, almost exactly the same with one minor difference," he said. "The Kansas police and I believed that one was a copycat of the Missouri case. But the police in Missouri disagreed and closed the case, saying the Kansas suspect was the killer."

"Are you sure he wasn't?" she asked.

"He couldn't have been the Missouri killer," Craig said. "The last Missouri death came just after the Kansas guy was arrested."

They were silent for a while. After that, he sipped the last of his coffee, and she drained her glass of milk. After a few moments, they gathered up the dishes and took them inside. He insisted on washing them and she dried and put them away.

"You need to keep anything I tell you about these deaths to yourself," he said as she drove back to the motel, this time in a different vehicle.

"I get it," she said. "You can trust me."

When she parked her Ford Taurus in the back of the motel, she turned to him.

"There's more to this, isn't there?" she asked. He nodded.

"We'll talk more later," he answered. "But I don't want to say anything more until I get some more facts to go on."

The only reunion activity scheduled for Monday was another gathering at the community center. Craig decided to go, but his heart wasn't enthusiastic about engaging in conversation. It was the same for his classmates as well. It was a somber gathering.

While much of the talk was reminiscences of Jane and Janine, Craig heard some whispers of concern from the women in the group. Some were speculating that since the two victims were from the same graduating class, were the rest of the class members targets? And since no men had been killed so far, did that mean the killer was only going after women? Were people who were in the class at one time but did not graduate with the Dubois group on the killer's target list?

Because they knew his background, some turned to him for answers. But he had nothing concrete to share with them. And he certainly wasn't going to share his suspicions.

"It is very early in the sheriff's department's investigation," he told those who asked. "I don't know that they have even classified these as murders."

The last comment was an evasion. Because the sheriff's office had not made an official announcement, he was technically telling the truth. But having been part of the discussion at the clinic, he knew that investigators were looking at the incidents as foul play deaths.

Fueling people's anxiety was the fact that two women from the graduating class were not in attendance at this activity, although everyone else, including the men and those who had been in the class but did not graduate with them, was at the community center.

"That's nothing to be concerned about," Craig had said, trying to be reassuring. "They might be up at the bar or visiting family."

One woman's elderly parents lived on the reservation, and the other's mother lived on a ranch north of town. That helped give some legitimacy to Craig's reassurances. However, he was not convinced of his own words.

The gathering finally started losing steam, and people scattered back to their homes, where they were staying for the week or to the bars. Craig had other ideas and made a quick phone call while walking from the center to his motel room.

O▬oo▬O

With the early afternoon sun starting its downward plunge toward the mountainous horizon to the west, Craig sat alongside Deputy Maple as the sheriff's department SUV navigated North Mountain View Road. They were headed for the homestead cabins. Craig wanted to examine the scenes where Jane and Janine were found. They decided to start with the first victim.

The drive through the treeless terrain took him back to his childhood. His family had visited the cabins numerous times before his father died. Being so young at the time, Craig only recalled bits and pieces of those trips. But he did remember fondly the few times his mother had taken the children back there for camping trips as they were growing up.

Rose had a difficult time adjusting after her husband's death, and Craig was seven before they returned to the camping trips, usually a couple of weekends a month, in different locations. At first, she avoided places they had gone to when Chester was alive. But eventually, she returned to her favorite spots -- the cabins, Bog Lake, Double Cabins, Wiggins Fork, and the three lakes.

"What's on your mind?" Maple asked as they neared the west rim of the small gorge that contained the Wiggins Fork and the cabins.

"Oh, just trippin' down memory lane," Craig answered.

"You raised around here?" Maple asked.

"All my life until I graduated high school," Craig responded.

"I'm an out-of-stater myself," Maple said and made a sharp turn onto the rocky road that led down to the cabins.

Fred inched the SUV down the narrow, bumpy roadway at a snail's pace. It was the only way to get down into the gorge except on foot, and neither man wanted to pack in any equipment. But one miscue at too fast a speed and a vehicle would roll down the side.

When they passed the rocky surface and the road turned into normal ground, the deputy took his foot off the brake and let the SUV roll to a stop near the northernmost cabin. After a short walk south, they were at the second cabin, still surrounded by yellow crime scene tape wrapped around trees.

Fred stood back while Craig gingerly stepped into the cabin. The scene had been photographed before and after Jane's body was removed and transported to the Dubois clinic. Fred had brought some of the photos along and Craig studied them during the drive from town.

At the cabin, he studied the site for himself. Not wanting to disturb the scene, he stood just one step inside the entry and played the flashlight Fred had given him over every inch of the inside, taking nearly a full minute on each section the light illuminated as he moved it from one area to the next. He then squatted down to study in more detail the exact area where the body was found. He spent several minutes staring intently at that specific area.

Finally, he stepped back out of the cabin.

"Let's head up to the airport," he told Maple.

During the drive back to and through town, Craig studied the photos of the scene where Janine was found, again before and after the body was removed. As Fred turned from Highway 26 onto Airport Road, Craig's mind again returned to memories of his childhood. He remembered a day when he was ten years old and was out hiking with a friend in the area of Warm Springs Road.

They began to hear something that sounded like an engine running. At first Craig thought it might be a hay baler or a tractor working a field on the plateau above the road to the west. The boys walked to a gully and followed it as it ascended to the plateau.

When they reached the top, almost directly in front of them, was the end of what they at first thought was a long paved street. But setting not far from the end facing away from them was a high-winged airplane. Now that they were at the same level, the plane's engine was roaring, so much so they could not hear each other's exclamations of surprise. Suddenly, the volume of the engine increased, and it began slowly rolling along the runway, picking up speed as it went. As it passed a cluster of buildings to the right of the runway, the nose wheel of the tricycle landing gear left the pavement, and the plane's tail dropped. Within a few feet, the main wheels lost touch with the ground, and the plane lifted into the air.

The boys stood and watched as the airplane continued to climb. Eventually, it leveled off and slowly got smaller as it flew northwest. Craig and his friend watched until it was out of sight, then walked to the buildings and found they were just four hangers with their doors closed and padlocked. There were no more planes visible.

That was how Craig discovered his small hometown had an airport. He later learned it had had one for some time, even before he was born. The original town airport had been on a flat hill above where the old school had been.

Fred completed the climb up Airport Road and parked the SUV several yards past the end of the runway where Craig had first found the airport. In the distance, the number of hangers had doubled since that day of discovery, and three other buildings had been added.

Airport Road snakes up the hill from Highway 26 and, when it reaches the top, splits at right angles, with one going to the buildings and the other through the gully connecting with Warm Springs Road. Across the split, the road continues but is called Fox Run.

Craig and the deputy walked to a point right behind the runway and just a few feet from Fox Run. There was an area about ten feet square staked out with crime scene tape stretched around the stakes. With the sun still a few hours from dropping below the mountains, there was plenty of light, so Craig did not step into the square. He simply looked over the interior very carefully as he slowly paced next to the tape until he had covered the entire square.

"How was the body found?" Craig asked. "Airport maintenance crew?"

"No. There is generally no one up here except the pilots when they come and go," Maple said. "Someone flying in spotted something that didn't look right as he was landing. He did a touch-and-go and came back around for another look. Then he drove down here to confirm what he thought he saw."

Craig took another quick look at the area within the taped-off square, this time staying in one place. He was silent for a long time.

"What are you thinking?" Fred asked.

"Have your detectives gone over these scenes?" Craig asked.

"We only have three detectives, and one is working a case out near Lysite," Maple said.

He went on to explain that the sheriff's office was divided into three districts -- Riverton, Lander and Dubois, with offices located in each community. One detective was assigned to each district.

"When one detective is out in the field, we rotate one of the other two into that vacated district office," Maple said. "Because we get fewer calls here, the Dubois detective is the one rotated most often."

That's about to change, Craig thought to himself.

The sheriff's department was also short-staffed on patrol deputies due to budget cuts. Fremont County is the second largest area in the state. The sheriff's staff is required to cover more than ten thousand square miles. That includes assisting the tribal police for the Wind River Indian Reservation, which was thirty-four hundred square miles of the county total. With the reduced staff, resources were stretched quite thin, Maple explained.

"I think we need to take a trip to Lander to talk to the sheriff tomorrow," Craig said.

"What for?" Fred asked.

"I have a suspicion there are going to be more deaths, and you all need to be prepared for it," Craig answered.

"Are we talking about a serial killer?" Maple asked nervously.

"I hope not, but…"

Chapter 7

Maple texted Craig that he was waiting outside the motel and ready for the trip to Lander. It was five-thirty in the morning.

Craig was ready, having been up since three o'clock after a restless night. He had been to Anna's for dinner the night before. They had dined on goulash and garlic bread with a generous slice of her homemade cherry pie for dessert.

They talked for several hours, although Craig kept the conversation away from the deaths of his classmates. They spent their time catching up with each other's lives and sharing old stories from school days. Their life shares were very general, with no real detail. She could tell he was somewhat distracted but did not press.

He left after the sun had gone down. They shared a tender kiss on her porch before he departed.

His sleep was interrupted mostly by the murders of his friends. But his mind was also occupied with Anna. He really enjoyed the time he was getting to spend with her. However, with the circumstances as they were, that time was not as much as he wanted. He was also nagged by the thought that he would eventually be leaving for his home in Kansas, and there was no telling when he would get to see her again.

He waded through the quagmire of those thoughts and the wide variety of emotions they brought with them as he and Maple traveled wordlessly along Highway 26. Maple finally broke the silence after they had passed Burris.

"So what was it like growing up around here?" he asked.

The deputy wanted to discuss the murder cases but remembered the previous day as they drove back to Dubois from the airport when he had asked Craig what he was thinking. Craig had said he preferred to wait until they met with the sheriff. He wanted time to collect his thoughts.

"Oh, it was great," Craig said. "I wouldn't trade it for anything."

"So why did you leave?" Fred asked.

"At that time, I had bigger ambitions than I thought this area had to offer," he answered.

"How did that work out?" Maple asked.

Craig took a few moments to think about it. Since his retirement from the Salina Police Department, he had not put much thought into his career choices and how they had worked out for him.

"I suppose it has worked out okay," he answered, not entirely convincing himself.

"Did you ever get that one big case that they say all cops are looking for?" Fred asked.

Craig thought back to the Kansas City serial killer case that he was called in to consult on. It had not been his case, but it had been a big one. And it had never been solved to his satisfaction, even though the Kansas City police considered it closed.

"Not really," he said, preferring to let him hear about the Kansas City case along with the sheriff. "But it looks like you got yours."

"Not quite the kind of cases I was hoping for," Maple said.

They were quiet again, which was okay with Craig. They drove past the old Crowheart School, and down the road a ways they stopped at the Crowheart Store. Maple topped off the SUV's gas tank, and they both bought a microwave breakfast burrito and soft drink.

They ate and drank in silence. The burritos were not the greatest, and Craig wished he was back in town sitting with Anna at her house or the popular cafe on Ramshorn Street, eating a hearty breakfast.

When they crossed over the Bull Lake Creek Bridge he looked to the left and saw the old bridge still in place.

"God, is that old bridge still used?" he asked. "We thought that should have been condemned when we were in high school."

Since then, the state has replaced the bridge about forty yards south in conjunction with a project to make the curve leading to and from the bridge more shallow.

Craig shared the story of the return from one football trip up north. It was late at night, and the head coach was driving to give the regular driver a break. He was eager to get back to town, and as they approached the bridge, those still awake could see a semi-truck coming from the opposite direction.

Everyone knew the bridge was too narrow for both to pass on it. But instead of slowing down, both drivers kept their speed. They met mid-bridge, and the grinding that followed made sure everyone on the bus was awake. When they all disembarked back in Dubois, they discovered that both side mirrors had been torn off, and there were scrape marks down both sides. It was a foregone conclusion that the semi-truck had the same damage.

"Holy crap," Fred said. "It's a wonder things weren't worse."

"I've got stories about going through Wind River Canyon that will make your balls retract into your body," Craig laughed.

Craig and Fred arrived at the Fremont County Sheriff's Office building on Railroad Street in Lander just after seven o'clock in the morning. Sheriff Sam Sharbono had not yet arrived, so Fred used his key to let them both inside.

The FCSO facility is a large brick structure that takes up nearly an entire city block. The building includes administrative offices, meeting rooms, booking facilities, the county jail and other rooms for various uses. Fred led Craig through the maze of rooms in the administrative area to a small break room.

"The sheriff usually gets in about eight o'clock, but he's coming in early today for us," Fred said. "He should be here soon."

Craig nodded and looked around. The room included a large refrigerator, a sink, counter space, cupboards both above and below the counter, and two round tables with five chairs circling each.

"This seems like a pretty nice facility," Craig said. "How many people do you have for the county?"

"We have forty deputies, including detention here at the jail, ten sergeants and three lieutenants, who are our detectives," Fred answered. "We should have about ten more deputies, but the commissioners cut our budget a few years ago during that economic downturn, and we haven't been able to recoup all those cuts."

Craig understood. In his last years at Salina, the department also suffered budget cuts. But, they did not face an additional obstacle for law enforcement agencies that was now prevalent.

"Even when we do try to hire, it's hard to find candidates because of the negative mood that seems to be building in this country against police," Fred explained. "Plus we lose some to attrition because they either want to get out of law enforcement or they are gobbled up by other departments that pay better."

"You're seeing people turning against police even here in Wyoming?" Craig asked.

The state leaned heavily on the conservative side of the political scale, which usually meant healthy respect for law and order, police and the military. So, to hear that seemed to be changing surprised and disappointed Craig.

"Yeah, those celebrities and the liberal gang that has taken over Jackson seems to be spreading," Maple said. "It's creeping into other areas of the state, including your hometown."

He hadn't been back in Dubois long enough to notice, but it had been subtly changing its makeup in other ways over the years. When he was in school, Craig did not see any art galleries in his hometown. But now there were two in the main section of downtown. There could be others. He just hadn't gotten to other parts of town yet. When he was quite young, he remembered visiting a stage theater in Dubois where plays were performed. But it lasted only a couple of years. The building was now the main grocery store in town.

"It's pretty quiet in here," Craig said to change the subject.

"Yeah, the support staff comes in at nine o'clock, and shift change is at eight, so that's when things will pick up," Fred explained.

Just then, they heard footsteps approaching. Sheriff Sam Sharbono stopped in the doorway to the break room.

"Hello, Craig, it's good to see you again," he said and also nodded a greeting to Maple. He then motioned for them to follow him.

Craig and Fred sat in chairs across the gray metal desk from the sheriff in his office. It was a small room with few items. In one corner was a bookshelf with a variety of three-ring binders and law books lining the shelves. A couple of framed scenic photos hung on the wall. Aside from that, there was little else.

Sharbono liked it that way. A modest, humble man, the sheriff did not flaunt his position or power, neither in the county nor within the department. But he was a decisive, clear leader. His personnel knew he was in charge, and they respected him. Most of all, they knew he had their backs at all times in all circumstances.

"So, I hear you are retired now," Sharbono said to Craig. "How is that going?"

"It's an adjustment, but I'm doing okay," he answered.

Sharbono was twenty-nine years Craig's junior, but they knew each other through the sheriff's father, Marvin. The elder Sharbono and Craig were one year apart in age, with Craig being younger. They had played against each other in high school sports from different schools. Marvin had been a standout football and track star at Wind River High School, about halfway between Dubois and Riverton.

More than that, they formed a friendship during the summers when Craig spent time at his grandparents' ranch south of Crowheart, adjacent to a smaller ranch Marvin's parents worked for the property owner who lived out of state. The Sharbono family lived in a modest home on the ranch property.

Marvin and Craig had kept in touch through letters and email when it became available, through the years. They had reconnected in person twenty-six years ago for the double funeral of Craig's grandparents after they were tragically killed when a drunk driver crossed the centerline on Highway 26 just west of the junction with Highway 287. It happened at a point where, following the natural terrain of the land, there was a sharp hump in the roadway that created a blind spot. That dangerous feature, in addition to three sharp turns on hills between there and Dubois, was corrected a few years later.

Marvin and Craig saw each other again during Craig's mother's funeral.

Since then, their electronic correspondence has become even more infrequent. But the friends had shared their work experiences. Marvin worked in Wyoming's oil fields, working his way up from a rigger to supervisor. In addition to information Craig shared about his work, Marvin had independently followed his friend's law enforcement career through Internet searches, especially after Sam went into law enforcement.

Craig had also vented to Marvin about his frustrations during his consultation service on the Kansas City killings. That prompted Marvin to suggest his son get Craig's advice after the second death in Dubois.

"Dad planned on going up to see you in Dubois later this week," Sam said. "He'll be peeved that I got to see you before him."

"How is Marvin?" Craig asked. "We haven't communicated in a few months."

"He's doing pretty well," Sam answered. "I'm glad he's not on the rigs full time. It was doing a number on his back."

"Yeah, it can do that. But if I know Marvin like I think I do, he finds a way to get out to a rig now and then," Craig laughed.

"You got that right," Sam said jokingly but with a bit of concern in his voice.

The conversation paused a moment while all three men collected their thoughts and began to focus on the business at hand.

"So tell me what you're thinking about these deaths up in your town," Sam finally said.

Craig winced a little inside, hoping it didn't show at Sam's reference to "your town." He had left Dubois in his wake many years ago, right after graduating from the high school there, in fact. He had rarely returned, his most recent appearances being to bury family members a quarter century ago. The memories of growing up there were still strong and mostly pleasurable. But he had cut nearly all ties to the town long ago.

He had always felt a small amount of guilt because of that. It was stronger now that he was older and since he had set foot in the community again after all those years of absence.

"Well, as your deputies, I'm sure, have deduced, the women were not killed at the sites they were found," he said with a nod toward Fred. "And they know the cause of death was strangulation."

Craig paused a moment, thinking back to his examination of the two dead women's bodies -- Jane's unofficially and Janine's at the request of the sheriff's deputies.

"I'm also sure you've determined these killings were done by the same person," Craig said.

Sam nodded, as did Fred.

"Both victims were in Dubois because of the reunion," Craig went on. "They were in the same graduating class. Now, is that a coincidence, or is there some kind of connection?"

"You knew both of these women, right?" Sam asked. "Is there something about them that made them targets? Were they close friends? Did they have any enemies in common?"

"When I knew them in school, they weren't close friends," Craig said. "As you know, small towns like Dubois didn't have many cliques in those days. I can't say any of us had enemies in the sense that anyone would want someone dead. Things may be different now."

"Dubois has a lot of tourists in the summer, more so now than when you went to school there," Fred said. "Do you think we're talking about some sicko just passing through?"

"The fact that there were only a few defensive wounds on either victim, just bruising and other marks caused, I believe, by being restrained, suggests they were comfortable, at least at first, with whoever did this," Craig said. "Whether it was someone they knew or someone they met and struck up a friendship with is hard to tell."

"What is your gut telling you?" Sam asked.

Craig was silent for a moment or two. He revisited his thoughts and suspicions of the past days since viewing Jane's body. Since there were so many similarities in the two women's deaths and similarities to another case very familiar to him, he decided it was time to share.

"My gut tells me this case is related to one I was part of in Kansas," he said.

"You're talking about that serial killer in Kansas City, right?" Sam asked. "But Kansas City PD said that case was solved. They had a guy, and, if I recall correctly, he was convicted and sentenced to multiple life terms in prison."

"That's what Kansas City PD believes. I disagree," Craig said.

He then filled in the sheriff and deputy on all the details of the killings in Missouri and the one in Kansas that seemed to end the case. He shared the fact that the sixth Missouri victim was killed shortly after the Kansas suspect was in custody.

"And it wasn't a case of the murder happening before the arrest and of the body being found after; the medical examiner certified the time of death as after the suspect was arrested," Craig concluded. "But Kansas City PD chose to disbelieve his findings."

The sheriff and deputy sat speechless for a few seconds. Sam finally broke the silence in the room.

"That was several years ago. Why would he start up again after all this time? And why here?"

The looks on the sheriff's and deputy's faces told Craig they had their suspicions about the reason for the change of killing ground, as had he.

However, before anyone could speak, a female deputy came into the break room and handed Sam a note. She stood by while he read it. A direct descendant of the Shoshone tribe that was indigenous to most of central Wyoming, Sam's reddish brown skin took on a lighter shade as the words on the paper sunk in.

"We've got another body up in Dubois," he whispered.

Chapter 8

Looking down on the Wyoming landscape from about three thousand feet, Craig marveled at the variety of terrain he could see. For the most part directly below it was bare dirt with sagebrush and scrub brush scattered here and there. There were thin greenways following the waterways and a wider greenbelt surrounding Ocean Lake, barely visible as he turned to look out the window to his right.

The sparseness of the landscape was nearly all within the boundaries of the Wind River Indian Reservation. It was typical of most Indian reservations. The Indian Removal Act of 1830 authorized the U.S. Government to negotiate treaties with Native American tribes for their removal from ancestral lands to designated reservation areas in the western portion of the country. Unfortunately for those tribes, the designated reservations were generally located in the most desolate parts of the areas where they were established.

The Wind River reservation, originally known as the Shoshone Indian Reservation, was established by the Fort Bridger Treaty of 1868, twenty-two years before Wyoming became a state. The 2.2-million-acre reservation is extremely smaller than the 44 million acres that comprised the Shoshone territory prior to the treaty. It spans portions of Fremont and Hot Springs counties.

Looking out the opposite window, past Sheriff Sharbobo, he could see the beginning of the higher reaches of the Wind River Mountain range. Ahead of them and to the north is the Absaroka Mountain range. Both ranges are studded with a selection of pine, larch, spruce, ash, elm, maple and hemlock trees. They provide a kaleidoscope of various shades of green and royal blue.

The rhythmic whop whop whop of the Robinson R66's single main rotor had Craig only slightly aware of the voice in the headset he wore because, up to this point, it had not been directed at him. The sheriff had been talking to the pilot, the helicopter's owner. He is the owner of a large Lander construction company with contracts throughout the state. He uses the aircraft to get to and from several job sites spread from Cheyenne to Cody and more sites in between. On occasions when the sheriff needs it, and it is not otherwise in use, the pilot lends the chopper and his services to the sheriff's department.

"Craig, look down below," Sharbono's voice broke Craig's concentration on the landscape. He looked down and saw a black vehicle making the turn from Highway 287 onto Highway 26 heading northwest.

"That's Deputy Maple heading back to Dubois," the sheriff said.

Craig looked again and saw, faintly from their altitude, red and blue flashes from the vehicle's windshield. From riding in his Chevy Tahoe to the sites where the two bodies were found in Dubois, he knew they were coming from the emergency light bar mounted on the vehicle's dash.

"So where was this new body found? Craig asked.

"Inside the geyser," Sam said.

"You mean 'THE geyser?'" Craig asked.

"That's the one," the sheriff answered.

Craig had been to the geyser many times during his days in high school. It was one of the party spots for the town's teenagers. Located west of the airport, right at the edge of the tree line, the geyser is a hole in the ground about ten feet across. The hole goes straight down about twenty-five feet to a small beach adjacent to a pool of warm water. To get to the beach, visitors climb down the nearly ninety-degree rocky edge above the beach.

"Was she in the water?" Craig asked.

"She," Sam said as he looked over at Craig. "What makes you think it's a woman?"

"It fits the pattern," he answered.

"You mean like the case in Missouri," Sam said. Craig only nodded in response.

"I think there's more you need to share with me," Sam said sternly.

Craig agreed, but he wasn't quite ready to do so while they flew to the new scene. What he had to say needed more consideration than was available in a noisy aircraft. Besides, he wanted to examine the latest scene to be certain in his own mind.

"Let's talk after we've been to the geyser," Craig offered.

Forty minutes after takeoff in Lander, the R66 dropped to one thousand feet and circled above the geyser at a respectable distance to keep rotor wash from sending dust and pebbles into the opening and spoiling the scene inside. There was another sheriff's office Tahoe parked about ten yards from the geyser opening and they could see Deputy Martin leaning against the front fender.

The pilot indicated a small clearing on the other side of a line of trees from the geyser. He brought the craft down, keeping the engine running. Craig and Sam, grabbing a tactical backpack, exited, and the sheriff said a few words to the pilot and then the chopper lifted off and began the flight back to Lander.

Craig and Sam walked through the trees and met Martin at the vehicle.

"Who found the body?" Sam asked.

"Three high school kids," Deputy Martin said. "They were up here hiking around, they said, and noticed it when they looked into the opening."

"Did they go down inside?" the sheriff asked.

"They said they didn't, and I couldn't see any indication from here that they did," Travis answered. "I didn't go down either. I wanted to wait until Fred got here."

"He's on his way and should be here in about forty-five minutes or less. We saw him at the junction," Sam said.

The sheriff began to move toward the hole in the clearing, and the other two men followed. They stood on the rim and looked down. A woman's body, completely nude, was lying on its stomach on the small bit of dry land next to a pool of water. The roughly circular pool was a yellowish tan under the first few feet of water, then changed to medium blue, growing darker farther out. Craig knew the pool extended back about fifty yards, but that was inside a cavern that could not be seen from where the men stood.

"Where are the kids?" Sam asked.

"I sent them home, said we'd be talking to them more later," Travis said.

"Did you get any information before then?" the sheriff asked.

"They had called dispatch on one of their cell phones from here, and I told them to stay here until I arrived," Travis explained. "They saw her down there and thought she was sleeping off a hangover. They dropped a couple of rocks down. When she didn't react, they yelled down, but she didn't answer."

Looking down at the body, all three men could tell it was not a teenager. But from the distance, they could not determine an age. The woman was a little chubby but not obese. Her reddish brown hair was cut in a six-inch pixie cut style. From their vantage point there were no signs the woman fell into the hole.

"And those kids said they were up here hiking?" the sheriff asked.

"That's what they said," Travis said. "I'm not sure that's the whole truth. But I'm sure they didn't have anything to do with this. They seemed genuinely shaken up."

"We'll see," Sam said. "We need to get down there and check this out. Travis, you stay up here and wait for Fred." The sheriff looked at

Craig. "You know your way around these parts. How do we get down there?"

The deputy was a little miffed to be left out of the initial investigative tasks, but his irritation was tempered somewhat by the fact that in his time serving in the Dubois area, this was one location he had not had the call to visit. However, since a civilian was being included instead of him, it was a blow to his ego.

"It's been quite a while, but I'm sure the climb down hasn't changed that much," he said, motioning the sheriff to follow.

They circled a few yards to their right and found a somewhat worn path on the rocky side of the opening. Using rock outcroppings and small ledges, Craig backed down the nearly ninety-degree incline with the sheriff following by a yard or two. When they reached the bottom, they were right next to the body's feet.

Before moving, they both scoured the area for footprints, clothing or any other clues. They found none. The sheriff took out his cell phone and began shooting the overall scene, then some closeups from where they stood. Sam then motioned Craig to take a position on the side of the body closest to the water, and he took a position on the other side. They both closely examined the body and the surrounding area.

Like the other victims, the woman was completely nude and lying on her stomach. The legs were stretched straight out and the arms against her sides with the palms of the hands facing upwards. Also, like the others, the skin still retained most of its natural color.

"This body has only been here twelve hours, fourteen at most," Sam said.

"But not dead that whole time," Craig muttered.

"How do you figure?" the sheriff asked.

Craig slowly took in the body and its immediate surroundings from his side. He then looked up and scanned the walls of the hole from top to bottom. Sam patiently waited.

"For one thing, I seriously doubt, unless the killer is an extremely skilled rock climber, that he was able to carry the body down here," Craig said. "And at first glance, I don't see any obvious signs the body was lowered down by rope."

He motioned across the body from neck to buttocks.

"Even if she was lowered down after death, there would be marks or bruising, even if she had clothes on at the time, from her dead weight against the rope," Craig explained.

"Are you saying the killing was done down here?" Sam asked.

"That would seem the most logical conclusion unless the ME finds something else to indicate otherwise," Craig said.

The sheriff took out his cell phone again.

"You climb on up and have Travis call in the ME," Sam said. "I'll get some more pictures of the scene, including the walls."

"I don't think your deputy would be too keen on taking orders from a civilian," Craig said, standing. "He seemed a little pissed that I'm down here instead of him."

"Don't worry about Travis, he'll do what you ask him to do," Sam said, already shooting closeup photos of the body, not looking at Craig. "Besides, I'll make you a deputy if I have to, like Festus."

"Well, I guess that would be better than Barney," Craig said as he started the climb out of the geyser hole.

⊙∞⊙

When Sam was done with his photos, he climbed up to find that Travis and Craig had staked off a perimeter around the geyser hole and strung crime scene tape around it. Fred had also arrived from his run from Lander. Sam had Fred stay at the scene until the medical examiner arrived, and he, Travis and Craig went back to town.

Craig asked to be taken to the motel.

"We'll drop you off, but I'd like to have you come up to the substation so we can talk about this," the sheriff said.

"I don't plan on being at the motel long; I just want to check in and see what's planned for today with the reunion," Craig said.

As he walked into the motel lobby, Anna motioned him over to the office door. She handed him a zip-lock snack bag. Inside was another index card, this one with the number "8" on it in the same style as the others.

"I only handled it by the edges and put it in that bag right away," she said.

Craig stared at it for a moment.

"That was the right thing to do," he said absently.

"What does this mean?" she asked.

"It means there's been another murder," he answered.

"I know, it's all over town already," Anna said. "But why is this happening, and why are you getting these cards?"

He thought about it before answering. Getting the third card confirmed a suspicion he had since the second card was delivered to him.

"I think it's a message to me," he said. "I think whoever is doing this is doing it because of me."

Anna's face went pale, and her eyelids opened wide. She stood stock still for a few seconds.

"Oh my God!" she exclaimed. "What the hell does that mean?"

"If it means what I think it does, there are a lot of women in danger," he said.

The look of fear on her face made Craig regret that he had shared that suspicion with her.

"I don't think you would be one of those women," he said quickly. "But still, I want you to be extra careful."

"Can you stay here for a while?" she asked. "I would feel safer with you around."

"The sheriff wants me to go up to the substation to talk about what's happening, and there are some things I need to share with him," Craig said. "But I don't think I'll be gone long."

She opened the half door and stepped out of the office. She threw her arms around him and snuggled her head into his chest.

"I'll wait here until you come back, no matter how long it takes," she said.

O••O

Much of the exteriors of business buildings in Dubois had an Old West appearance. In fact, some of them were original structures built after the turn of the century. Two of the oldest in town were the general store on Ramshorn Street, just east of Craig's lodgings at the motel, and the stone bank next to the store.

The bank had been operating when Craig was in school. In fact, he had his first savings account there. But the bank was now closed, and the windows boarded up with plywood. The store was now only open for business on certain days, a requirement to keep its listing on the National Register of Historic Buildings.

But the town hall was different. Built in the late-1970s, the town hall had a more modern look. In a split-level design, the facility was built in a location where the ground begins to slope upward toward the flat-topped plateau on top of which had been located the old airport.

The town hall was built while Craig was away at college. He had toured it once during one of his visits prior to his mother's death. The interior was just as modern looking as the outside, but there were hints in the architecture of the town's western heritage.

The new town hall provided major improvements over the former facility, located within the town's former single volunteer fire department station on Horse Creek Road just off Ramshorn Street. The town hall portion was little more than a meeting room and an office for the mayor.

The new building now housed all aspects of the town administration, including the municipal court, mayor and council offices, the water and street maintenance departments, the parks department and the sanitation department. It also provided space for the county sheriff's office substation in Dubois. That is where Craig found himself, along with Sam Sharbono and his Dubois deputies.

"We've got three victims now with what appears to be the same MO, so this is officially a serial killer we're dealing with," the sheriff said to the group scattered around a small conference table. "I've called the FBI since they will have to be involved."

He paused for a moment.

"But the Denver and Salt Lake field offices are overwhelmed with cases right now, so it could be next week before any of their agents can get up here," he continued. "So, for the time being, we are on our own."

Fred and Travis looked at each other and then back to the sheriff.

"This is the biggest thing we've ever dealt with," Fred said. "We're a little out of our depth."

"I know, but I have confidence in you guys," Sam said, then looked toward Craig. "Plus, we do have another resource if he's willing."

Craig pulled the snack bag from his shirt pocket. It now contained all three index cards. He put it in the middle of the table.

"I'll help in any way I can," he said. "Since I'm kind of involved."

Chapter 9

Sheriff Sharbono and his deputies stared at the cards in the sandwich bag with puzzled looks on their faces. In unison, they looked up at Craig. Their facial expressions had changed to ones demanding answers.

"These cards showed up at my motel after each killing," Craig explained. "The first two I found propped on the doorknob of my room, and the third one was found there by the motel owner this morning while I was in Lander."

Sam reached out and pulled the bag toward him. He picked it up with his thumb and index finger on one corner. He held it up and examined it for several seconds.

"You can see they are numbered," Craig said. "The first one is '6' followed by '7' and '8'"

"What does that mean?" Sam asked, lowering the bag and setting it gently on the table. "And why did you get them?"

"It means these killings are a continuation of a series of murders in Missouri I consulted on a few years ago," Craig explained.

He then briefed the officers on the Missouri case, the one similar killing in Kansas and the Missouri police's position that their case was solved with the arrest and confession of the Kansas victim's killer. He also told them he did not agree the Missouri case was solved and why. However, the Missouri police position was strengthened when no further killings with the same MO occurred following the Kansas suspect's arrest.

"If our murders were done by the same guy, wouldn't he start his count here at seven since the Kansas murder was the sixth?" Travis asked. The three sheriff's officers looked at Craig in anticipation.

"There were five murders in Missouri. Since he started the cards here at six, that means he won't take credit for the Kansas murder," Craig said.

"Why wouldn't he?' Fred asked.

"Most serial killers are proud and possessive of their deeds," Craig said. "And they won't take credit for someone else's killing, even if the MO is the same, or even similar with minor differences."

Craig let that sink in a moment.

"Also, the fifth Missouri murder was after the Kansas guy confessed," he added. "This means he is acknowledging the fifth Missouri murder was his also."

"So why didn't he start up again somewhere else after a cooling-off period?" Travis asked.

"He might have, except that I was pretty vocal, including in the media, about my disagreement that the Missouri case was solved," Craig said. "He couldn't start up anywhere near that area any time soon after the case was considered solved without proving me right, and that would mean the Kansas City police would have to reopen the case, and that would also have brought more attention down on the case and him."

The sheriff's face took on an expression as if a light bulb had suddenly come on above his head, like in the comics when a character gets an idea.

"So this is his way of getting back at you," he said. "He wants to show you in a very up close and personal way that he's smarter than you and the rest of law enforcement."

"I'm afraid that's exactly what is going on," Craig said, sadness beginning to fill his heart. "And it has cost some friends their lives."

The four of them were silent for a moment or two.

"But how can we be sure it is the same guy and not a clever copycat?" Fred asked. "I mean, years have gone by. Why wait so long?"

"Because to do this, he needed time to do a lot of research and planning," Craig said. "A complete stranger couldn't do this on short notice."

He took a deep breath.

"And I saw things that were exactly -- not just similar -- but exactly like the cases in Missouri," he finally said. "Things that weren't released to the public, even after the case was closed by Missouri."

"Such as?" Sam asked.

"The bodies were found at dump sites, not where the killings were done; that the bodies were all face down; that while all the women appeared to be raped, no semen, fibers, hair or other DNA was found on the bodies," Craig said.

"If his pattern continues here, there is a connection between the victims," Sam said. "Was that also the case in the Missouri killings?"

"Yes, but not quite as obvious," Craig said. "In Missouri, all the victims were from the same socio-economic group. They were all working-class women who had jobs slightly above the minimum wage. I think he picked those women because they were of below-average intelligence and easily taken in."

"So, in the first two murders here, the victims were members of your graduating class," Fred said. "And both were women. Now, we have another female victim. If she was in your class that would make the pattern ironclad."

"But at the geyser, you said you believed the woman was killed at that location," Sam said. "That means it wasn't a dump site. It was the death site. That's a break in the pattern."

Craig thought for a moment while the sheriff and deputies stared in anticipation.

"Yes, but each site where bodies were found had some personal connection to me," Craig said. He explained that his family sometimes camped at the homestead cabins, his discovery of the airport as a young boy and that the geyser was a popular party spot for high schoolers.

"He could have used threats to get her to climb down into the geyser," he continued. "Or I could be wrong about her being lowered down by rope."

At that moment, Fred's cell phone chirped. He checked the text that had just come in.

"The ME wants us down at the clinic," he reported. "Dr. Hall can't identify this victim as one of his patients."

They all stood and began to leave the room.

"This could break the pattern," Travis said. "It could be a random tourist."

⊶⊷

Gathered in an unused exam room at the clinic just large enough for the three sheriff's officers and Craig to sit and stand comfortably, they begin their discussion following the wordless examination of the latest body under the watchful eye of Dr. Hall.

"This is no random tourist," Craig said, emotion cracking his voice.

"How do you know?" Travis asked.

"Because I know her, she is one of my classmates," Craig answered. "Her name is... was Valerie Morton."

There was silence in the room for a moment. Craig worked to compose himself. For most of his junior year in high school, he had actually dated Valerie. Now that he was looking over her lifeless body in a professional manner, the memories of their time together came flooding back.

Craig had thought the relationship would last. But toward the end of that school year, Valerie appeared to be losing interest in it. Eventually, they had a heart-to-heart talk and mutually decided to see other people. They remained friends, although somewhat strained from Craig's point of view.

Craig explained to the officers that he observed the same attributes with Valerie as he had seen with Jane and Janine -- strangulation, brown and gold fibers and the rest.

"So, the pattern continues," Sam said. "There is no doubt we have a serial killer here."

While the sheriff's department handled a wide variety of crimes in the county, it had never had a serial killing to deal with. Certainly not in the past several decades.

"Since we likely won't have the FBI's help for a while, you're the closest we've got to someone experienced with serial killings," Sam said to Craig. "What's our next move?"

Craig hesitated. His first instinct was to warn all the women in his class. But he wondered whether that instinct was based on emotion and his personal connection to the victims and the potential victims. He was also concerned about starting a panic, not only among his classmates but throughout the town. After all, word travels fast in a small, tight-knit community.

"I think we need to talk to my classmates, let them in on what's happening," he finally said.

"Do you think that is wise?" Travis asked, looking both at Craig and Sam. "We really don't know exactly what is going on."

"We have a responsibility to them, to let them make some decisions," Sam said before Craig could answer.

"Most of these people came in from out of town," Craig chimed in. "They may want to head back home where they are more likely to be out of the line of fire, so to speak."

"So how do we do this?" Fred asked.

"We need to get everyone from my class, whether they graduated here or not, together, and then we just lay it out for them," Craig explained.

"Just the women, since that seems to be the ones he's going after," Sam said.

"No, we should tell them all," Craig said. "The married women are going to tell their husbands, so we need to tell the single guys, too. There aren't many besides me."

Sam had a worried look on his face. Craig guessed what he was thinking.

"How are we going to keep this from spreading all over town?" Craig asked rhetorically. "We have to stress that what we tell them stays within this group and trust that they will understand."

"Good luck with that," Fred exclaimed. "I've been working small towns long enough to know that will have a snowball's chance in hell."

"There's no way we're going to get everyone in town together to share this information," Travis said.

The four of them sat silently for a couple of moments. The enormity of their challenge was hitting them like an avalanche on Grand Teton.

"We're just going to have to start with this small group and figure out the rest as we go," Sam finally said.

It was not a hard task to get the class together as by the afternoon, most were at the tavern on Ramshorn Street. Some were at the bar near Anna's motel, and a few others were scattered at different homes visiting friends and family. They were all told to meet at the tavern at four o'clock.

The tougher task was finding a location where they could all meet privately. Sam insisted it is a location as much out of public access as possible to keep others from hearing the discussions.

The community center was out of the question, and so was the school. They couldn't cordon those locations off without drawing attention to the meeting. There were few other places in town that were large enough and fit the bill for solitude. Craig suggested the general store. But Fred vetoed that idea because there was still merchandise in place throughout, and the group would be too spread out.

The solution was the old stone bank next to the store. The difficulty was how to get inside. That was solved by Tom Kincade. The fire department had a key to the empty building, and as town mayor and a volunteer fireman, he was able to get the key.

As Craig led the twenty-one remaining members of the graduating class and the six class members who had graduated elsewhere westward on the boardwalk headed for the bank, they drew some curious looks. But for those people who lived in town it was not unusual to see a group of people moving from watering hole to watering hole, even in such a large group and even during a weekday.

The more things changed, the more they stayed the same in some respects.

Kincade, the sheriff and his deputies were waiting inside the bank building. The officers and mayor had also brought some work lights from the fire station since the bank had no power connected to it, and the windows were boarded up. There was some coughing and sneezing once everyone was inside, and there was a slight haze in the bright work lights from the dust stirred up by the activity.

Sam briefed the crowd on the three deaths, sharing the names and the fact they were all part of the class in town for the reunion. He did not share the details of how the victims were killed and that they were found nude. He also left out all the other details of evidence they had gathered so far. He knew most if not all, in attendance, had already heard some of the details through town gossip. But he believed there was nothing to be gained by repeating them.

He could see that nearly every one of the class members had questions. But before he opened the meeting for them, he brought Craig to the front of the gathering.

"I'm sure you all know Craig Reilly and that he was a police officer in Kansas," Sam said. "The FBI will be joining us in this case, but most likely not until next week. In the meantime, Craig has agreed to work with us, even though he is now retired."

Craig gave a nod to his friends.

"Now, if any of you have questions, we'll try to answer them," Sam said, holding up his hand as some started to ask questions. "But please keep in mind that since this is an ongoing investigation, there is little we can say about it."

"Also, nothing we tell you should leave this room," Craig said quickly as he saw a couple of people bring up their cell phones. "We don't want to start a panic in town."

Kincade, who had only been told by the sheriff there needed to be a meeting in isolation with the class members but not the content, was the first to speak.

"What does this mean for us?" he asked. "What do we do to protect ourselves?"

"Those of you who live out of town can go home. We don't think this killer will follow you there," Sam said.

"What makes you so sure?" Roger Davis asked.

"There are no guarantees, but if we are dealing with a single killer, he most likely will stick to the area," Sam said.

"Why is that?" Kay Wallace asked.

"Because this kind of killer stakes out a territory to work in," Craig explained. "He becomes, or is already familiar with it and doesn't want to have to learn a new territory all over again."

"But why here?" Kincade asked.

Craig and the sheriff exchanged glances, and there was an awkward silence.

"We're not really sure at this point," Craig finally answered.

"Why were these particular people killed?" Karen Bullock, at the front of the group, whispered.

"That we're also not sure of," Craig said.

"Judging by the things you have said, it sounds like you expect this killer to strike again," Kincade said.

"That is a possibility," Sam said. There was a murmur that passed from the class members as a group. "But it's also a possibly that there will be no more," Craig said. "We're hoping for the best but trying to prepare for the worst."

"Since the first victims were all women, does that mean this guy is targeting only women?" Wallace asked the question that was going through all their minds.

"That's what it looks like from what we have been able to gather so far," Sam said. "But that does not mean the pattern won't change -- if it does, in fact, continue."

The room went quiet for a moment.

"You all need to make up your own minds about what to do," Craig said. "We're going to keep working the clues as we find them. We want to find this guy and put him away as quickly as possible."

"Now, if there are no more questions, we'll let you do whatever you decide to do," Sam said.

Kincade looked each of his classmates in the eye, then turned to Craig and the three law enforcement officers.

"Can you give us a few minutes alone here?" he asked. "I want to talk to everyone."

"Sure," Sam said, and the four of them started toward the door.

"Craig, please stay," the mayor said. "You are a part of this class, too, and we want you here for this."

Craig nodded and watched the sheriff and his deputies leave the bank building.

"We'll wait up by the bridge," Sam said as he shut the bank door.

Chapter 10

The steady gurgling of Horse Creek just a few feet away had Craig deep in memories from long ago. He sat motionless on the cushion of the lounge chair on Anna's deck behind the garage.

Just downstream a few yards was the site of the rip-rap half-dam held in place by a cable secured to a tree on the east bank. When his family had lived several blocks northeast of this location, he had shinnied down the cable to the thick collection of tree trunks and other debris that slowed the flow of water as it plowed south to eventually empty into the Wind River that ran through the south side of town. Once across the creek, he would climb the hill next to Horse Creek Road and descend the other side to the school.

In the coldest part of winter, the dam was unnecessary because the creek would freeze with ice thick enough to walk upon.

But the dam was gone now. Sometime after he left town, someone decided there was no real need to slow the creek down, and it was removed. In addition, a block south of where the dam had been, they built a bridge across the creek at Clendening Street. These two changes ruined the character of the neighborhood for Craig. They made the trips to school, and if it had remained in the same location, he remembered it much more convenient for youngsters of this day and age. Crossing a bridge and rounding the hill at ground level just took the sense of adventure out of it, he thought.

However, sitting on Anna's deck with the sound of the flowing water made it better. Or was it that she was sitting in a chair next to him, with her hand laying atop his, that made it better. Perhaps it was both.

"Hello, are you still with me?"

Anna's voice and her hand tapping his suddenly broke through his wall of memories. He looked over and saw her brown eyes drilling holes through his forehead as if trying to find his inner thoughts. The sun had just gone behind the hill next to the school, but there was still enough of its light to make her cascading hair take on a reddish color.

Craig hesitated, wanting to take in the sight a bit longer, to commit it to memory. She was as beautiful as he remembered, maybe even more so. Or was that just the years of separation and their sudden closeness that was making her seem so?

"I'm sorry. I remembered the old times in the neighborhood," he finally said.

Anna rolled over onto her right side. The movement exposed a great deal of cleavage in the loose-fitting white tank top she was wearing. Craig gave it a quick glance, burning that image into his brain as well.

"I was asking if you could tell me what is going on with the murders of those women," she said. "There are so many rumors going around town."

That was no surprise. Even in a vacuum of real information, small-town residents start building their own realities.

"I can't really talk about specifics of what the police have found," he answered. "I can only say it looks like it could be a serial killer."

"Jesus! Here in Dubois? That's pretty scary," Anna said, a look of fear clouding her face.

They had dinner at her house about ninety minutes ago -- a full salad followed by her home-baked apple pie -- and Craig had told her he was helping the sheriff's department with the investigation until the FBI could get agents in town. She knew how law enforcement agencies keep information close to the vest with ongoing cases and did not press during dinner. But now that they were relaxed, curiosity got the better of her.

"What are they going to do to protect people?" she asked. "Only women have been killed. Does that mean that's all the killer will go after? Will it just be women in your class?"

Craig was somewhat surprised at her knowledge of the victims in the case. But on the other hand, it was not that surprising considering the way word travels in small towns. In addition, Anna was no dummy. While she had lived most of her life in Dubois, she had gone to community college in Riverton for a couple of years and earned an associate degree. Riverton was considered a small town by most, but it was more than fifteen times the size of Dubois, and the college drew students from throughout the country. So, Anna was exposed to a larger world and a larger volume of knowledge.

"Well, that seems to be the pattern so far, but anything can change at any time," Craig said. "This could even be the end of it, but the police can't count on that."

He paused for a few moments. The first part of her question was a bit harder to answer.

"There's not a lot the police or the town can do to make sure people are protected," he said. "We had a meeting of the class and it was suggested those people who lived out of town could go home. There's little chance the killer would follow them there."

"Who is leaving?" Anna wanted to know.

"None of them," he explained. "They all decided to stay here. They all figured being together would be the best protection. They decided not to go anywhere alone, there would always be groups."

"I hope some of the guys will hang around with the women," Anna said.

"That was the idea," Craig said, then turned to look up at the darkening sky.

There were scattered clouds, but for the most part, it was clear. He was looking forward to seeing the stars. Despite the town's lights at night, it wasn't like a large city where one could barely make them out. In this rural setting, the millions of pinpricks of light were starkly visible on moonless nights. That was especially true when he spent time on his grandparents' ranch. With no town lights, more stars could be made out and constellations were clearly identifiable.

Anna continued to lie on her side, staring at him. He wore jeans and a black T-shirt with the Salina Police Department logo on the left chest. The shirt fits loosely as if he had been more buff at one time. In reality, he just preferred his shirts to fit loosely. His brown hair was thinner than when she saw him last, but there was only a hint of a bald spot at the top of his head. His facial profile reminded her of an actor she had seen in many supporting roles in movies and television programs. She remembered the actor's dimples, and during the walk with Craig from the cafe to the motel, she marveled at how similar his dimples were to the actor's.

"I would feel safer if you stayed here with me tonight," she heard herself saying before she could stop it from coming out of her mouth. He slowly turned his head to face her.

They looked deeply into each other's eyes for a moment. He was searching to see if she really meant it. Having made the request, Anna did not regret it. She was looking for a hint that would indicate his answer. He sat up and swung his legs off the lounger. He reached out and took her hand.

"I'll do whatever you would like me to do," he said softly.

⌾⋯⊙

They stayed out on the deck for another three hours. They spent much of that time talking, getting reacquainted. He already knew that Anna had been married twice before but divorced from her second husband shortly after Craig's mother's death. Both husbands were physically abusive, a common theme in those days before domestic violence was taken much more seriously by law enforcement and society at large. Craig had not known about Anna's suffering at the time. Anna was good at hiding it. But because she lived in a small town, everyone in Dubois knew.

In the twenty-two years since the divorce, Anna had dated a few men off and on but had vowed not to get involved in another romantic relationship. A couple of times, it came close when she became intimate. But she broke it off each time when the men became clingy.

She had returned to Dubois after earning her college degree and began working at the motel her parents owned. After ten years, they named her the manager, and ten years after that, she bought a third of the business. Her parents remained active in the business until they were in their late seventies, at which time they sold the remainder of the business to their daughter. They bought a large motorhome and began to travel the country. They both died within weeks of each other the previous year. Craig had heard about her parents' deaths, but not until weeks after the second passing. He had sent a sympathy card and received a thank you card in response.

Anna was a hard worker, but she also liked to play hard. She was heavily active in the town's social activities and events. She was a frequent visitor of both bars on Ramshorn Street after things had quieted down at the motel, although she took care to limit herself to two drinks -- or beers, depending on her mood -- a night. She was there for the social interaction more than the alcohol.

Craig had little to share about his life after high school that Anna did not already know. Through his mother, she kept abreast of his career. By the time she died, the Internet and email were her links. She contacted him through his work email, which she got by visiting the Salina website at least twice a year. He answered, but mostly just to say hello and say things were going well for him. He rarely asked about her. Not that he was uninterested; he just didn't want to be intrusive.

They had also seen each other during his infrequent visits to Dubois prior to his mother's death. Each time, Anna had wanted to tell him how she had always felt about him. But she never got up the courage, and then there were her two marriages. She had almost spoken to him about it twenty-three years ago when he was home for his mom's funeral, but she did not think that was the appropriate time.

And then he never returned, and she believed sharing that information through an email was too impersonal.

"I really want to thank you for your frequent visits with Mom," he said after more than two hours of reminiscing. "I feel like an idiot for not telling you that years ago."

They were lying on their sides on their loungers, facing each other. She grabbed both his hands and squeezed them affectionately.

"I was happy to do it. I loved your Mom," Anna said. "Besides, I was a little selfish about it. That was a way to know what was going on in your life."

They shared a chuckle.

"I wish we had talked like this a long time ago," Craig said.

"But we are now," she answered. "Besides, you can wish in one hand and crap in the other and see which one fills up first."

They sat up, with her still grasping his hands. With the loungers so close together, his feet and knees straddled hers. They locked eyes for a few seconds, then simultaneously began to lean into each other. Their lips met tentatively then they pulled back a few inches. After an instant, they locked lips, this time heavily for a long, delicious kiss.

Craig felt his heart beat against his rib cage. He couldn't help but wonder if she was feeling the same. As if they shared a brain, she pulled his hand toward her and placed it between her ample breasts. He could feel her heart beating like a drum.

Message given and received, she let go of his hands, threw her arms around his neck and pulled him in for another long, lustful kiss. He put his arms around her waist and pulled her toward him while he adjusted closer to her so they weren't bending at the waist quite so much.

"I have wanted to do that for so long," Anna said when the kiss finally ended.

"It was something I dreamed about back in the day," he answered.

"So why didn't you?" she asked.

"I was kind of shy, and I figured you were out of my league," he said, blushing a bit in the darkness.

She threw her head back and let out a hearty laugh with that sexy, husky tone that made Craig shiver with delight.

"What a pair we are," Anna said when the laughter faded. "And what could have been."

"Well, there's that thing with the hands you mentioned," Craig said deadpan.

"Let's take this inside," Anna said, getting up and taking one of his hands. She led him up to the house.

They made love for the next two hours. It was a bit clumsy at first. Neither had had sex in some years, so now it was like they were doing it for the first time. Craig apologized several times for his clumsiness, but she just put her index finger to his lips, and they went on.

⌾

The sun was at least thirty minutes from topping the hills east of town. But enough light streamed in from the sheer curtains on the eastern-facing bedroom window that it provided dim light in the white-painted room. Anna lay on her right side with Craig snuggled up tightly to her back with his arms tightly around her. His left arm was draped over her side and cupping her bare right breast.

His eyes fluttered open, and he realized where he was. His nose was buried in her hair, and he breathed in deeply and took in the remnants of her perfume mixed with the leftover smell of their lovemaking. His right arm was under her shoulder, and he became aware that he could not feel it from the elbow to the fingertips.

Craig tried to wriggle his finders, but they didn't move much. It was more than the numbness. He could tell there was something obstructing their movement. He could feel Anna twitch, and then she slowly untangled her fingers from his and rolled over to face him. Suddenly, he could make at least a partial fist.

"She was holding my hand," he thought.

"Good morning," she said.

"I'm sorry I woke you," he said as he bent his right arm upward. The feeling was starting to return as the full blood flow was restored.

"It's okay. I need to get up anyway," she said. "I've got to get down to the motel soon." She glanced over his shoulder at the clock and saw it was six-thirteen. The room was brightening as the seconds ticked by.

He stroked her hair with his right hand, the fingertips still tingling a little bit. He gently stroked her cheek with his other hand. Anna rubbed his side and then around his shoulder. She pulled him in for another kiss. As she pulled away, something on his forearm caught her eye. She fingered a patch of bare skin about two inches long among the thin forest of hair that covered his arm.

"What's this?" she asked. He glanced at the spot as she slowly caressed it lengthwise.

"Oh, that's a knife wound I got trying to break up a riot on the University of Colorado campus in my first job," he said.

She craned her head and gently kissed the scar.

"I got a really bad taser burn on my butt once, too," he said deadpan.

Anna propped herself up on her elbow and started to roll him onto his stomach. She pulled up the waistband of his blue briefs and began to move toward his closest butt cheek. She heard a stifled giggle, got the joke and playfully slapped his ass.

"Thank you, sir. May I have another?" she heard him say into the pillow.

She lay back on her side next to him.

"You're gonna have to earn it, mister," she said, just as deadpan as he had originally been.

Craig rolled back up on his side. He looked her over from the top of her head down to her waist, where the bedclothes still covered her legs. She had broad shoulders for a short woman, indicative of someone who did a lot of lifting. Her arms were muscular but still dainty. Her breasts were still firm, although they were starting to show a slight sag. She had large nipples surrounded by dark olive areola. Her waist was still as thin as Craig remembered, but she was showing the very beginnings of a small paunch. She was in very good shape for a woman her age.

He pulled her body into his. Her bare breasts flattened into his chest, and he gently rubbed her behind. Her silk panties felt as soft as the skin underneath. They kissed for a long moment.

"Thank you," he said when they disengaged their lips.

"For what?" she asked innocently.

"For spending this time with me," he said. There seemed to be a finality to the statement that saddened Anna.

"It doesn't have to end here," she said, running her finger across his lips.

Craig began to say something but was interrupted by the rattling of his silenced cell phone as it vibrated on the wooden nightstand. He rolled over, grabbed the phone, and pressed the "accept" button.

"We've got another victim," he heard the sheriff say excitedly. "This one is still alive."

Chapter 11

The bridge over Horse Creek in the middle of town looked much the same as Craig remembered it from his school days, even though it had been replaced when the highway was widened. As he recalled it, the bridge seemed the same width as in his youth, but in fact, it had been extended on both sides to accommodate the four lanes of traffic rather than two. The only way he could tell was the sidewalks leading to the walkways on either side were straighter rather than angled more sharply.

Except for the yellow crime scene tape under the east end, the underside of the bridge looked the same as he remembered. It was here in his freshman year he and his friends came to drink a few beers. The following year, he was there again one summer night with a couple of classmates who smoked. They urged him to try it. That was the one and only time he put a cigarette in his mouth. He finished it, but it left his throat so dry and a sooty taste on his tongue for two days. And then pot started going around in his junior year, and it was back to the bridge, among other places, to get high. The mellow buzz he got from the ganja made smoking it okay. Besides, he didn't have to inhale the smoke into his lungs to get the effects.

When he went to school in Dubois, there was very little for young people to do outside of school and related activities. There was no arcade, except for a pinball machine or two in the two food joints where the teens hung out; no bowling alley; no theater, except for short flirtations with old movies in the school cafeteria, the banquet hall at the tavern and the silent movies in the tent in a vacant lot at the corner of Riverton and Welty streets. And all of those had gone by the wayside by the time he was in high school.

So, drinking alcohol became the teen pastime, much as it was for the adults. They did it out of boredom, probably in some way to emulate the adults and because of the thrill of doing something one was not supposed to. The adults knew their kids were drinking but, for the most part, turned a blind eye to it unless it created problems they could not ignore.

Once he reached the legal drinking age in Wyoming, which at that time was nineteen, the fun was gone, and he tapered off quite a bit. He also lost the desire to get high once he was out of high school and decided on a path into law enforcement.

Now Craig was back under that bridge where he had dabbled in those taboos. But this time, he was there for a more sinister reason.

Another person was attacked and nearly killed. As he walked along the creek bank toward the knot of people -- the sheriff, his two deputies and the town's mayor -- he did not know who it was that had been assaulted. Tom Kincade cleared it up as he stepped to meet Craig.

"It was another one of us," he whispered, in case there were people on the bridge walkways who could hear. "It is DeAnn Paxton. She was life-flighted to Riverton about a half hour ago."

Craig remembered hearing something during the early morning hours. But he was so deep in sleep he couldn't identify whether it was something in a dream or reality. Now he learned it was the life flight helicopter roaring over Anna's house to land on the old football field on the other side of the hill adjacent to Horse Creek Road. DeAnn had been placed on a backboard and put in the back of one of the FCSO Tahoes to be driven the short distance to the landing zone.

Before Tom could say anything else, Craig rushed over to where the officers were huddled. On the rocky ground just below where the bridge and the upper edge of the creek bank met was a small oblong string of crime scene tape wrapped around stakes that marked a perimeter.

"She was found up there by a couple of kids who came down here for a smoke," the sheriff said. "She was naked and laying on her belly."

A chill went down Craig's spine. At that instant, his cell phone ringer went off, echoing against the steel girders under the roadway. He grabbed it and took the call from Anna.

"There is another card here, Craig," she said before he could get another word out. "It is the same as the others, and this one has the number '9' on it."

"Shit!" Craig said. If there had been any doubt in his mind, this was confirmation the same killer had struck again.

"Where are you? I can bring it to you," she asked.

Craig quickly told Sam and he dispatched Travis to go get it.

"Just put it in a baggie. A deputy is on his way to pick it up," Craig told Anna.

"Who is it, Craig? Are you alright?" she asked, worry in her voice.

"I'm fine," he said, thankful for her concern. "I can't say anything about this," he added for the sheriff's benefit, then ended the call.

"We took some real quick photos of the scene before they took her," Sam explained. "She was marked up more than the others. It looks like she put up more of a fight. But that didn't happen here."

Craig remembered DeAnn from school. She was an athletically built six-footer who played volleyball and basketball and competed in weight events in track for the Rams' fledgling girls' sports programs. Seeing her at the reunion activities the last few days showed she had stayed in pretty good shape. She was a very outgoing woman, then and now, and had played basketball in college.

"You said she was alive. Did she say anything, give a description of her attacker or anything else?" Craig asked.

"No, she was unconscious," Sam answered. "The medics said she was barely hanging on. They weren't sure she'd make it from here to the helicopter, let alone to Riverton."

"Dammit!" Craig yelled with more emotion than he intended.

"The Dubois detective was rotated to Riverton a few days ago and I've sent him to the hospital. He'll keep us posted and be there to question her if she survives the flight and regains consciousness," Sam said.

Craig sat at the dining room table at his sister Kathleen's house on the south bank of the Wind River just west of the bridge. It was a large house, too large for one person. There were two large master suites upstairs, each with its own bathroom, and a smaller suite downstairs. It was a ranch-style home with a wrap-around porch and a large wooden deck facing the river.

She had remained there following her divorce from Paul Austin several years ago because she got it in the settlement. Two years ago she had met and married Charlie Young, a career U.S. Marine Corps officer. He was stationed outside the continental United States, but Kathleen was not willing to give up her job with the town to move with him to his posting, especially since it could change at any time. So he came to stay with her when he had leave and she went to stay with him when she had vacation time. It was, more than anything, a marriage of convenience.

Craig had called his sister the previous Sunday morning to let her know he was in town, and she and Daniel had breakfast with him. He had not told her or his brother in advance that he was coming.

Kathleen came in from the kitchen and sat down near her brother. She had been getting lunch prepared while they waited for Daniel to arrive. There was very little for him to do with the sheriff and his deputies while they waited for word from Riverton about DeAnn's medical condition, so he went to his sister's earlier than they had agreed.

Prior to heading across the river he helped Anna at the motel prepare for the day. With some guests checking out during the day and others coming in to take their place, rooms needed to be cleaned and gotten ready for the new guests. New linens were stacked, and cleaning supplies were loaded on carts. When this was done, they had time to sit and talk.

"You know you don't have to stay at the motel," she said. "You can stay with me."

Craig was not surprised that Anna's bluntness had survived all these years. He thought about the offer for a moment before responding.

"That's a tempting offer," he finally said. "But that might not be the best idea."

"Why the hell not?" she asked, a little hurt that he would even consider saying no.

"Well, I don't want people all over town thinking less of you because you've got some guy living in your house," he said. It was kind of lame, he knew, but it was the first thing that came to his mind. And there was some truth to it. He cared about her and didn't want anything to blow back on her.

"What makes you think there haven't been other guys living with me?" she shot at him. In the moment she wanted to make him feel bad for his refusal. It was a feeble swipe, as there had never been a man living in any home she had since she left her second husband. But she was certain Craig did not know that.

Her attempt to sting him was only slightly successful. Craig was a little disappointed that she had been with someone else before him. However, he decided that was an unreasonable expectation. While he had not been with a woman, except for casual dates here and there, since college, to expect others to live the same lifestyle was not realistic.

"Besides, you would kind of be doing me a favor by freeing up another room at the motel," she said, regretting her implication of having other men share her bed.

"Well, when you put it that way, I'd be happy to help," he said.

As he replayed that conversation in his mind sitting at his sister's table, he suddenly realized she was talking to him.

"I'm sorry, what was that?" he asked.

"I was asking about these deaths that are happening in town," she said. "I hear you are helping the sheriff's department with their investigation."

"That's true," he said. "But I can't say much about it."

"Yeah, I know, I watch TV enough to know you can't talk about ongoing investigations," she said.

"Not just on TV," he said with a smile. "That's one thing they actually get right."

She smiled and put her hand on top of his.

"Then tell me about you and Anna," she cooed.

"Damn this small-town gossip," he thought.

"We're just getting reacquainted," he lied.

"Oh, come on, it's no secret, to me at least, that you really liked her in high school," Kathleen said.

She had been a freshman during Craig's senior year and had the chance to see how he looked at Anna and hear how he talked about her in such glowing terms. When she would confront him about it at that time, he would deny it vehemently. But even that young, she could see right through him.

"And she always asked about you all these years," she said.

Craig was a little surprised to hear that last statement. Neither Kathleen nor Daniel, in their communications with him over the years, had said anything to him about her inquiries about him. And certainly Anna never mentioned it in their infrequent emails.

"I don't know what to tell you. Right now, we're just getting reacquainted," he said.

A knock at the door interrupted their conversation. She motioned for him to answer it while she returned to the kitchen. Craig found Daniel standing on the porch when he opened the door. They hugged briefly, and Daniel came inside.

"So, how are you and Anna getting along?" was his brother's first words.

"Oh, for crying out loud in the afternoon," Craig whined. Daniel laughed, lightly punched him on the shoulder and headed for the kitchen.

⭕⚊⚊⭕

Tom Kincade's home was situated on the hill overlooking the old football field to the southeast. When Craig first arrived at the mayor's house, he walked to the hedge on the south side of the property and looked down on the field. The grass portion was still maintained, as was the running track around it, which had not been there when he was in school.

Looking down on the field, the memories of those playing days came flooding back. He and Tom had been linemen on the offense while on defense Craig had played end and Tom a linebacker. Of course, being the better athlete, Tom had seen plenty of playing time as a freshman and then was a three-year starter. Craig became a starter on offense in his junior year and played some on defense, but by his senior year, he started on both sides of the line.

He and Tom were friendly enough in high school but not real close friends. Tom had always been something of a big fish in a small pond. Handsome in a boyish kind of way but built like an athlete. In contrast, Craig was what some would call wiry. In the intervening years, Craig had filled out while Tom had lost some of his athletic form and had a pretty healthy paunch.

"Remembering the good old days?" Craig heard Tom say as he walked up beside him at the hedge.

"Yep," was all Craig said.

The two men stood for a few minutes, replaying in their minds some of the games they had participated in on the field below them.

"Come on inside, we need to talk," Tom finally said.

Craig sat in a plush armchair in Tom's and Lara's large living room. He was facing west through the large picture window with a view of the

96

western end of town and the Wind River Mountains beyond. There were two other plush chairs and a fluffy cloth-covered sofa also in the room. They were arranged around a glass-topped coffee table with intertwined polished driftwood serving as a stand. There were ornately carved end tables on each end of the sofa and matching tables to the left of each chair.

Lara was left-handed, so it was clear to Craig she had done the layout for the room.

The walls were polished native wood paneling, except for the west wall with the picture window. It was sheetrock painted white, and the large window and smaller vertical ones to either side were framed in the same polished native wood. A variety of scenic paintings adorned the walls.

Tom entered the room from the short hallway that contained a wet bar. He had tall glasses in each hand filled nearly to the top with an amber liquid and some ice cubes. He handed one to Craig and then sat in the chair to Craig's right.

"I'll come right to the point, Craig," Tom said, taking a long pull on his drink. "We've got to get the women in our class out of town."

Craig took a modest sip of his drink. The bite of some very old, very good bourbon tingled down his throat and into his stomach.

"Why is that?" Craig asked innocently.

"For their safety," Tom said calmly.

"How is disrupting the lives of these women, especially those who live and work here, going to make them safe? And why just the women in our class?" Craig asked, taking another small sip.

"We need to get them out of the line of fire, so to speak," Tom said, raising his voice just a little. He took down a heavy gulp of his drink, leaving the tall glass half full. "And all four victims have been women in our class. I'm not stupid, Craig. This is a pattern. Serial killers have victimology patterns."

"You heard them, Tom, in that meeting at the bank," Craig said. "No one wants to leave town. Even the out-of-towners said they would extend their stay until the sheriff gets a handle on this thing."

"But these women are targets," Tom said angrily. "We can't have any more killings here."

"So is it their safety you're most concerned about or the town's image?" Craig said.

Tom threw back his glass, sending another quarter of the iced bourbon down his throat.

"That's bullshit, Craig, and I resent that," he yelled. "I'm just as worried about their safety as I am about the town. But surely you can see what this will do to the businesses here. Some of the motel owners are already telling me people are canceling their reservations."

There was silence in the room for a few moments. Craig was well aware of how a killing spree affected the economy of a community. The two Kansas Cities were just now recovering from the serial killings that had happened there years before. So Tom's arguments weren't totally out of line.

"If the women aren't here, this killer will go try to find them, and we won't have the problem anymore," Tom said.

Craig took another small sip of his drink.

"Say we do get all the women in our class to leave town. Who's to say this killer won't go after other women," Craig said. "Then will you want to get all the women out of town? And if we do, what's to say the killer won't start going after men? Then we're talking about total evacuation. What will that do to the town's image?"

Tom guzzled the rest of his drink and sat sullenly for a few seconds like a schoolboy being lectured about not doing his homework.

"Serial killers are about territory and methodology," Craig explained. "This guy has staked out this town as his territory, and his method of assaulting and killing these women is well established. It is doubtful he will go chasing after the specific type of victim to who knows where. That would take more work and more resources."

He paused to let that sink in. But it didn't appear Tom was ready yet to give up on his line of thinking.

"I'll talk to the sheriff about it, but I believe it is more likely that if we start chasing people out of town, we'll just be putting more people at risk," Craig said as he stood up, leaving the rest of his nearly full drink on the coaster. "And besides, if all the women do leave and the killer goes looking for them and finds them, all we've done is pass the buck to some other community or multiple communities."

Getting no response from Tom, Craig turned and headed for the front door. The mayor was still sitting in the plush chair, staring at his feet, when Craig backed out of the driveway and headed for town hall just a few blocks away.

Chapter 12

Craig stopped at the motel to see if Anna was available for lunch. She was and suggested pizza at the shop on Ramshorn Street.

"That's okay, but let's get it to go," he told her. She was puzzled but agreed. Craig had things he wanted to talk about without prying ears eavesdropping.

Though it was a beautiful day with only scattered clouds and the temperature near eighty degrees, Craig insisted they eat inside.

"What's up?" Anna asked as they sat at the table and began to eat their pepperoni and sausage pizza.

"I just talked to Tom Kincade," Craig said after swallowing his first mouthful. "He wants to get all the women in our class out of town."

"That seems to make sense since all the victims so far have been from your class," Anna said. But she knew he did not agree. Otherwise, he would not have raised the issue.

Craig explained to her all the reasons he had thrown at Tom that moving the women out of town was not the best idea. By the time he was finished, they had each polished off one large slice of the pizza, but their appetite for more had vanished.

"I can certainly see the logic in your arguments," she said. "But as long as they stay here, they will be targets, right?"

He nodded thoughtfully but did not respond verbally.

"What does the sheriff think?" she asked as she got up and cleared the table. The remaining pizza was slipped into the refrigerator to be available for another meal.

They left the dining area next to the modest ranch kitchen and adjourned to the living room. It was not large and modestly furnished with a couch, recliner, coffee table and two end tables, one at the couch and the other at the recliner. In the opposite corner to the left of the couch was a fifty-five-inch flatscreen television mounted to the beige-painted walls. Anna had several framed photos of herself with friends from high school and beyond, and some framed scenic photos. She was a very good photographer and had taken the scenery pictures herself.

Craig sat next to Anna on the couch. He had not yet answered her question about the sheriff as he was mulling it over in his mind. Because of Sam's inexperience with serial killer cases, Craig was certain the sheriff would defer to his judgment.

"I haven't talked to him yet," Craig finally said. "I should go see him before Tom does. I probably should have gone there first. I started to, but then came here."

"Are you going to tell him not to get the women out of town?" she asked. She draped her arm around his neck and pulled him closer to her.

"I think that's the best thing," he answered, then gave her a kiss on the forehead. "If we do try to force them to leave, that could start a panic."

"You know, Tom is very controlling when it comes to this town," Anna said. "It seems to me that he looks on it like his own little kingdom. He's on his third term as mayor, and I suspect he'll run again and win."

While he had not kept up with the town politics over the years, this was not a surprise to Craig. Tom had always been controlling, in a subtle way, during their school years. He had never left Dubois, not even to attend college, since their high school graduation. He had offers of scholarships to play football, including from Wyoming and two national power schools. But he turned them all down.

Instead, he had gone to work at his father's construction company, starting as a laborer and moving through all other positions. Eventually, he took over management when his father retired and became the de facto owner two years ago when the effects of Alzheimer's began to affect his dad's ability to operate the company.

Anna told him Tom had spent several years on the town council before winning the mayor's seat on his first attempt.

"It seems, from our conversation, that he is more interested in the town's image than the people who could be in danger," Craig said.

Before Anna could respond, the ringtone on Craig's cell phone went off. He pulled the device from the holster on his belt and looked at the caller ID. It was the sheriff. He pushed the "accept call" button and raised it to his ear. Before he could say hello, he heard the sheriff's agitated voice.

"Get up to town hall," he ordered. "I've got Tom Kincade up my ass about evacuating the town."

"Give me five minutes," Craig said, then ended the call.

"Shit!" he hollered as he pulled away from Anna and stood up. She followed, a look of worry on her face.

"Is there another victim?" Anna asked, her face as pale as a ghost.

"No, your asshole mayor is raising a stink that could really screw things up," he answered.

Craig saw the color return to Anna's face. In fact, it took on an angry shade of pink. He put both hands on either side of her face and pulled her in for a long kiss.

"I've got to go, but I'll keep you posted," he said as he headed for the door.

Anna watched anxiously from the front window. Craig went to the passenger side of his truck, opened the door, reached in and brought out an ankle holster. She watched as he strapped it on, then pulled a handgun from the truck and put it in the holster, pulling his pant leg down over it. Having grown up and lived in Dubois nearly all her life, Anna was very familiar with firearms. She recognized it as a Sig P365. He then shoved a Glock 17 into a clip holster and anchored it on his belt in front of his cell phone holster. His shirt was untucked but remained behind those two implements. They were visible for all to see.

Anna's anxiety rose as he jumped in the driver's side and, backed out of the driveway and roared down the street.

⌗

When Craig walked into the town hall lobby, Kathleen was there waiting for him.

"I heard Sam call you, so I came down to wait for you," she said. "They are all in the council chambers."

Until he had come to the sheriff's substation days before, Craig had never been in the new town hall. He gave his sister a questioning look, and she motioned for him to follow.

"What's going on?" she asked as they hurried toward the stairs to the second level. "They are yelling back and forth in there."

"Your mayor wants people to leave town," he answered automatically. He suddenly stopped and looked around. No one else was within earshot.

"Keep that to yourself, okay." he requested. She nodded. He gave her a hug, and she pointed toward the council chambers doorway and he went inside.

Sam and Tom were in the middle of a full-throated argument as Craig shut the door behind him and walked toward them. The two deputies were standing side-by-side, watching the exchange. The bickering stopped as Craig drew near. Tom rolled his eyes and threw a disgusted look at the newcomer.

"Can you please talk some sense into this guy?" Sam said, turning toward Craig and pointing toward the mayor.

"I thought I had," Craig responded, looking at Tom.

"We have to think of the safety of our people," the mayor said sheepishly, hanging his head.

103

The group stood in front of the council dais. The only light in the empty room was a single fixture from behind the slightly curved wooden backdrop pointed up to the white ceiling to provide reflected lighting.

"Evacuating this whole town simply is not going to happen," Sam said with finality. "For starters, the sheriff's department does not have the manpower to make that happen. And frankly, we don't have the authority to order it."

"Who does?" Tom asked, raising his head with a little hope in his eyes.

"Theoretically, the governor could order it by declaring a state of emergency," Sam explained. "Which this is not," he added forcefully when Tom raised his index finger and began to speak.

"And if you think the business owners in town are going to close up shop and leave, you're nuts," Craig said. "The only way they will go is by force."

"And no one, not the governor, not the county commissioners and certainly not me, wants that," Sam said.

"Then what the hell are we supposed to do? Live in fear?" Tom asked.

Sam heaved a heavy sigh and subconsciously put his hands on his hips, his right hand coming to rest on the butt of the Glock 19 in its holster. It was a stance he made multiple times a day without even thinking about it. It was not meant to be a gesture of intimidation or aggression, just a natural movement for him.

Tom noticed the placement of the sheriff's hand and took it in a totally different way. He glanced at the deputies to his right. Travis stood with his arms crossed on his chest, a holstered Glock on his belt. Fred had his right hand holding his utility belt just in front of his holstered Glock and the left hand in a similar position on the other side. The mayor turned toward Craig and, for the first time, noticed the weapon on his hip.

The horrified look on Tom's face made Sam follow his gaze and the sheriff also noticed for the first time that Craig was armed. His expression remained poker-faced, but he made a mental note to talk with Craig about that later.

"So, that's what it's come to? Are we going to be a real Wild West town? Vigilantes everywhere," Tom whined.

The mayor was not as into guns as a lot of people in and around Dubois. That area of Fremont County was known for its big game hunting, both for locals and out-of-staters. Tom owned only one gun, a Winchester Model 70 that he used for hunting deer and elk, and only hunting. For many in the small town, hunting the big bulls and bucks was less about sport and trophies and more about stocking the freezers with meat for the winter, especially with the cost of groceries continually climbing the ladder.

"No, this is not going to become the Wild West," Sam said, then added only half sarcastically, "Unless your rantings about evacuation get people so stirred up that it leads to that."

Tom's face turned a bright pink.

"So you need to not say another word about that subject," Sam ordered. "And if the subject does come up, you treat it like a joke or a slip of the tongue."

"Wyoming is still an open carry state, is it not?" Craig asked, looking straight at the mayor, knowing full well the answer. Tom did not answer. Craig looked toward Sam, who nodded.

"Your rantings about evacuating will cause a panic and create that vigilante ball rolling," Craig said.

"I have only spoken to you and the sheriff about this," Tom protested.

"This room is not completely soundproof," Craig said. "My sister heard you guys arguing in here. Who knows who else might have heard it and even picked up on what you were saying."

"Oh great," Sam said in disgust.

With that, the sheriff turned on his heel and headed for the door, with a quick glance at Craig that said, "Follow me." The two deputies trailed their boss and Craig out the main door to the council chambers.

Tom stood in the semi-lit room for several minutes, alternating between anger and embarrassment.

⊶

Sam sent the deputies out to perform their regular patrols and to answer a few calls that had come in during the heated discussion in the council chambers. Once they had departed, Sam motioned for Craig to follow him. They got into Craig's truck, and the sheriff instructed him to drive up to the old airport on the plateau above the town hall. They parked at the far east end facing west on the worn track that was once a dirt runway but now served as the raceway for the annual chariot races. The truck was running to allow the air conditioner to keep them cool.

"First things first, it probably isn't a good idea to be parading around town with a visible pistol on your hip," Sam said. "Open carry state or not, that could also start a panic."

"Sam, I know this town," Craig started to say, but the sheriff interrupted.

"You knew this town, but that was a long time ago. Things change," he said.

"One thing about this town that never changes is everyone knows everyone's business eventually," Craig said. "I've heard it said that if you go for a walk in the woods, everyone in town will know where you went and what you were doing before you got back."

"And gossip will have twisted the story so badly that you would have screwed a few wood nymphs while you were out there," Sam said. "I've heard that, too."

Craig chuckled a little, and Sam joined in. Through all the years he had lived in Dubois, Craig had heard that story retold so many times it was embedded into his brain. Except he'd never heard the wood nymph version before.

"In all the time I spent in the woods around this town, if only I'd run across some wood nymphs," Craig said.

"Yeah, knowing my luck, if I found one, she's be fat and ugly," Sam said.

The two men laughed out loud, which seemed a bit morbid considering what had been happening in the town the last several days. But when people get caught up in very tense situations, a little levity always helps to keep one's thoughts on an even keel.

"Seriously, though, we've got to figure out what to do if this mayor's paranoia starts seeping out," Sam said as their laughter subsided. "People start hearing things like evacuation, and all kinds of emotions are going to erupt. Hell, with three women killed and another one nearly so, it amazes me we haven't seen that already."

"I think most people are in a little bit of shock and a lot of denial," Craig said. "In bigger cities, this is almost a routine thing, but it is almost unheard of in small towns."

"I don't know, there is always that Starkweather case," Sam said.

Charles Starkweather was nineteen years old when he killed eleven people in Nebraska and Wyoming between November 1957 and January 1958. Most of the murders were committed in Nebraska, but he and his accused accomplice, Caril Fugate, fled that state into Wyoming. His last victim was a traveling salesman, killed near Douglas, Wyoming, east of Casper and two hundred forty-three miles from Dubois.

"That was a long time ago, and most people now don't even remember it or know anything about it unless they look it up on the Internet," Craig said.

"Which they might," Sam said.

Craig agreed that was a possibility. But he thought it would be insignificant. Starkweather's last victim was killed a long way from Dubois, and the case was very different than the one they now faced. Still, it had to be factored into the equation.

"So you think this mayor will back down on this evacuation thing and keep his mouth shut?" Sam asked.

"I don't know," Craig said. "I didn't know him that well in high school, except that he liked being important and the attention it brought him."

They sat in silence for a few moments. Both deep in his own thoughts.

"Well, we're just going to have to play things by ear," Sam said. "I don't know what we can do to keep a lid on the mayor except lock him up in Lander, and that just won't fly."

Craig turned the knob to put the Ram into drive and began to roll down the chariot track.

"Listen, I think I need to stay here at least until the FBI gets here," Sam said. "But I need a place to stay and some way of getting around. My deputies only have two cars here, and I don't want them tied down."

"I think I can help with both of those needs," Craig said.

Chapter 13

Anna was delighted when Craig called the motel. Of course, she was glad to hear his voice. But that excitement was enhanced when she was informed she would be getting another guest.

So far, she had no registered quests canceling the remainder of their stays and leaving town. But she was also not getting any additional bookings. Sheriff Sam Sharbono was booked into the room that Craig had vacated. It would not only be a place for him to lay his head at night -- if there was any sleep to be had, that is -- but as a secondary office. The booking was open-ended and paid for by the county.

Sam assured Anna that the county would pay extra for the room to allow him to use the laundry facilities. He had brought a "go bag" with him on the helicopter with toiletries and a couple of days' change of clothing. But he wanted to be able to wash his clothes if his stay was extended more than overnight.

"You just give me any clothes you need done, and I'll put it in with the rest of the daily stuff," Anna told him when he checked in.

"Thank you," he said. "But the county will still pay the extra for your trouble."

She told him it would be no trouble, but he insisted. Anna offered another half-hearted refusal to take the money, but when he persisted, she accepted.

The sheriff also had some wheels for getting around town and the surrounding area, thanks to Craig's call to his sister at town hall. She arranged to allow Sam to drive one of the town's volunteer fire department's four-wheel-drive crew cab pickup trucks used as a command vehicle during fire events. It was a reserve vehicle and was equipped with a powerful two-way radio, emergency lights and a siren.

Sam also insisted the county pay to use the truck. Kathleen did not protest.

"Thanks for helping get me set up," Sam said as he and Craig walked out of the motel. "This will help me stay on top of things here."

"Not a problem," Craig said as both men began walking toward the fire station a couple of blocks away on 3rd Street. "It's good to have contacts, even after all this time."

They walked in silence the rest of the way to the station. Once they were inside and had gotten the truck keys, Sam detoured Craig to a small room. He gestured for Craig to take a seat, and he sat opposite him.

"I've got to talk to you about this," he said, pointing to Craig's right hip where the Glock rested in its holster. Craig glanced down and then back at the sheriff.

"Why all of a sudden do you feel you need to be armed?" he asked.

"You mean besides the fact that there is a serial killer loose in my hometown killing my classmates?" Craig asked with a sprinkling of sarcasm.

"I know you were in law enforcement, but even if you weren't retired, you would be out of your jurisdiction," the sheriff said.

"I thought you wanted my help in this investigation," Craig said.

"I do, as a consultant," the sheriff said. "But you need to leave that part," pointing to the gun, "to the duly sworn officers."

Craig bolted out of his chair, turned his back on Sam and paced three steps to the wall. He paused there for a moment, then whirled on his friend.

"I have the right of personal protection, just like everyone else," he said. "And I'm not just talking about myself."

"Yes, your brother and sister, I know," Sam said. "And Anna."

Craig tried to shoot daggers out of his eyes at Sam, but they came out more like Nerf darts.

"Why bring her up?" he asked.

"Oh, give me a break," Sam said. "I knew how you felt about her way back then. You weren't bashful about telling my dad all about it."

Craig blushed a little. When he felt the warmth in his cheeks, he took a deep breath to calm his embarrassment.

"I know you were staying in the motel because she called about that card that was left at your door. But she also told me, when you were out of earshot when I checked in, that I was in your original room," Sam said. "Where are you staying now? Not with your sister, I'll bet."

Craig's blush returned, but this time, he made no attempt to try and hide it.

"I don't want things to get out of hand because you are too close to this," Sam said.

Craig slapped his open hand on the table. It echoed in the nearly empty room. But Sam half expected it, so it didn't startle him.

"You don't think I'm professional enough to keep my cool in a crisis?" he asked. His tone indicated to Sam that he was stung by the implication.

"I trust you, and I trust your professionalism," Sam said. "It's the rest of this town I have a problem with."

"The rest of this town?" Craig asked, a little confused.

"You saw how the mayor reacted. He is in panic mode. You know that can't help but be seen and spread," the sheriff said. "And when people see you -- or anyone -- waltzing around with a gun on their hip, there will be more. And pretty soon, this will be just like an old west town with vigilantes behind every sagebrush."

Craig thought about that for a few moments while Sam patiently waited. He remembered how things were back in the day. At that time, just about every pickup in town had a gun rack hung over the back window with at least two rifles in it. People showed off their handguns in public, bragging and exercising some oneupmanship. You show me yours and I'll show you mine kind of thing.

But at that time, school and other mass shootings were almost unheard of. Now, they were so common, and there was such a push to disarm even the everyday citizen that even seeing a gun in public could start a riot. Craig could not bring to mind even one pickup he had seen since coming back to town with gun racks in the back windows.

However, he knew there were enough residents in the community who had grown up there during those simpler, more innocent times that those attitudes were just below the surface. Besides, there are many ways to carry firearms in a vehicle besides displaying them in a gun rack in the back window.

"The more things change, the more they stay the same, I suppose," he said out loud. Sam did not respond.

"I won't give up my rights under the law," Craig said. "But I'll compromise."

He reached down and lifted his shirttail from behind the grip of his weapon and dropped it on the other side. The shirt was long enough to cover the pistol and the holster. He spread his arms out with his palms up in a "ta-da" gesture.

"I can live with that," the sheriff said.

After a brief dinner at her home, Anna and Craig went to the tavern where nearly all of Craig's class, along with many other residents and tourists, had gathered for another night of drinking and swapping stories. Since it was the middle of the week, the amount of residents in attendance was smaller than the weekend crowd.

Craig's group stayed together for the most part. Many of them were curious about the murder investigation. Because word had spread that he was consulting with the sheriff's department, large knots of his classmates gathered around him and peppered him with questions -- some subtle, some not so much.

"I really can't talk about it in detail, only to tell you what you already know," he had said more times than he could count.

Because the establishment would be crowded, the chances of someone bumping into him and noticing a gun on his hip were high, he left the Glock in his truck. However, the Sig remained in its holster strapped to his right ankle.

Craig did notice two of his classmates, Roger Davis and Austin Adams, were openly carrying firearms, a Smith and Wesson 686 Plus Deluxe in a western-style holster and a Smith and Wesson Model 327 in an open-top belt holster, respectively. Both men occasionally drew stares from people Craig could see were out-of-staters while residents didn't take notice of the pistols.

It was closing in on nine o'clock in the evening when Craig, caught in another of those knots of classmates fielding questions he could not answer, met the eyes of Anna across the room. She had stayed at Craig's side most of the night but, from time to time, went to say hello to some of her friends, only a few of which Craig knew from school. She was in just such a gathering when his eyes locked with hers. She smiled toward him, but he could see it was a strained smile. Without moving her head away from him, her eyes darted to the left toward the tavern's main entrance. Craig nodded and excused himself from the group that surrounded him.

As he moved toward the door, he could see her disengage from her friends and head for the same destination. They met just outside on the boardwalk. She slipped her arm through his and turned him toward the intersection of Ramshorn and 1st streets. Without a word, they crossed the street, first waiting for three cars to pass, going in opposite directions.

"I needed to get out of there," Anna finally said as they started walking west on the north side of Ramshorn. Their pace was slow and leisurely.

"Thank you for that," Craig said, squeezing her arm, thus pulling her closer to him. "Everyone kept asking me about the murders and what I knew about the investigation. But I can't share most of what I know."

She looked up at him as they continued to walk. She felt somewhat privileged because he had shared a few details with her that she knew he had not with others. Without seeing her gaze, he somehow knew she was looking at him. He turned his head and looked down into her beautiful face. Simultaneously, they stopped walking, and he leaned down and kissed her.

She was wearing cutoff jean shorts, a little frayed at the cut, and a short-sleeved light pink blouse. The top two buttons were undone, and he could see the light bra she was wearing barely contained her breasts. Her long auburn hair was trailing down her back. Her brown eyes seemed more like a golden color, and there was a shimmering to them as if they were covered in glitter.

"You have the prettiest green eyes," she said as they stood staring at each other directly across the street from the tavern entrance. "I have never seen a man with green eyes."

He turned his head to look straight ahead and resumed the slow walk, hoping she did not see him blush.

As they walked, several people came out of the tavern and briskly traveled west on the south side of the street. Craig guessed they were people switching bars, as often happened. The town's other bar was only two-and-a-half football fields west on Ramshorn Street. An easy walk, even for those who were drunk. He did not recognize any of them, so he assumed they were tourists, but they could just as well have been residents he had never met. Other than that group, the streets were empty of pedestrians.

"Are you scared of what's going on in town?" Anna suddenly asked.

Craig considered the question until they were in front of the pizza restaurant a block from the bridge. It was a new establishment, not the one he remembered from his youth that was one of the teen hangouts. The lights were off in the main part of the building, but he could see some lights in the back as the employees were finishing the tasks of closing it up for the night.

"I suppose in a way I am," he finally answered. "But I'm more concerned than scared."

"Concerned about what?" she asked.

"I'm concerned that we are not anywhere near figuring out who is doing the killing," he said, giving her more information than he had anyone else during the night but without sharing specific details.

"That's what scares me, too," Anna said.

"I wouldn't worry too much if I were you," he said gently, then lowering his voice. "So far the pattern is he is going after only the women in my class. You should be safe."

"But will that always be the case?" she asked as they took three steps downward from the elevated boardwalk in front of a souvenir shop and were steps away from the bridge's pedestrian walkway. "I've read enough and seen enough on TV to know that could change."

"TV shows are not reality," he said as they stepped onto the bridge. He was keenly aware they had found the latest victim just that morning, only feet below where they were walking.

"I'm not talking about TV shows. I've seen this on news programs and read it in true-life crime stories," she said.

As they continued across the bridge, Craig listened to Horse Creek babble its way to its meeting with the Wind River. The mountain snowmelt had long since faded and the creek was at its normal levels. During the peak flood season in May and June, there were times you could hardly hear someone right next to you speak while on the bridge. The flow of water was so noisy. And it spilled out of its banks in certain spots.

"Well then, it could happen that the killer could change his victim pattern," he said. "But I believe that would only happen if his preferred targets were not available."

"You mean if Tom got his way and got your classmates to leave town," she said.

"That's right," he confirmed.

"Well," she sighed, "That doesn't make me less scared."

Craig was of the same mind but did not share that with Anna.

As they passed the other bar, with its door propped open, they could see inside that it was only about half full. This bar had a darker atmosphere than the tavern, both literally and figuratively. Even though the lighting inside was darker, Craig spotted the knot of people he had seen leave the tavern and head this way. They were sitting at a table in the middle of the room, deep in what appeared to be serious conversation. He caught a glimpse of a handgun on one man's hip, but he could not tell the type.

When Craig and Anna got to the motel, she went inside to check on things. When she returned, they got into her Jeep Wrangler and drove to her house.

As they passed the bar, a man was standing in the main doorway. He had gone there once Craig and Anna had passed by on foot and watched their progress. He continued his vigil while Craig stood out in front of the motel, and Anna went inside, then watched her emerge. They went around the corner of the building, and moments later, the Jeep pulled out onto Ramshorn Street.

After the vehicle went by the bar, the man turned and looked at his comrades, another man and a woman, sitting at the table in the center of the room. He nodded to them, and they both stood and walked toward the front door.

Chapter 14

Craig's eyes fluttered open. He found himself lying naked against a bare, warm, soft body. They were both on their left sides. Craig's right arm was wrapped around her body, with her left breast cupped firmly in his hand. His left arm was under her neck and outstretched on the other side. Her arms hugged his right arm tightly.

He could feel her heavy breathing and a quiet, steady snore escaping her nose with each inhale.

Not a speck of light peeked in through the tiny gaps at the ends of the closed blinds and curtains covering the window. That told him that sunrise was still a ways off. But just how much he could not tell. He wanted to glance over Anna at the digital alarm clock on the nightstand but resisted because he did not want to wake her. She needed the sleep. Besides, he was so comfortable with her clamped tightly to him he did not want it to end. He tried to picture this happening for the rest of his life. But the realities of the past few days kept interrupting those pleasant thoughts.

There was something about these murders in Dubois that had puzzled him almost from the start. There were so many similarities to the Kansas City murders he had consulted on a few years ago it was hard not to believe they were connected in some way. He had entertained the idea that the killer in both cases was the same and had shared that with the sheriff and his deputies.

But that was hard to reconcile because of the time and the distance between the crimes. It was not necessarily unusual for a spree killer to go dormant for a period of time and then start again. Precedent had also established that serial killers could change locations. However, it was rare for a killer to go dormant and then start again and change locations.

But it had been done, so Craig had to admit it was possible this was the same killer as in Kansas City. Remote, maybe, but still possible.

It was odd that the killer would go from a large city to a small rural environment. That would reduce the targets considerably. The Kansas City killer, like in Dubois, had targeted only women. But there were so many more in a metropolitan area. And the Dubois killer had further reduced the targets by, so far, killing only women in a specific high school graduating class.

In the back of Craig's mind, the theory continued to grow that he, in fact, was somehow the link between the two sprees. But why?

Until he had some firm answers, he did not want to share his entire theory with the sheriff. He wanted Sam's full focus on following what clues they had in hopes they would eventually lead them to the killer.

As he lay there thinking, Craig had also geared his mind to receiving another phone call telling of another attack or successful killing. But after some time passed -- he guessed about an hour -- there had been no phone call.

It was at that point that Anna's snoring halted, and her breathing became lighter. She loosened her grip on his arms and slowly rolled toward him until she was lying on her back. He leaned down and kissed her.

"Good morning, beautiful," he said in a low and raspy voice that was typical for him until he'd had water or coffee.

"God, you sound so sexy in the morning," she responded in her own husky, sensual tone.

She pulled him over on top of her, and they repeated the lovemaking performance they had played out just four hours ago.

Anna showered first after they grudgingly tore apart from each other. Craig emerged from the shower to find a hearty breakfast of fried eggs, biscuits, gravy, and bacon and toast waiting for him on the dining table. It was still steaming. Anna placed a smaller portion on the oak table and sat down around the corner of the square from him. They ate in silence for a few moments.

"What's on your agenda today?" Anna finally asked when she had only a few bites of breakfast left.

Craig was in the middle of taking a few gulps of grapefruit juice to wash down his latest mouthful. He still had about half his helpings left to eat.

"Well, I'll probably go see what the sheriff has in the way of new information," he said after swallowing. "I didn't get a call this morning, so I'm assuming we don't have a new victim."

Anna shuddered visibly as she finished her last bite of bacon.

"I still find it hard to believe that three people have been killed and another one's near death," she said. "That's just unheard of here."

The same sense of disbelief had filtered through Craig's mind. But mixed with those thoughts were the memories of seeing the bodies of all the dead women. And to make it worse, they were women he knew. That brought the same sense of hybrid fantasy/reality into his thoughts.

"I just don't understand how a person can do those things to another human being," she said.

"There are a lot of strange and sick people out there, Anna," Craig said.

"But never in my wildest dreams did I imagine this could happen here," she said. "We've never had anything like this. It has never been perfect, but it has been relatively crime-free."

Pangs of guilt began to rise up in Craig, a new sensation that had not come to him when he first began forming his theory that he was the connection between the Kansas City and Dubois murders. He started to feel nauseous, and he pushed away his plate with remnants of egg, biscuits, gravy, bacon and toast still aboard. Anna was a little surprised, as she had never seen him leave any part of a meal unfinished, both during their school days together and since he had been back in town.

Craig's guilt came from his growing theory that he might somehow be the connection between the Kansas City and Dubois murders. If he was correct, the lives of three women -- and nearly a fourth -- were snuffed out because of him. And how many more might there be? How could he stop this cycle of killing in his hometown, among the people he knew and cared about?

More importantly, how could he live the rest of his life knowing that he had caused these deaths?

He began to tremble. So much so that Anna reached out her hand and placed it on his that was grasping his knee. She could see his eyes were watery, just on the verge of dropping tears down his cheeks. He stared straight ahead and did not react to her touch.

"What's wrong, Craig?" she asked worriedly.

"Nothing," he stammered after a few seconds of hesitation. She knew it was a lie.

"Don't give me that 'nothing' shit," she said firmly, squeezing his hand. "I know something's wrong. What is it?"

He slowly turned his head to face her. He had gone pale, and his eyes were still moist. He was trembling even harder. Anna could tell he was preparing to say something. But the pained look on his face told her he either did not want to share it or it was difficult for him to find the right words.

"Come on, you can tell me. You are safe with me," she said in a softer, coaxing tone.

He opened his mouth as if to speak but then closed it again. The anguish grew deeper. She squeezed his hand again.

"I think I'm the reason these women are dead," he suddenly spewed.

Anna was taken aback for a moment, not sure she heard him correctly. She stared at him. The color began to return to his face, but the pained expression remained.

"What do you mean?" she asked, still gripping his hand. "You didn't kill anyone."

"I didn't do the actual killing, but I am the reason they are dead," he said.

Anna shook her head.

"I don't understand," she said.

"I am the connection between the Kansas City murders and the ones here," he said.

"How do you know that?" she said. "How could you know that for sure?"

Slowly and carefully, Craig shared all the details of the Kansas City murders and that investigation with Anna. He explained how the Kansas City authorities had found no physical evidence that pointed to a suspect, how they had closed the case after the one murder across the river that was almost the same but not quite. He also told her how he had disagreed with their decision and that he had been quite vocal about it.

"The killings stopped there, probably because the killer wanted to make it look like the police were right and they had caught the guy," Craig said. He was a little more under control of his emotions, but the guilt still nagged at him.

"But he wanted to keep on killing. He knew that if he started up again, they would have reopened the case," Craig said. "I suspect he was scouting out new locations and then he somehow found out about this reunion."

"But you told me you made the decision to come at the last minute," Anna said. "You didn't even tell your brother and sister you were coming."

"He wouldn't have known I might not have come, but he could have gone ahead hoping some killings would draw me here," Craig said. "And he would have been right, and I would have come once I heard what was happening."

He then shared with Anna all the details of the Dubois killings and how they were mirror images of the Kansas City killings.

"It has to be the same guy," he said. "And the only reason he would have chosen Dubois is because of my connection here."

"It could be a coincidence," Anna said, not even sure she believed that was possible.

"That would be, I believe, the most wild-ass coincidence in the world, don't you?" he asked. She slowly nodded.

Craig's demeanor changed a little. Anna could tell guilt was still hammering at his brain.

"Whether this nut job came here because of you or not, those deaths are not your doing," she said, reaching for his other hand and pulling his body around in the chair to face her fully. "You did not kill those women. He did. It was his sick-ass choice to do it, not yours."

Her words soothed him a bit, although the guilt did not fully leave him. She stood and pulled him out of his chair. She looked deeply into his eyes, then threw her arms around him and squeezed as tight as she could, her face buried into his chest.

"I believe in you," she said, then added, "I love you."

Those last three words shocked him a bit but, at the same time, warmed his heart.

"I love you, too," he said and felt a tear roll down his cheek. He could feel the front of his T-shirt start to get damp then heard Anna softly sobbing. They stood that way for a few moments, and when he took her shoulders and pushed her away from his chest, but with her arms still wrapped around him, he looked down at her. He wiped the tears from her face.

"Why did it take this long?" he asked.

"Because you ran off to be a cop," she said with a little chuckle.

"True, that is my fault," he said.

"Asshole," she said.

"Bitch," he responded.

They burst out laughing.

⊙—⊙

"Now, you have to promise me you won't repeat anything I said to you about these two cases, not to anyone," he said as he stood by the front door, preparing to leave.

"I won't," she said. "You can count on me."

They shared a long kiss, and then he opened the door, stepped out onto the porch, and began walking toward the driveway. He heard the door shut behind him. She also needed to get on with her day.

The front porch extended to the corner of the house, where three steps led to the driveway. The porch wrapped around the house to the small deck in the back. As Craig passed the corner just a few feet away from the steps, he felt a sharp pain in the side of his head, and some strong grips took hold of his arms. With his right ear ringing and his head throbbing, he was forced around to the back deck.

Once there, he was thrust up against the house. Facing it, he smelled the peeled logs that covered the walls. He could not see who it was that had him held captive, but he could tell there was a man on either side of him. He suddenly felt a third person jam something into his lower back. He recognized it as a pistol barrel.

"You're going to tell us who is killing the women around here," he heard a female voice snarl into his left ear. He could tell from the way her chin rested on his shoulder that she was a few inches shorter them him.

123

At the same time, he felt the woman kick each of his ankles in turn outward so that he was spread eagle.

"I have no idea who it is," Craig said.

He felt the unmistakable pain in his groin as the woman brought her knew up sharply into his balls. The pain radiated upward into his belly, and he felt a little dizzy.

"This ain't no dainty city girl," he thought through the pain. *"This is a farm girl. These aren't tourists."*

"We're not stupid," she said. "You're working with the cops. They know, so that means you know."

"That is where you are mistaken," Craig said, forcing each word out against the continued pain in his crotch and tensed to be ready for another crack of his nuts.

Before it came, however, he felt the man to his right loosen his grip slightly. Craig turned his head against the smooth logs so he was now facing to his right. He noticed the man's face was as white as a ghost, and beyond it, he could see the barrel of a Browning break action over-under shotgun pressed against the man's cheek.

"Let him go," he heard Anna's voice from around the corner of the house.

The man loosened his grip a little more and looked back with his eyes without turning his head toward the woman behind Craig.

"I've got a gun on his spine," the woman said.

"And I've got a shotgun to this guy's head," Anna said. "If I pull the trigger, it will blow his head clean off, and the next barrel will be for you."

"I'm letting go," the man said, terror dripping from his lips.

"Slide sideways," Anna said, keeping the shotgun barrel on his cheek and remaining unseen around the corner. The man, tall and skinny, obeyed. "Now on your knees." He complied again, with the shotgun pushing his head around so he was facing the remaining three.

"Now toss your gun to the back of the deck," Anna ordered.

The woman hesitated. Craig's guess was correct. She was a farm girl. She was stocky with muscular arms and legs. Her torso was built like a man's -- no hourglass figure and a barrel chest with smaller breasts.

"Do it for God's sake," the man hollered. She dropped the weapon straight down on the wood planks of the deck.

Just then, they all heard a faint siren coming from downtown. It began to grow louder as it came up Horse Creek Road. The man to Craig's left, who was similar in build to the farm girl, loosened the grip on his arm, and Craig shoved him aside and whirled around to face the woman. He grabbed her by the throat with his left hand and drew his Glock, which they had not noticed under his untucked shirt. He put the barrel to her forehead.

"Jesus Christ," he heard the man to his left say. But he stayed where he was.

Craig backed the woman up and sat her on one of the lounge chairs. He turned to the man to his left and motioned for him to take a seat next to the woman. He complied meekly.

Anna motioned the other man to sit with the others, which he did. Anna and Craig kept their guns leveled on them. The siren had made the turn onto the upper creek bridge and was now near Anna's house. The three attackers were younger than Craig and Anna, in their late twenties or early thirties, he guessed.

They sat on the lounge chair with their hands on their laps. They looked to Craig like the famous three monkeys, only they were definitely not making the "hear no evil, see no evil, speak no evil" gestures.

Chapter 15

Sheriff Sharbono was in the conference room at the town hall with Anna. The two of them were alone in the large room with the big oval oak table and twelve chairs evenly spaced on both sides. It made the table and chairs seem excessive. It also made the town staffers who had their meeting interrupted a bit peeved now that they were transplanted to the council chambers.

But he wanted her to be where she would feel comfortable, or more comfortable than the cramped quarters of the sheriff's tiny rooms. He didn't want her to feel like she was in an interrogation room, like on television shows such as "Homicide Hunter," which were about real-life murder cases.

He had done the same when he interviewed Craig about the incident at Anna's house. The sheriff, though, had no such compassion for the three suspects. Each was being interviewed individually in rotation by Fred in the sheriff's break room while the other two sat handcuffed in the small squad room under Travis' watchful eye. The squawk of the police radio combined with the sound of the small TV tuned to a news channel kept the waiting pair from hearing clearly any of the conversations from the adjoining break room.

"How did you know there was a problem outside?" Sam asked Anna after she related her version of events.

"I thought I heard Craig holler at me," she said. "I thought he might have forgotten something. I started to go out the front door but heard footsteps on the porch heading for the back."

Sam had his notepad and a pen out, but he was not writing anything down. Her version matched Craig's almost identically, although he could not explain what Anna had heard or seen inside the house.

"I grabbed my phone and called 9-1-1 and told the dispatcher my location and that I thought someone was trying to break into the house," she explained. "I got the shotgun out of the closet and went out the front. As I went along the side of the house and got closer to the deck, I could hear what they were saying, and I saw the guy holding Craig on that side."

"Which side was that?" Sam asked.

"It was just around the corner of the house," she said. "They had him pinned with his front to the house, so I would have been to his right side."

"Did you relay that to the dispatcher?" the sheriff asked.

"I didn't want them to hear me, so I left the connection open and put the phone here," she said, pointing to her cleavage.

Sam followed her gesture, then blushed when he realized he had kept his gaze there longer than necessary. Anna's mouth curled up on the left in a small yet somewhat satisfied smirk.

"Men," she thought.

"And that's when you stuck the shotgun barrel into that guy's face?" he asked, mostly to cover his embarrassment.

"Yep, and then we took them down just like I said before," she said.

"But why call 9-1-1 and get a weapon before you knew for sure there was a problem?" he asked. "It could just as well have been Craig going back to the deck for some reason."

She shook her head.

"I knew something was wrong because I could tell by the noise on the wood deck that there was more than one person there," she answered. "I grabbed the shotgun because who knows what was going on, what with these women dying in town."

Anna was careful not to use the word "murders." She didn't want the sheriff to know that Craig had been sharing details of the case with her. But Sam guessed that Craig was supplying her with information. It made little difference to him, though. He was confident in Craig's professionalism and that he was not sharing with anyone other than Anna, a woman he was so close to and trying to protect. Through his father, he also knew Anna well enough to know she was not involved in town gossip and could be trusted to keep what information Craig gave up to herself.

The Sheriff nodded, satisfied that he had heard the truth from both of them. He also felt some admiration for the courage shown by that attractive, sexy woman sitting across the table from him. She was clearly someone not to be trifled with.

Sam stood, and she followed suit. He extended his hand, and she took it. The grip was firm, but at the same time, it felt dainty. He held the door for her, and they exited the room. Craig met her in the lower-level lobby.

"How did it go?" he asked. "Are you alright?"

"It was fine, and I am fine," she said, grabbing one of his hands and squeezing it lovingly.

"I'm going to stick around and talk to Sam," Craig said. "But let's have lunch when I'm done."

She pulled on his hand, and he bent down. She planted a long, sensuous kiss on his lips.

"You got it, cowboy," she said, then sauntered out the front door. The wiggle of her plump, firm ass almost drags him along with her.

Craig sat at the small table in the sheriff's office break room in the Dubois town hall, stirring a large mug full of coffee. He wasn't much of a coffee drinker and didn't care for the bitterness. But he did drink it sparingly for the boost from the caffeine. But he wondered just how effective it was for him since he put so much creamer in to kill the bitter taste.

He had already had a cup with breakfast, and that was his usual limit, with some exceptions. But after the rush of adrenaline from the attack at Anna's house wore off, he felt he needed another boost.

Sam set his own mug down on the table and settled into a chair opposite Craig. He took a long sip of his steaming drink before speaking.

"Well, it has started. Now the question is how fast will it spread and how do we contain it?" the sheriff asked.

Craig shook himself out of his own thoughts -- recalling the morning's activity, the murder cases, whether he should have a third cup of coffee -- and looked across at his friend.

"If you mean the vigilante stuff, I don't see how we can contain it," he said. "People are going to do what they are going to do."

"But I can't keep arresting people when things like this happen," Sam said. "For one thing, there is not enough room to hold them all because you know as well as I do that this will start snowballing if we don't stop these killings damned soon."

The two men and the woman who had threatened Craig were in custody in town until they could be transported to the county jail in Lander. When the new fire hall was built on 3rd Street, the old facility on Horse Creek Road was fitted with crude cells in the bay where the fire vehicles used to be parked. They served as temporary holding cells. For the most part, they were used for drunks who had gotten a little too rowdy and needed to sleep it off for a few hours or overnight. From time to time, more serious offenders were kept there until a county jail detention officer could drive up to transport them down to Lander.

"Those three from this morning will be taken to Lander by this afternoon," Sam said. "But if we have to keep arresting people, that's going to fill up the county jail so fast we'll have to house them in a tent city like they did down in Arizona. And I'm sure you know how much grief that caused."

"I could just not press charges," Craig said half-heartedly.

"Well, whether you did or not, they will face charges," Sam said. "We need to do that to set an example and put the fear of jail into people. Maybe that will calm things down a bit."

Craig offered no protest. He could see Sam's point.

Before either man could speak again, Heather Strain, the young woman who served as receptionist for the sheriff's substation, poked her head into the room.

"Sheriff, there are a couple of women here who would like to speak to you," she said.

"Did they say what it was about?" he asked.

"They wanted to talk about some odd behavior they noticed from someone last night," she answered.

Sam excused himself and followed the woman out. Craig remained seated, but within a few minutes, Sam was back at the break room doorway, motioning Craig to follow him to the substation's small squad room. They joined Karen Bullock and Lea Curtis. Karen had shoulder-length grey hair and was overweight. Some might call it obese. Craig saw that she was still kind of cute in the face, as she always had been. Lea was attractive and petite with short brown hair.

Both women were married, Karen to her second husband and Lea to a man she had met in college. Karen lived in Dubois and worked in one of the art galleries on Ramshorn Street, while Lea was in from a city in New Mexico where she was a legal aide. Craig had been friends with both in school.

"The ladies tell me they experienced some odd behavior from one of your classmates at the bar last night," Sam said.

"It was Grace," Karen offered. Now Craig knew why he was being included in this conversation.

Grace Metcalf was a "plain Jane" with an average build and figure. She had been a tomboy during the time Craig knew her in school. She seemed to have no real close friends among her classmates. Craig found her difficult to make friends with because she spoke very little and mostly kept to herself.

"Tell me what was so odd about her behavior," Sam said.

The two women looked at each other for a few seconds before responding.

"Well, she seemed to be a lot more social than I remember," Lea said.

"People change over time. Maybe that's what you were seeing," Sam said.

"It was more than that," Karen said. "She was asking questions and saying other things that were kind of awkward."

"Like what?" the sheriff asked.

"Like asking what kind of sexual positions were our favorites," Lea said, and Karen blushed.

"She asked me if I ever had anything inside me besides a man's penis," Karen said hesitantly, her blush deepening.

Sam and Craig looked at each other. Neither was entirely comfortable with the conversation at this point. Sam had dealt with some cases in his career where similar conversations had been reported, with the complainant accusing someone of lewd behavior and even rape. But none had panned out. Most times, the accused claimed they were simply misunderstood, and with no hard evidence to point to any crime or intent of criminal activity, the matters had been dropped, and he heard nothing further from those complainants.

Craig remembered Grace as being very socially awkward. The few times she did speak to him or anyone else, what she said was out of context for the moment or so weird as to be a conversation stopper. He also knew that she never dated in high school. Perhaps, after all these years, she was trying to improve on her social ineptitude but failing as she always had.

Seeing that the men seemed unmoved, Karen spoke up again.

"She was also talking a lot about the murders that have taken place here," she said.

"I'm sure that's a topic in a lot of conversations in town right now," Craig said. "People are concerned and afraid."

"But it was different than that," Lea said.

"How so?" the sheriff asked.

"It's hard to explain," Karen said. "But she didn't seem concerned or afraid. It was more like she was trying to scare us."

"And there was something else," Lea said before the men could react. "I kept catching a whiff of a strange smell, kind of like a doctor's office, but also kind of sweet. It made me sneeze, and Grace pulled out a handkerchief from her jacket, and the smell got stronger."

"Did she put it up to your face?" Craig asked.

"No, I made her put it away," Lea said.

"Were there other people around to hear and see all this?" Sam asked.

"Not really, we were outside near the intersection," Karen said.

It was at that moment that Heather knocked on the closed squad room door.

"You have a call from the medical examiner on line one," she told Sam.

After thanking the two women for their time and watching them exit the squad room, Craig and Sam sat close to the phone. Sam pushed the blinking light for line one and put the phone on speaker so they could both hear.

"Hello, John, this is Sheriff Sharbono and with me is Craig Reilly, a retired detective I have consulting on this case. What's up?" the sheriff said.

"I have finished full examinations of the first two victims and have some information that might be helpful to you," said John DeLaney, the veteran Fremont County coroner.

Sam had a steno notebook open on the table and was poised with his pen.

"First, both women were definitely killed by strangulation," DeLaney explained. "We found brown and yellow fibers embedded in the ligature marks on their necks."

"That jibes with what our doctor here found," Sam said. "He also found bruising on the bodies."

"That is confirmed," DeLaney said. "I can also tell you they were sexually assaulted. But there are a couple of odd things I found."

"What is that, John?" Sam asked.

"First, there was definitely penetration involved," the doctor said. "But I found no semen or DNA inside or outside the vaginas. None anywhere on either body."

He paused a moment to consult his notes.

"There is also no trace of latex, polyurethane, polyisoprene or animal intestine, so a condom was not used," the coroner said. "There was also no sign of the lubricant the rubbers are coated in."

"Was there anything that indicated what was used for penetration?" Sam asked.

"There were some traces of a substance, but I had trouble identifying until I ran several tests," DeLaney said. "I can't be exactly sure, but my best guess is plastic."

"What type of plastic? From what?" Craig asked his first question.

"It's very hard to say, but I do have a theory based on something else I found on both victims and something on the second," the doctor said, then paused.

"Well, what were they?" Sam asked.

"On both victims, there were tiny marks high up on their inner thighs. Under testing, it proved to be Glovolium," DeLaney said.

"What's that?" Craig asked.

"It's used to treat baseball gloves. Leather baseball gloves," the doctor said. "But it can be used on most leathers, including straps."

"And the other thing on the second victim?" Sam said.

"Detergent," the doctor said. "Most likely used to clean the penetration tool after the first assault, if these killings are done by the same person."

Craig and Sam looked at each other. They both had puzzled looks on their faces.

"Do you have a computer handy?" the doctor asked.

Sam wheeled over to a desktop unit and answered in the affirmative. He gave the sheriff a website to input. The sheriff waited a few seconds for the search to complete. Suddenly, his mouth opened, and if his lower jaw had not been attached, it would have fallen on the computer keyboard. Craig saw his look and walked over behind him and looked. He involuntarily put his hand on his chin and closed his astonished open mouth.

On the computer screen were several pictures of dildos with leather harnesses.

Chapter 16

A little exhausted after the morning's events and the questioning by the sheriff, Anna had stopped by the motel to check on things before heading home to relax. The cleaners were busy redressing the rooms, a few vacant but others still with guests.

"Is everything okay?" she asked Carlotta, her friend who gave her a break when needed.

She was an older woman, a widow, who had inherited a small fortune from her late husband but was bored sitting at home all the time. She had met Anna several years ago while sitting in front of the motel, watching the floats and military vehicles from the nearby museum roll by during the annual Fourth of July parade. When she learned Anna owned the motel, she asked if there was a part-time job available. There really wasn't, but Anna could tell from what she heard of Carlotta's story that she wanted something to make her feel useful. They worked out an agreement in which Carlotta could fill in for any of Anna's employees who called in sick or took vacations and for Anna whenever she wanted a break.

Anna had called Carlotta right after the police arrived at her home following the attack that morning and asked her to watch the front desk for a while as the night person was due to go home. She readily agreed.

"Everything's fine," Carlotta answered.

Anna had called her while Craig was being interviewed at town hall to give her a more detailed explanation of what had happened and why she needed to fill in. Carlotta could tell the younger woman was still a little shaken from the morning's activity.

"You should go home and rest," she told Anna. "Take the rest of the day if you need. I can stay. God knows I have nothing else to do."

Anna was grateful for this stately woman. Carlotta always refused to be paid for the time she spent at the motel. She had more than enough money to live on, and she was thrilled to be busy from time to time and it gave her a sense of usefulness. But Anna always found a way to reward her for her efforts.

"Thank you, Carlotta," Anna said. "I'm having lunch with Craig later, and I'll be back after that."

"You like this boy, don't you," Carlotta said with a mischievous grin.

Anna gave her a dismissive wave, but her blush told Carlotta she had hit the nail right on the head.

At her home, Anna had just dozed off on her living room sofa when she was roughly reawakened by a loud knock on her front door. In that brief period when the body was still half asleep and struggling to become fully conscious, Anna staggered upright and moved slowly to the door as a second round of knocking began.

"I'm coming," she mumbled loudly, sure she wasn't heard, or if she was, it was not understood.

She turned the knob on the door and started to pull it open. Suddenly, the door was pushed aside and Anna caught a glimpse of a shadowy figure backlighted by the late morning sun before something soft was jammed into her face. She felt a hand on the back of her head that kept her from moving away. She remembered a strong, sweet smell before everything went grey.

O๐oๆO

Craig and Sam were still in the sheriff's break room mulling over the ramifications that DeLaney had revealed when Heather stuck her head in again.

"Sheriff, it's Pat on line two," she informed him.

Patrick Kroll was the detective assigned to Dubois, but who had been rotated to Riverton, then assigned to keep watch over DeAnn Paxton, the fourth victim who was still alive but unconscious. He had been ordered to report if she ever regained consciousness.

"Sheriff, she's awake," Patrick said when Sam punched the line and put the handset to his ear.

"What is her condition?" the sheriff asked.

"The doctors believe she will make a full recovery, but she'll have to stay in the hospital for a few days while they monitor her progress," the detective answered.

"Has she said anything?" Sam asked.

"Just one word over and over," Patrick answered. "Grace."

"Alright, keep us posted," Sam said, then hung up the phone.

He relayed all that information to Craig.

"He said she kept saying grace?" Craig asked, mostly rhetorically. "What does that mean?"

"Maybe she was thanking God for her survival or wanting people to pray for her," Sam said.

Both men sat in silent contemplation for a few seconds. Suddenly, Craig sat bolt upright. His eyes as wide as half dollars. He then jumped to his feet. The move caught the sheriff off guard, and he stood up as well, not expecting what might come next.

"Holy shit, Sam. What DeLaney told us could indicate that a woman was doing these killings!" Craig yelled. "The woman that exhibited the odd behavior last night, the one those women just told us about! They said her name was Grace, and she was in my class."

The sheriff held up his hands, palms out.

"Let's not jump to conclusions, Craig," he said. "There was nothing definitive in what John told us that would identify the killer as a woman."

Craig shook his head rapidly.

"No, Sam. If it was a man, why would he use a fake dick to rape them? Why wouldn't he use his own?" Craig asked, still in a state of agitation.

"You know as well as I do that some killers get off just on the pain they cause," Sam said. "Maybe this guy's impotent, and that's why he used a dildo. That could also be what is fueling his desire to do these things to these women."

Craig wasn't buying it at all.

"But he wouldn't strap the thing on himself, his cock and balls would be in the way, and I can't say from experience, but even if he did strap it on, he would be hurting himself," he said.

Sam thought about that for a moment. It made sense to him. But he still wasn't convinced.

"Okay, we need to look at every possibility, no matter how improbable," he said. "I think the first thing we need to do is get ahold of Grace and see if she can account for her whereabouts during the most probable times these crimes were committed."

As they headed for the main entrance door, they saw Kathleen also leaving the building.

"Calling it a day already," Craig called out to her.

"No. Somebody called and said they heard beeping coming from inside my house. I need to go check it out," she answered.

"I can send one of my guys over to check it out for you," Sam offered.

"Don't bother them. I'm sure they have more important things to do," Kathleen said. "Besides, it's probably my alarm clock. It's been acting up lately. Or a smoke detector battery died. I can take care of it," she added as she headed for the main entrance door.

○──○

As she crossed the 3rd Street Bridge over the Wind River and prepared to turn right onto Birch Street, Kathleen saw a minivan under a tree on the southeast corner of her property. It was on the north side of the tree, so it was off the street. She made a mental note to talk to her neighbor to the east about parking on her property, something she had to do almost on a monthly basis.

When she pulled into her driveway, she looked over at the minivan. It was dark green in color and dusty. She figured that was from driving around Dubois, where most of the streets, besides Ramshorn and 1st streets, were graded gravel, not paved. She also noticed it had Wyoming license plates, but the county number was twenty-two, not ten.

"He doesn't have a Teton County registered vehicle," she thought as she headed for the front door. She decided when she was done here and back at the office, she would ask the sheriff's department to check it out instead of calling her neighbor.

As Kathleen reached for the doorknob to her front door, she heard the crunch of a foot stepping lightly on gravel behind her. Before she could turn around, a hand was thrust into her face, and a soft cloth pressed over her mouth and nose. The last thing she remembered was a sweet smell.

Craig and Sam spent several hours visiting the town's motels, campgrounds and RV parks looking for Grace Metcalf. But none of those establishments had anyone by that name staying there. In between stops, Craig used his cell phone to call those establishments not within the town limits -- as far west as Brooks Lake and Togwotee lodges and as far east as Red Rock Lodge. He got the same results.

They also stopped at the bar and tavern, even the VFW Club just south of the Episcopal Church. Not finding her there, they canvassed the stores on Ramshorn, each walking on different sides of the street. Then, they drove out to the stores west of Anna's motel. But Grace seemed nowhere to be found. Finding most of Craig's classmates in various locations on their search, they asked when they had seen Grace last. Nearly all had said the night before at the tavern. She was reported to be there until it closed at two o'clock in the morning.

"This is not looking good for Grace," Sam said when they returned to the town hall at twelve-thirty. "But there is one other place to check."

"And that would be?" Sam asked.

"Her parents have a ranch up off Horse Creek Road," Craig said. "She might be there. We should head up there."

When he was not on the phone or talking to store personnel or his classmates, Craig said nothing. But Sam could tell there was something clouding his mind.

"What are you thinking?" Sam asked.

Craig shook his head and looked at his friend's son with a dull, puzzled expression on his face.

"I never in a million years would have thought about a woman killer," he said absently.

"Well, that makes two of us," Sam said.

"I don't mean just here," Craig said. "I never would have thought of it in Missouri. It had never entered my mind."

Sam cocked his head and stared at Craig with a questioning look, like a dog when someone makes a noise he doesn't understand. Craig looked at the sheriff for a few seconds, knowing what he had to do now.

"The Missouri case and this one are connected," he said. "And I'm the catalyst. I'm sure of it now."

He then launched into all the details of the Missouri case and the similarities to the one they were investigating.

Craig was completely drained when he got to Anna's just before one o'clock. The day so far had been a lot to handle, and he was not looking forward to explaining to her why he had bugged out on their lunch date. In the back of his mind, he wondered why she had not called to see what was keeping him. He and the sheriff had been so busy with their search that he had forgotten to call her.

He and Sam were going to head for Grace's parents' ranch, but he wanted to make this one-stop to check on Anna first.

He climbed down out of the truck and walked slowly around it and past her Jeep parked alongside. He was just mounting the first steps to the wrap-around porch when he heard a shaky voice behind him.

"Is Anna alright?"

He turned to find a woman who must have been in her seventies. She was short and as frail looking as her shaky voice implied.

"She's alright," Craig said. "She might be mad at me for skipping lunch today, but when I explain, she'll understand."

"Are you going to see her now?" the lady asked. "Tell her Irene said hello, and I'm sorry for whatever happened."

Craig was a bit puzzled.

"Well, I'm sure she wouldn't mind if you came in and told her yourself," he said, pointing toward the house.

"But she's not there," Irene said.

Craig turned to look at her Jeep and then back at the woman.

"Someone came earlier and picked her up," Irene explained. "I could tell something was wrong because she was a little unsteady on her feet, and the person who picked her up was holding a hanky for her to blow her nose."

"When was this?" Craig asked, starting to get a little concerned.

"Oh, about eight o'clock this morning," Irene said.

Craig's body tensed a little. That was shortly after they both left town hall. He was certain she would have called him if something had happened.

"What did the person who picked her up look like?" Craig asked.

"She was about Anna's age, maybe a few years older," Irene said. "She seemed kind of familiar like she had gone to school here at one time."

"Have you lived here long?" Craig asked.

"I graduated from high school here fifty-six years ago," she said. "I've lived here ever since. Worked at the school as a cook until three years ago."

Craig pulled out his cell phone and dialed the sheriff's cell. When he answered, Craig relayed the information Irene had given him.

"I'm at the substation," Sam said. "Travis is over at your sister's house. Neighbors there called in something suspicious earlier. No one is there, and Travis found her keys on the porch at the front door."

"I'm on my way," Craig said and went to the driver's side of the truck. "Thank you for the information, ma'am," he added as he climbed in.

"Be sure to tell her what I said," she yelled as Craig backed away from the house and took off down the street.

The trip to Grace's parents' was completely forgotten.

Chapter 17

Craig was feeling frantic as he went through his sister's home. He was looking for anything that might suggest what had happened to Kathleen. He could not remember ever having the level of anxiety he was feeling at this moment.

While he had rarely been back to Dubois to visit his siblings much, they were close in a way that might not be recognized by others. They kept in touch by phone, email and social media on a fairly regular basis. Their conversations were not deep. Very little, if any, politics, worldview, current events or the meaning of life. They mostly talked about what was happening with each of them and the good old days when they were growing up, which was the majority of their topics.

He could not even imagine what life would be like without his sister. But it was more than that. He did not want to think about such a possibility.

However, there was something else fueling his anxiety -- Anna. It was a double whammy. When he became aware Kathleen and Anna disappeared within hours of each other, it was hard not to come to the conclusion that they had each been taken against their will.

It was then that the reality of his feelings for Anna hit Craig like a head-on collision between semi-trucks.

In his search of Kathleen's house, he found nothing that seemed out of place since the last time he was there. After he and Daniel had lunch with her, she had given him the dime tour of the home. All seemed to him like it should be.

"So it appears that whoever took her did not get into the house," Sam said after Craig reported the results of his search of the house. "Since her keys were right at the front door, it seems clear she was surprised and taken at that spot."

"What about that vehicle the neighbor reported parked under that tree?" Craig asked.

"We followed up with the license plate number he gave us. It is registered to a rental agency at the Jackson Hole airport," the sheriff informed him. "The van was rented by Grace exactly a week ago."

The sheriff paused for a minute while Craig stared at him in anticipation. He was about to prod his friend for more information when Sam spoke up.

"Grace had flown in that day on a Delta flight," he said. "It originated in Kansas City, Missouri and had one stop in Denver."

Craig felt a dullness in his chest like his heart skipped several beats.

"Can you track down where she lives?" he asked.

"Already did. A Kansas City suburb called Fairway," Sam answered.

The sheriff let that sink in.

"It is beginning to look like your theory about these crimes being connected is correct," the sheriff said with a touch of sadness.

"Shit, Sam, that means three women are dead, a fourth nearly so, and two more could be because of me," Craig said. As soon as the words were out of his mouth, his emotions burst like a cracked dam holding back millions of cubic feet of water.

He pounded his head with both fists as a stream of obscenities exploded out of his mouth that shattered the quiet of the neighborhood. Several residents waiting to be interviewed by Travis and Fred turned their heads to look in his direction. The deputies also turned their attention to the commotion. They weren't shocked by the words but more so by the actions. Craig stopped hitting himself and dropped to his knees, leaning his body forward. He looked utterly drained.

Sam motioned for his deputies to go on with their interviews then knelt down at Craig's side.

"This is not your fault, Craig," he said softly. "No friggin' way."

Craig was so drained of emotion he was barely breathing. Sam quietly encouraged him to take some deep breaths. After a few moments, he did just that. Shortly, he was breathing normally. He pulled one foot out from underneath himself and planted it firmly on the ground. He straightened up and stayed on one knee. He finally held out his hand, and Sam took it and pulled him up to a standing position.

"I'm sorry about that outburst, Sam," Craig said loud enough for the nearby neighbors and deputies to hear.

"Don't worry about it," the sheriff assured him.

"I know it was someone else that killed those women, but I am the focal point," Craig said. "The fact that she broke her pattern and took two people I care a great deal about proves that."

Sam agreed. But he couldn't help but notice that Craig had included Anna as a person he cared a great deal about. Clearly, she was more than just an acquaintance, a schoolmate, a friend. It was something Sam had suspected. His father had mentioned it to him a few times when he shared with his son stories of his own high school days.

"Let's go back to the substation and talk about where we go from here," Sam said, guiding Craig by the arm to his truck.

⊙══⊙

Four victims in, the Dubois killer's outlook went from satisfied to frustrated. The actions were not getting the desired results from people in town -- especially one person in particular. There was an expectation of panic from the residents. But from the killer's observations, there was none. Business continued as usual.

Of course, the killer did not count the mayor flipping out. He was a known quantity, and his reaction was predictable.

As for that particular person, the expectations were uncertain. It was known he was now retired from law enforcement. But once he started putting the pieces together, making the connection to Kansas City, there was some desire for him to join the panic that was expected from the rest of the residents. Since none of that happened to any great extent, frustration set in.

Then came the anger.

The Dubois grapevine revealed the fourth victim had survived the attempt to kill her. Since the killer was connected to the grapevine, it was not hard to get that news.

After the initial burst of anger, the killer's analytical mind kicked in. Attempts to get another victim fell through, and again, the grapevine got the word around that the killer's newest intended victims had gone to the sheriff, who was working with that particular person to try and stop the killings and solve the case.

With the most recent developments, the killer decided it would be difficult to secure any more victims from the desired target group. There now must be a direct assault on that particular person. The killer was not interested in seeing that person dead. It was more a case of wanting to make him suffer. And the killer was not interested in changing one aspect of the target group.

It was time to hit Craig Reilly, where it hurt the most.

The killer knew where to find the first target. Not only was it known where she lived, but careful observation had shown that Craig Reilly was smitten with her. His distinctive copper-colored Dodge Ram was seen at her home several nights now. The killer parked the minivan a block east on Watson Street facing Horse Creek. That gave a clear sight line to Anna's house.

Imagine the killer's surprise and initial frustration when the morning attack on Reilly played out. When Anna came out of the house with a shotgun and helped Craig take down the attackers, there was some relief. The target could still be in play, and Reilly could still be vulnerable.

After the sheriff's deputies took the suspects away, Anna and Craig got in their respective vehicles and followed them. The killer knew where they would go, so waited thirty minutes then drove across town and took up observation near enough town hall to see when Anna and Craig left.

Anna came out alone and got in her Jeep. The killer followed at a respectable distance until Anna stopped at the motel. The killer parked across from the bar forty yards from the motel and waited. In a matter of minutes, Anna drove east on Ramshorn, and the killer followed after seeing her make a left turn on 1st Street. Clearly, she was headed home.

Parking next to Anna's Jeep, the killer walked to the door and knocked. With no immediate answer, there was a second knock. When the door opened, the killer moved forward quickly and placed the white washcloth soaked in chloroform into Anna's face and used the second hand to push her head into it even tighter.

Anna was still half conscious when the killer quickly let the back of her head go to shut the door and then wrapped it around her shoulder and neck. In that way, Anna was guided down the steps to the passenger side of the minivan. By that time, she was nearly unconscious. The killer got her into the seat and fastened her seat belt. The washcloth was held in place until it was clear Anna was completely unconscious.

Rounding the front of the vehicle and sliding into the driver's seat, the killer backed out and began to head for the south end of town. Parking next to the tree alongside Birch Street, the killer quickly called town hall.

"I need to leave a message for my neighbor, Kathleen Young. There is a beeping coming from her house. It doesn't sound right. She should come and check it out."

Ten minutes later, Kathleen pulled into her driveway. The killer saw her as she turned her Ford Mustang onto Birch Street. The killer was out of the van at the same time Kathleen exited her car. The killer took the three concrete steps up to the wrap-around porch, caught up with Kathleen right at the front door, and reached around and pressed the freshly soaked washcloth into her face. She was too surprised to struggle, and the killer literally dragged her back to the van. Kathleen was pushed into the bench seat behind the driver and passenger bucket seats, and the killer slammed the sliding side door.

Getting back into the driver's seat, the killer brought the van to life, rounded the tree, got to 3rd Street, zoomed up to Ramshorn and zig-zagged onto Horse Creek Road. A half mile up the road, the killer stopped long enough to secure her targets' hands and feet with zip ties and gagged them with lightly soaked chloroform cloths. Then, the trip north continued.

⊷⊶

In a town as small as Dubois, it did not take long to search for a specific vehicle. Between the sheriff, his two deputies and Craig, they covered it in thirty minutes. In that time, Sam had the Dubois detective pursue another search avenue.

"The minivan is not within the town limits," Sam, back at the substation, told the detective by phone. "And the ways out of town are limited."

He instructed the detective to issue an all-points bulletin for the minivan. Roadblock check stations were to be set up on Togwotee Pass to the west and at the Lander-Riverton junction to the east on Highway 26. Sam briefed the deputies and Craig on the measures being taken.

Dubois Detective Patrick Kroll convinced the car rental company to share the identification and password for the global positioning satellite tracker on the minivan rented by Grace. When the information was input into the laptop computer in Fred's patrol cruiser, it showed the vehicle's exact location. It was moving about thirty miles per hour on Horse Creek Road, about twenty miles north of town.

"It's been a little over an hour since we left your sister's place," the sheriff told Craig. "She should be farther out than that."

Fred made a few clicks on the laptop and brought up a history of travel for the vehicle. He began at the point where the vehicle was shown at Kathleen's house. He scrolled through the history until he came to

148

the point where the vehicle had stopped shortly after beginning the journey up Horse Creek Road. A second, longer stop was also recorded a couple of miles past the first stop.

"She stopped about seven miles up the road," Fred explained. "It shows the van was motionless for about forty minutes."

"Get a fix on that exact position," Sam ordered.

"Don't bother," Craig said. "I'm pretty sure what is there. We need to get there as fast as we can."

He headed for his truck, but Sam stopped him. He handed him a portable radio.

"We're going to talk on the way," he said.

Sam was on the radio before Craig could get his truck into gear. Using one hand to drive and the other to operate the portable, their conversation began.

"What are we going to find when we get there?" Sam asked as he flipped on the light bar to the borrowed fire department pickup. Craig was in the lead, with Sam behind and Fred trailing with his lights and siren blazing.

"This is where Grace's parents had a small horse ranch when we were in school," Craig responded. "They still live there and have some horses, but it's not a working ranch anymore. Grace mentioned that during that first get-together at the community center earlier this week."

"What do you suppose she stopped there for?" Sam asked.

Instead of answering the sheriff, Craig directed a question to Fred.

"Fred, does that minivan she's driving have a tow package?"

After a couple of seconds, the deputy answered in the affirmative.

"Shit!" Craig said. Then he pressed the transmit button on the radio.

"I think she's planning on going up into the high country," he told the officers.

Sam quickly changed frequencies on his radio and called the state police.

"We're going to need some air support north of Dubois," he said when he reached the local commander. He glanced out his window at the sky. There was still plenty of daylight, but they would start losing it in about five hours.

"We've got a bird up in Jackson and can have it there in about an hour," the state police captain said.

It was then that Craig turned off the main road and into a short gravel driveway and up to a modest farmhouse. The sheriff followed him in but he instructed Fred to continue on.

A woman in her late eighties answered the door when the sheriff knocked for the third time. She was very frail and shaky.

"Are you Grace Metcalf's mother?" Sam asked. The woman nodded. "We'd like to ask you some questions about your daughter."

"She was here a while ago," the woman said as she shuffled out the door and slowly sat in a rocking chair on the porch.

"Why was she here?" Sam asked.

"Well, she wanted to borrow some horses," the old woman said slowly. "She had a couple of friends she wanted to take riding."

"Did you see these friends?" Craig asked. "Did you recognize them?"

The woman shook her head.

"They stayed in the car while Grace hooked up the trailer and loaded the horses and tack," she explained. "My husband offered to help her, but she said no. Just as well. He's ninety-one and can barely walk."

"How many horses?' Craig asked.

"Just two, a quarter horse and the Appaloosa," Grace's mother said. "I don't think she could have pulled the big trailer with that little toy car she was driving. We offered her the pickup, but she didn't want it."

Craig knew why. Grace would not want to risk her parents seeing her load two unconscious women from the minivan to another vehicle.

Sam thanked the old lady, and he and Craig returned to their trucks. They left a cloud of dust and a spray of gravel as they zoomed out of the driveway and back onto Horse Creek Road, this time with Sam in the lead.

The old woman waved the dust away from her face.

"Damned fool kids and their trucks. Always in such a God-awful hurry," she muttered as she sat and watched them disappear up the road.

Chapter 18

Racing north on Horse Creek Road behind the sheriff in his borrowed fire department truck, Craig's anxiety was building. The safety of Anna and Kathleen was uppermost in his mind. Neither he nor the sheriff knew whether the two women were in Grace's rented minivan. They had to go on the assumption that they were.

According to the GPS tracker Fred was monitoring as he also sped north, the van had made only the two stops. While Grace's mother said she had not seen the two women during that stop, her description of Grace hooking up the trailer to the van and loading two horses and all the necessary tack made it unlikely she had time to kill one or both women.

Unlikely but not impossible.

Sam radioed Travis and ordered him to go question the parents further. He was also told to search the property for anybody or bodies. Under the changed circumstances, it was conceivable Grace abandoned her method of killing and quickly dispatched either Anna or Kathleen -- or both -- in the time she had. With his knowledge of spree killers -- through research and his own experience -- Craig thought that the possibility was slim.

Again, slim but not impossible.

The two vehicles were more than halfway to the Double Cabins Campground, 28 miles north of town, when the radio crackled to life after being silent since Sam had called Travis.

"I found the van," Fred said. "It's just short of the campground pulled off into the trees to the left side of the road. I didn't see it until I passed it and saw it in the side mirror."

"Is she there?" Sam asked. "What about the women?"

"There is no one here. The horse trailer is empty, too," Fred answered.

"They've gone wilderness," Craig said into his portable radio.

"I don't think she had planned to mount the horses this soon," Fred said. "The van is smoking real bad. I think she burned up all her oil trying to haul that trailer up here faster than the van was meant to go with a tow."

His assessment was sound because it was unseasonably hot that August, and even at the higher elevation from the town's 6,946 feet above sea level, the temperature was hovering around ninety-five degrees.

Because Horse Creek Road ends at the campground, Craig speculated that Grace may have planned to go as far past the end of the road as possible before abandoning the vehicle. From there, she could make her way, with or without her victims, through the mountain valleys to Meeteetse and from there to Cody. However, taking Anna and Kathleen into other towns would have raised suspicions. So Craig expected she would kill them in the wilderness and make for Cody to execute an escape, most likely into Canada.

Grace had gone off plan when she abducted Anna and Kathleen but she had quickly adjusted to a new plan. Now, she apparently needed to alter the plan again, but only in a timeline. Now that she was heading into the high country on horseback, it would be harder to track her. And would she still try to make it for Cody? And with only two horses, would she kill one of the women before starting out?

"I found two sets of horse tracks. They are heading west through the timber," Fred radioed. "I'm going to follow them. They can't be that far ahead."

"No, wait until we get there," Sam said.

"Sheriff, these tracks seem very recent," Fred said. "She had to take time to gear up the horses and load the women aboard. They can't be that far ahead."

It was hard to argue the deputy's logic. However, the sheriff needed the deputy to ascertain whether Grace had both women with her or had dispatched one -- or both -- of them to help speed her escape.

"Alright, go ahead," he said. "But keep the van in sight until we get there. We're not far away. And look for signs that one or both of the women are still with her."

But Sam was still concerned. His training told him there was safety in numbers, and the standard procedure was never to go into a potentially hostile situation without backup.

Craig saw Sam's truck jump forward, and he pressed down on the accelerator of his Ram to keep pace.

⌾‑∘∘‑⌾

Grace slowed down to make the turn off Horse Creek Road into the short driveway that led to her parents' house. She had been staying with them on the ranch while she was in town for the reunion, but with all the activities she was involved in, she did little more than sleep a few hours there, coming home late and leaving early.

Her mother, Helen, and father, Jerome, had not seen her in person for three years. But they kept in almost daily contact by phone. They were close and had gotten even closer after her brother, Herbert, was killed in a vehicle accident twenty-one years ago. The Metcalfs had no other children, so they clung to whatever attention they could get from their daughter.

Grace went to the front door to let her parents know she would be taking horses and a trailer. Her mother encouraged her to come inside and have a bite to eat, but Grace politely refused.

"I can't stay, Mom. I want to take some friends riding up in the high country, and if we don't get going now, we'll lose the light," she said.

"Are these friends from your class?" Helen asked. "I'd like to say hello."

"No, Mom, they're waiting in the car," Grace said.

"Alright then," Helen said, a little perturbed. "George is out in the field mending fences, but I'll see if your father can help you hook up and load."

George was the one ranch hand the Metcalfs had hired to perform maintenance on the property. While it was no longer a working ranch, the elderly couple would not allow it to be run down.

Grace grabbed her mother's arm as she turned to speak to Jerome. Her grip was tighter than she expected it would be, and her mother grimaced.

"I'm sorry, Mom," Grace said, letting go of her mother's arm. "Don't bother Dad. He can barely walk. I can do it myself."

"Well, you're only going to be able to take the small trailer. The bigger one has a couple of flat tires," Helen lied. She had seen the minivan her daughter arrived in and knew it couldn't handle the four-horse trailer. "George hasn't gotten around to fixing it yet."

Grace wrapped her arms around Helen and gave her a long, warm hug. She then let her go and headed for the barn where she had parked the minivan. Helen went to the kitchen window and watched as her daughter hitched the two-horse trailer to the van, then led the appaloosa and the quarter horse into it. She then loaded up full tack gear for the horses. Grace also put one bedroll into the trailer. Helen thought that was odd since her daughter had said she was taking multiple friends riding, and when Grace had talked about losing daylight her mother assumed she planned to be back off the mountains before the sun went down.

Once back on Horse Creek Road, Grace put her foot down on the accelerator and got the van and its heavy load up to sixty-five miles per hour. For the next ten miles, the road was mostly straight and fairly level and she was able to hold that speed. But the engine was working overtime trying to move nearly four tons at a speed of twenty-five miles per hour, faster than the recommended amount for towing.

Past that ten-mile point the road began to get a bit steeper in climb, and curves were popping up. This was not unexpected, as Grace had been up this route many times in her youth and during visits to the area since. But, except for the need to slow down for the curves, she continued to push the van past its limits.

Eventually she came to the fork in the road where Parque Creek Road branches off to the left and Horse Creek Road continues right. But immediately past the fork, the road angle goes up sharply and curves one hundred eighty degrees, and Grace could only get fifteen miles per hour from the van until she went through a trio of curves, and then the road leveled off, heading east. She coasted down a slight downgrade for several hundred yards. That allowed the motor to take a break of sorts.

Up to that point, the terrain had been flat land, with small hills back from the road. But when the road turned back north, the timber came closer to the road with open meadows spaced here and there. As she continued up the mountain, the road angle continued to increase, putting more of a load on the van's engine. Small trails branched off the main road from time to time, and after passing one such trail, the lush green pines flanked the road closely on both sides.

Grace noticed the engine temperature gauge inching toward the red zone. But she pushed on. After a few miles, a long meadow appeared on her left. Just past it, the van dropped down into a small valley via a series of switchbacks. She had to navigate them at five miles per hour, but even before that, she could only coax the van to thirty miles per hour. The same was true once she got into the small valley. She had to take a single switchback at five mph that took her up out of the little valley.

The switchback valley respite revived the van enough that Grace was able to maintain thirty mph for a few miles, but the temperature gauge continued to move until it was touching the red mark, and her speed dropped by one mile for every half mile traveled.

Finally, she was barely able to maintain ten mph when the flanking timber opened up ahead into another meadow. By this time, the van's engine was smoking like a five-pack-a-day smoker and clunking like a blacksmith pounding an anvil. She was able to pull the van and trailer off the road to the left and, hugging the tree line, parked in a small opening in the thick trees, just large enough to squeeze the vehicle into and still be able to open the doors.

Grace was about one mile south of the Double Cabins Campground, the terminus of Horse Creek Road, her intended destination.

First, she checked on her prisoners. Anna and Kathleen were still unconscious. But Grace could see signs they were on the verge of coming out of the effects of the chloroform. So, she needed to work fast. One by one, she took the horses out of the trailer and geared them up. She put a blanket and western saddle on the appaloosa, then fitted the bridle over its snout and head. The horse gently mouthed the bit to get comfortable with it. Grace tied the bridle to a nearby tree, then tied the bedroll behind the saddle. She then put a lead halter on the quarter horse and tied it to a tree.

Grace then went to the back of the van and took out a Browning BAR semiautomatic hunting rifle fitted with a Vortex Viper scope. She slid it into a scabbard and tied it to the right side of the saddle on the Appaloosa. She then got a Colt Python revolver from the van, shoved it into a belted hip holster and strapped it on.

Snatching a small leather bag, she hung it on the saddle horn.

Moving to the van's sliding door, she pulled Anna out by the arms and dragged her to the quarter horse. Lifting her under her armpits, she got her head and shoulders, face down, onto the horse's back, then pushed her the rest of the way up until she was draped over the animal bent at the waist, her feet on one side and her head on the other. She repeated the procedure with Kathleen, although her feet and head were on opposite sides to Anna's. The horse side stepped a couple of times to steady itself under the load. Grace then secured the two women's hands and feet together, and using leather straps around their waists, under the horse's belly much like a saddle and fastened to buckles at the top. She hoped this would keep them from sliding off the horse's back and under its belly.

Grace untied the rope on the lead halter and then secured it to the saddle on the appaloosa. She untied the appaloosa's reins from the tree and mounted the horse. Taking a look around to make sure no one was within eyesight, she prodded her horse forward and began a trek due west.

Chapter 19

Sam and Craig got to the spot where Grace had parked the van a little more than twenty minutes after leaving the Metcalfs' ranch. With all they had done since Craig discovered Anna and Kathleen were missing, it was after four o'clock. He looked to the south and saw the sun's position. They had just under five hours of daylight left in the day, with the last thirty minutes almost useless as the sun sank behind the mountains to the west.

Feeling anxiety start to build up in him, Craig found the impressions left in the ground by the horse hooves and began to follow them.

"Hey, wait a minute," Sam hollered after him. "Don't go running off half-cocked. We need to figure out what we are doing."

Craig stopped and turned back to his friend.

"I know what I'm doing," he said, with a hint of anger in his voice. "I'm going to find my sister and Anna." He turned and took a step forward.

"Dammit, Craig, wait," Sam shouted.

Craig turned back and strutted right up to the sheriff.

"The longer we stand here and make plans, the farther away she gets with people I care a lot about," he said into Sam's face. "So you either stand here like a pussy or come with me. I'm going."

Sam grabbed Craig's arm as he started to turn back west. Craig whirled around, aiming a roundhouse punch at the sheriff's head. Sam was prepared for the move and ducked under the punch, but not quite enough. Craig's fist caught him just above the left ear, and it glanced off the top of his head, knocking his light brown cowboy hat off his head. At the same time, Sam unholstered his Glock 19 service pistol and pointed it at Craig's gut.

Craig shook off the sheriff's grip on his arm and backed up a step.

"Whoa, hold on," he said. "There's no need for that."

"Then you need to settle your ass down and quit letting your emotions get the better of you," Sam said. "You've been a police officer, for Christ's sake."

Craig knew he was right. He had seen it too many times when police officers with a personal stake in the outcome of cases had either screwed up the case allowing the perpetrator to walk away free, or gotten someone hurt because they couldn't control their emotions.

"You're right, I'm sorry," Craig said. "But that's my sister up there, and I care a lot about Anna."

"I know," the sheriff said. "I want this resolved so that they come back safely, too. But we need to go into this with our heads screwed on straight."

At that second, the portable radio on the sheriff's belt came to life.

"Sheriff, are you at the van yet?" came Fred's hushed voice.

"We just got here," Sam told the deputy. "Where are you?"

I'm about one hundred yards from where the van is," Fred answered. "I can still see it through the trees, but just barely."

Sam looked at Craig.

"Do you have Grace in sight?" the sheriff asked.

"No, but she's still moving west," the deputy responded.

"Does she still have the two horses?" Sam asked.

"Yes, there are two distinct sets of tracks," Fred explained. "It's hot out, but the ground is still spongy enough that the hooves are sinking in about a quarter of an inch."

"Have you seen anything to indicate she has both women with her?" the sheriff asked.

"Nothing definitive," Fred answered.

"Alright, keep tracking her, but go a little slowly, and we'll catch up," Sam said. "Do you have your bear spray?"

Fred said he had the spray. Sam then went to his vehicle and pulled a Mossberg 590 shotgun he had placed between the bucket seats of the Ford pickup from the fire department before they left town and handed it to Craig. He grabbed from the side rack behind the driver's seat a Remington 700 rifle. He also got two cans of bear spray and tossed one to Craig.

They made a quick search of the horse trailer. There was nothing inside except a horse blanket and a western saddle.

"She's using one of the horses as a pack animal," Sam said. "Kathleen and Anna could be on that horse. She's probably got them tied up and secured on the horse."

An alternative flashed into Craig's mind. It was that Grace had already killed the two women, and the pack horse was carrying provisions for a long stay in the wilderness. That alternative was too painful to think about, so he tried to push it out of his mind.

"That could slow her progress, leading a pack horse," Craig said. "She'll also probably have to stop from time to time to make sure the women are secured tightly."

Locating the hoof prints left by the horses taken from the trailer, along with Fred's barely detectable boot prints, the two men began jogging west through the pines.

O═o═O

Grace had followed breaks in the trees -- mostly Lodgepole pine, Douglas fir and Engelmann spruce -- that formed quasi-trails through the otherwise thick forest growth. She kept the horses moving at a brisk walk, checking every so often to make sure the subdued women on the quarter horse had not shifted.

After a few hundred yards of travel, she noticed that both women were showing signs of consciousness. They had been loaded so that their heads hung down on opposite sides of the horse and were facing each other. They began to struggle against their restraints, but they had been applied tight enough that there was no way to move. Grace could see their faces were starting to turn pink as the blood moved toward their heads.

She stopped the two-horse caravan, dismounted and tied the animals' bridle and lead rope to a tree. She cared little about their welfare and initially would have been happy if their prolonged position on the horse caused aneurysms or even death. She planned to kill them anyway with her usual method. That's why she had the strap-on and the yellow and brown scarf in the leather bag hung from her saddle.

But as she rode farther into the woods, she began to think the two women might be useful if they remained alive, at least for a while. Instead of thinking of her own pleasure in the killings, as she had with all the others, her own survival instinct kicked in. She might be able to use them as leverage if she was ever cornered.

She knelt down so she could face the hanging women. She undid the straps that kept them tight to the horse's back, then snipped the zip ties that connected the women's hands and feet to each other. Welts had already formed on their wrists and ankles from those and the individual ties. Grace removed the ties that bound Anna's feet together. She then pushed her up by the hips and threw one leg over the other side of the horse, so she was now in a normal riding position. She was a little lightheaded from the blood rushing to her head, so she offered no resistance. Leaving her hands bound, Grace laid her down on the horse's neck with her arms and head off to the left and used a strap wrapped around her and the horse's chest to secure her. She then repeated the procedure with Kathleen with her leaning forward onto Anna's back with her arms and head to the right of the horse's neck. Grace then remounted the Appaloosa and continued on her way with the quarter horse's lead rope tied to her saddle.

Craig and Sam caught up with Fred within ten minutes. They took a few minutes to catch their breath and confer with the deputy.

"It looks like she's headed for the rockier ground up near Cathedral Peak," Fred explained. "She'll be harder to track that way."

"Have you had her in sight at any time?" the sheriff asked.

Fred shook his head.

"I can't tell how far ahead she is, but she seems to be moving steadily," he said. "There has been no indication so far that she has stopped for anything."

The trio looked up ahead of them. From the van the incline had been a bit shallow. But it increased rapidly until they were climbing at about a forty-five-degree angle. Sam and Fred were close to the same age, with the sheriff two years Fred's senior, but Craig was more than twenty years older. Craig had stayed in shape, and the climb had not affected him so far.

However, since leaving the police department in Salina, Craig's workout routines had diminished some. He knew if he continued to climb at this angle for too much longer, he would start to lag behind the others. But he knew he had to find the inner strength to keep going. Knowing Anna and Kathleen were in severe danger had pushed him so far. He hoped his concern for them would continue to fuel his reserves.

"We've got to keep moving," he told the others, and they trudged on.

They hadn't gone far when their portable radios came alive with a voice.

"Sheriff Sharbono, do you read me?"

Sam keyed the mic and said he could.

"This is Sergeant Linsky with the state police. We have our chopper in the air," the voice said. "It's just passing over the Tie Hack memorial on Highway 26. Where do you want it?"

"We are a few hundred yards west of Horse Creek Road, just south of Double Cabins Campground," Sam instructed. "Our suspect is somewhere ahead of us, not sure how far, headed toward Cathedral Peak."

"Roger. Will relay to the aircraft."

A few minutes later, the three walked out of the cover of the trees and into a small clearing. They were walking three abreast and advanced into the open about ten yards when they heard the unmistakable crack of a rifle shot. Simultaneous with the shot, Fred, walking on the right flank, spun three hundred-sixty degrees around and plunged to the ground, coming to rest on his back.

Craig and Sam froze for a full second, then dived to their left and hurriedly crawled to cover within a small stand of trees. They heard a second shot and saw a dirt geyser shoot up right between Fred's spread legs within inches of his crotch. Sam, who was the closest to him, dashed out and, grabbed his left wrist and quickly dragged him into the trees a split second before a third bullet tore up the ground right where his belly would have been.

Sam sat him up with his back to a tree facing away from the direction from which the shots had come. With another tree uphill from Fred's rest shielding his movements, Sam checked the deputy. He was conscious but a little dazed. There was a small pool of blood on his uniform shirt just above and to the right of the left armpit. Sam pushed him forward and saw the back of his shirt saturated with blood mixed with dirt and grass from when he had been drug into the trees.

"It was a through and through," Sam said as Craig looked on from behind a tree to Fred's right. Sam yanked a large bandana from a pouch on his utility belt. He unbuttoned Fred's shirt about halfway down and stuffed most of the bandana over the exit wound on his back and the rest, looped under his armpit, over the entry. He then took the belt off Fred's trousers and used it to compress the makeshift bandage, looping it under his armpit and threading the belt through the buckle on top of his shoulder.

"Fred, take the end of your belt and pull down real hard," he instructed. The deputy did so with his right hand and flinched. "Keep it tight," the sheriff said.

Sam keyed his radio and called for Travis back in Dubois. He told him to send an ambulance to their location. He also told the deputy to drop anything he was doing and get there himself.

"That dressing isn't going to completely stop the bleeding, and the ambulance won't be here for probably an hour and a half," Craig said.

"Don't worry about me," Fred said groggily. "You guys need to keep going, or she'll get up there where she can't be tracked, and we'll never know where she is."

Craig and Sam looked at each other. Neither one wanted to leave the deputy, but they knew he was right. At that moment, they heard a faint whop whop whop.

"That's the state police helicopter," Sam said. "Hopefully, they will spot her before she gets too far away."

They heard the helicopter noise grow louder. They could tell it was tracing the route of Horse Creek Road. When they heard the noise change slightly, Sam guessed they had spotted all the vehicles off the road and made the turn due west. The high-speed slapping of the rotors increased quickly, and suddenly, it was nearly on top of them. They felt the rotor wash come pouring down on them, and it showered them with pine needles and pine cones as the craft passed about ten feet above the tallest trees.

"Are we near you?" Sam faintly heard over the engine roar.

"You're almost on top of us," he hollered into the radio.

The chopper slowly moved west, staying just above the trees. It had traveled just a few yards when the trio heard faint pops mixed with the whop whop whop of the chopper.

"We're taking fire," their radios blared.

They looked around the trees and saw the helicopter bank sharply to the right and zoom away in the direction of the campground. They heard two more pops, louder this time now that the aircraft was moving away. Craig saw sparks flare out from the metal on the boom just aft of the main cabin. But no smoke followed.

"They took a hit, but it must have just bounced off," he told the others.

The noise of the chopper was faint, and they could tell it was hovering near the campground.

"They're probably checking to make sure they didn't take any damage that would affect flight," Sam said.

Then, the radios came to life again.

"We saw muzzle flashes," they heard. "Your suspect is about one hundred twenty yards west of you."

"You guys get going," Fred said, still a little dazed.

⊂∙∙⊃

In the forest, human voices cannot be heard over long distances when people talk in normal tones. Only when they yell will the sound carry.

But the grating sound of static and the almost metallic click of man-made devices will carry further than a voice. When Grace heard both of those, she knew she had pursuers, and they were much closer than she was comfortable with.

She had passed out of the heaviest collection of trees a few minutes previously. She was now in an area where the trees were thinning, and the landscape was littered with rocks and small boulders that had jarred loose from the granite peak above and rolled down the sloping hill as far as they would go before the dense forest brought them to a halt.

She tied the horses to a tree, took the rifle out of the scabbard and looked around. She needed a large boulder that jutted up from the ground. She found one a few yards away and, scurried up one side and perched on the top. She sighted through the scope due east, in the direction she knew the pursuers would be coming.

It was difficult to see much, even from her high vantage point, through the green pines. But after a few minutes, she caught sight of a light brown color between two trees. It could have been a patch of dirt on the forest floor, but as she held the scope on that spot, the color suddenly disappeared, and it was light green between the darker green of the pine trees.

She knew her horses would have left prints in the slightly spongy earth, so she knew the track they would follow. She repositioned the scope to the small clearing she had passed through about fifteen minutes earlier. Grace sighted the opening in the trees where she had entered the clearing and waited.

Moments later, she saw three men come out into the clear. With her high power scope, it wasn't hard to make out details from where she was. The men were walking quickly, three abreast. The one on her left and the one in the middle were wearing county sheriff uniforms, while the other man was in civilian clothing -- jeans and a long-sleeved shirt that looked to be a light yellow color. Not the best color to be wearing in the woods if one is trying to be camouflaged. The two uniformed men wore light brown cowboy hats and were looking at the ground, following the hoof prints. The other man had a red ball cap on his head, the bill covering his face. Again, not the best color for stealthy woodland travel.

"Craig Reilly, you son-of-a-bitch," Grace thought.

She rolled down onto her belly on the rounded top of the rock letting her legs lay down the back. Moving her feet back and forth, she found one crevice and planted her right foot into it. She brought the butt of the rifle's stock to rest on her right shoulder and wrapped her right hand around the grip, and laced her finger around the trigger. She steadied the barrel with her left hand and gingerly placed her left elbow on the rock's surface.

She positioned the crosshairs in the scope on Craig's belt buckle. She estimated the distance at a little more than one hundred yards. Accounting for his forward movement as he stepped, she figured aiming at the belt line would mean the bullet would strike him square in the chest. At this distance, it would have been an easy shot.

Remembering her father's instructions when she was a teenager, and they were hunting deer, she took two deep breaths and let them out slowly. Just as the last of the second breath left her mouth, Craig raised his head, and she saw a Kansas City Chiefs logo on the front of his cap. He seemed to be looking right at her when she squeezed the trigger.

A split second before she had put enough pressure on the trigger to fire the weapon, she felt her right foot start to slide on some sand in the crevice where she had placed it for stability. She felt the recoil bite into her shoulder. It felt different than she remembered.

Grace jammed her foot into the crevice and put her eye on the scope again. She saw one of the uniformed men lying spread eagle on the ground. She aimed for his chest and fired again. Dirt and grass flew upright between his spread legs.

"Damn, squeezed the trigger too hard," she thought.

She saw a hand enter her vision through the scope, and she pulled the trigger again, this time with just the slightest pressure. When she pulled the rifle away from her eye, she saw no one in the clearing.

"Dammit," she whispered.

A quick sighting through the scope drew no results. She slid down off the rock and ran back to where the horses were secured to the tree. She looked at the women strapped to the quarter horse's back. They both had a mixture of anger and fear showing clearly on their faces.

She was about to untie the horses when she heard the same whop whop whop that Craig, Sam and Fred had heard. She knew what it was instantly. She stood for a few moments and listened to the sound as it got louder. It seemed to be passing from right to left as she looked downhill. Then she spotted it. The helicopter was indeed coming from right to left. But then it banked and headed straight in her direction.

Grace hurried down into the thicker trees and listened as the chopper drew closer. Suddenly it was passing slowly right over her position. She raised the rifle, pointed it straight up at the craft's belly and fired two shots dead center. But the down draft from the rotors kept her from balancing her body in a good shooting position and sent the bullets off course. But the occupants must have seen her or the horses tied up several yards up the hill, and it sharply banked away and sped off. She fired two more shots, sure she had missed again.

Chapter 20

After a quick discussion, Craig and Sam decided to advance up the hill toward Cathedral Peak. They believed it would be best if they continued to go due west but on separate tracks in an attempt to flank Grace on both sides. The separate tracks would also put them in positions to detect her if she deviated south or north. She would eventually have to change course in any direction but west, as there was no way she could navigate up the nearly vertical wall of the peak. Certainly not with her horses and hostages.

Sam told Fred to stay where he was and wait for help to come to him. The sheriff knew that put the deputy at more risk as the makeshift field dressing he had applied would not halt the bleeding completely. And even if the ambulance got to the point where their vehicles were parked, it might take medics another thirty minutes to get to him, trudging uphill with their equipment and possibly a stretcher, in tow.

Fred listlessly nodded his head in acknowledgment. But Craig and Sam had been gone only two minutes when the deputy put his own plan into motion.

He pressed his back against the tree, bent his legs, and began squirming upward. He could feel the tree bark scratching his back through the light uniform shirt and the T-shirt underneath. As he got his torso higher, he repositioned his feet until they were right under him, and he was standing upright but still using the tree for support. He took a step forward and felt a little unsteady. He wasn't dizzy, just a little weaker than normal. He took another step and remained upright.

"I can do this," he thought, his right hand still holding the belt tight around the bandana, keeping most of the blood inside his body. But his shoulder felt wet and sticky, and he could feel a thin stream of blood trickling down his side. He glanced down and saw the stream had reached his waistline, and a small dark red pool was forming on his pants.

Fred took several more tentative steps forward. With his right arm occupied with the belt and his left arm hanging uselessly at his side, it was difficult to keep his balance on the branch and twig-strewn ground under the trees.

"I've got to get out of the trees where the ground is more even," he whispered aloud. He adjusted his direction only slightly to head for the small clearing but, at the same time, continued on a downhill route. After several steps, he found himself in the clearing under the late afternoon sun. He was thankful he wore his hat tight enough that it had stayed on his head through the shot and being drug into the trees. At this point he was also thankful that in their rush to follow Grace, he nor the sheriff or Craig had put on kevlar vests. The extra weight would have been an extra strain on his body already being taxed by the blood loss.

But at the same time, he began to worry about his comrades up the hill without the extra protection against gunshots the vests provided.

He cleared the small stand of trees in which they had taken shelter and was on the trail they had taken on the way up. Now, he was able to walk a little faster, but only just a fraction.

"This is better," he said to himself. "I'm going to make it."

He was so focused on his journey that he was oblivious to anything else around him. He didn't hear the gentle breeze blowing through the pine needles, the birds chirping back and forth, nor did he hear the state police helicopter pass over him, the shots fired at it, the chopper hovering over the campground and then rev up and move back up the hill.

Sam's and Craig's strategy of splitting up in an attempt to flank Grace in her getaway up the mountain had its disadvantages. Now with Fred injured and left behind, there was no one to continue following the horses' tracks to make sure she continued on a westerly course. It also left them a man short, which meant Grace would have only two targets to worry about. It also left a route unguarded if she doubled back on her own path and with no one following the horse tracks. If Grace veered to either side, with the dense timber it might not be noticed until she had slipped past either flanking man.

However, as she continued up the hill, the trees started to thin out. In addition, the terrain became rockier. While two men could travel over the rocky ground at a pace faster than a walk, someone on horseback would have to go slower to allow the mount to find the most stable spot to plant each hoof. It would slow the rider even more if they were leading another horse. Especially if that horse was carrying not one but two riders.

Another advantage Craig and Sam had was air support.

Sam heard the JetRanger rev up from the hover mode and knew it was headed their way. There was no need for him to radio the pilot. He had instructed them as they were leaving the small stand of trees that he and Craig were splitting up. In addition, the pilot would return to the location he had initially pinpointed as the suspect's location.

As the craft traveled toward the peak, Sam glanced up and noticed it was at a higher altitude. Being on the right flank, he was also looking south, which gave him a chance to see the sun's position. It was dipping lower in the sky. He guessed they had two hours of good daylight left, with continually dimming twilight after that for about an hour more.

He also knew the helicopter's increased altitude was to widen the range from Grace in case she decided to shoot at the helo again. But he knew enough about helicopters to know that the higher it went, the harder the engine had to work to stay aloft in the thinner air. Cathedral Peak was more than twelve thousand feet above sea level. Sam guessed the helicopter was at about the ten thousand foot mark compared to the peak's height and climbing as it advanced westward. How long would it be before the craft reached the point where it would have to return to base? The time on station could be extended if, when they got to that point, they went to Dubois to refuel rather than all the way back to Jackson, the sheriff thought.

Craig was thinking much the same as he watched the helicopter pass up to his right.

He and the sheriff were about one hundred yards apart and could see each other occasionally through small breaks in the timber. They had kept pace with each other, give or take a few feet. They had just gotten to the point where the trees began to thin out when they heard a rifle shot.

They looked uphill but didn't see anything at ground level. But in the sky, they saw the helicopter hovering about one hundred yards ahead and almost in a straight line in front of Sam. Two more shots rang out. Sam and Craig saw something small exit the helo's left side door and travel in an arch trailing yellow smoke.

A smoke grenade.

O─○

When Grace returned to the horses secured to the tree, she found Anna and Kathleen struggling against their restraints. She saw the leather strap had loosened some and that the women were continuing to work on it with their heads turned away from her. She rushed over to the quarter horse and slammed the butt of her rifle into Kathleen's left side. Because she was smaller and secured below Kathleen, less of Anna was exposed. But Grace smashed the rifle butt into her elbow as Anna brought her tied hands back up underneath her chest when she heard Kathleen scream from the pain of the blow to her side.

The attack startled the horse, and it sidestepped away from the blows. The sudden move and the looseness of the straps allowed the women to slide to the left along the horse's side. With their hands and feet tied together, they had no way of stopping the momentum from taking them over the side. They tried to close their hands around the straps as they slid, but they could not get a solid grip. Not that it would have helped. The straps had become so loose that even if they had been able to grab them, they would simply have slipped along with them.

They continued to fall until the straps caught them like a hammock under the horse's belly. That frightened the horse anew, and it took several more steps to the right. That movement further loosened the knots in the straps, and they fell away, dropping the women, now inverted so they were facing up to the ground. Although it was a distance of about three feet to the ground, they fell on several jagged rocks. Because she was now on the bottom, Kathleen took the brunt of the impact.

She screamed in pain again. Although she was also in extreme pain from the blow to her elbow, Anna rolled off Kathleen to the right and scrambled to her knees. With her feet and hands tied, she could not stand up. Instead, she put her hands straight up and gently touched the horse's side, then lightly rubbed her hands back and forth until the horse calmed down. It was then that she became aware again of the agonizing pain in her left elbow. She brought her hands down.

"Shit!" Grace yelled as the women slid down the horse's side. She took a step back and could only watch as the women hit the ground. She watched Anna calm the quarter horse, then stepped close to Kathleen lying on her back, struggling to catch her breath. Grace thought she had just had the wind knocked out of her. But the reality was that the rifle to the side had broken two ribs, and the fall to the ground had cracked a vertebra in her upper back. She watched for a few seconds as Kathleen continued to wheeze and grimace.

Grace then walked to the Appaloosa, which had skittered as far away from the action as it could and retrieved the Colt Python from the belt holster she had earlier tied to the rifle scabbard. She walked right up to Kathleen and stood looking straight down into her face. Now, the pain and effort to breathe that was apparent on her face was replaced with sheer terror. Grace pointed the Python directly at her nose.

"You're no use to me now," she said.

"No!" Anna screamed, which didn't distract Grace at all. But another sound did.

Grace slowly turned to look slightly northeast, and she saw the helicopter climbing back in her direction. She dashed back to the Appaloosa, replaced the Python in the holster and, with the Browning rifle still in her left hand, walked a few yards away from the horses and raised the scope to her eye. She fired two quick shots with the pilot in the scope's crosshairs. Just as she pulled the trigger, the helo banked sharply, and something was thrown out the side door. Grace was sure one of her shots struck home.

The small item flew through the air in a graceful arc and landed several feet in front of her. It began to emit yellow smoke. Grace ran over, set the rifle on the ground and tried to pick the smoke grenade up to toss it away, but the canister was too hot, and it burned her fingers.

⊙╌⊙

Fred staggered along the well-defined trails within the timber, heading what he believed to be due east. In reality, he was headed in a slightly southeasterly direction, more sharply at first. Then, there was a short change to slightly northeasterly. He came out into a very small clearing.

The sudden appearance of the open space momentarily confused him. In his dazed state from the slow but continued loss of blood, he was certain he would see no open space in the timber until he got to the point just off Horse Creek Road where the van, horse trailer, sheriff's borrowed fire department pickup, Craig's truck and his own sheriff's marked Chevy Tahoe were parked.

Fred stood in the center of the clearing and tried to think. He was not sure how far he had walked since leaving the stand of trees where the sheriff had told him to stay. Staying very quiet, he turned his head one-hundred eighty degrees from right to left, taking in as much detail as his fuzzy brain could process. There was no need to turn and take in the other one-hundred-eighty degrees. As slow as his mind was becoming, he knew he did not want to backtrack.

The deputy heard, faintly, the steady sound of water rolling over a rocky surface. The noise was coming from in front of him; that much was clear.

"That's got to be Wiggins Fork. I'm heading in the right direction," he said aloud.

To his left was an almost unbroken wall of pine trees. To his right was an opening a few yards wide. He turned in that direction and, on wobbly legs, walked toward it. Once there, he saw the opening in the woods extended to the left, back in an easterly direction. He turned and took a few steps. Fred saw that what he took to be a trail ended just a few yards away. But he was certain that was the direction he needed to go.

"If I have to go through the trees, I'll just have to," he said.

He got up to what looked to be an impassable barrier. But the more he stared at it, it came into focus for what it was -- a dense clump of trees with narrow spaces in between. He took slow steps forward and squeezed through the tree trunks. After a few steps, he lost his balance and slammed his left shoulder into a thick pine. Intense pain shot through his shoulder and up into his neck, but he stayed upright.

He continued to lean against the tree until he was able to get his feet squarely under himself. The pain continued in intensity. But as it turned out, it was a good thing. The pain cleared his head somewhat and restored some of his resolve. Fred felt a small trickle of blood rolling down his back. He yanked the belt tighter. The blood continued to roll down his back, but it stopped just above the belt line on his pants. Fred carefully squeezed through three more tightly spaced trees and suddenly found himself in a narrow track of open space within the timber.

It was a seldom-used walking trail. But it was certainly better than trying to slip through dense timber. The path appeared to lead in that slightly northeast direction. After what he guessed was about twenty yards, the trail curved ever so slightly, so it was now leading him due east. The noise of the water was becoming louder in his ears. Did that mean he was getting closer to it? He was not certain but thought it likely.

Fred could feel his legs becoming weaker with each step. He felt no more blood tickling his side or back. Had the bleeding stopped?

"I sure hope so, but I can't count on that," he said and continued taking slow, small steps.

Chapter 21

As the yellow smoke billowed up from the forest floor, Sam got on the radio.

"She'll be coming toward you," he said, meant for Craig. "She'll move away from the helo."

He replaced the radio on his belt and continued up the hill. But he quickened his pace as much as he could over the uneven, rocky terrain. He had to get even with the smoke in case he was wrong.

Craig also pushed himself to move faster. Instead of moving straight up the hillside, Craig altered his course to the left and advanced at a forty-five-degree angle from his previous track. If Grace started to move to the south, away from the helicopter, she would move past him. He had to take an angle of attack not to where she was but where she would be. His training in football, all those years ago, was dictating his approach.

Unbeknownst to him, it was an approach that would put him out of position to intercept her.

⊶⊷

Grace ran the few yards back to the horses and the two women. Kathleen was still on the ground, flat on her back. She had tried to roll over in an effort to stand up. But the pain shot from two points, her back and ribs, to points throughout her body. But since the pain was felt everywhere, it was clear to her that she was not paralyzed.

Anna was still on her knees next to the quarter horse. With her hands down and her arms motionless, the pain in her elbow was reduced to a dull throb.

Ignoring Kathleen, Grace went straight to Anna and cut through the zip ties binding her feet. But she left her hands securely tied.

"Stand up," Grace demanded. Anna complied clumsily because she could not use her arms for balance, and Grace did not help her.

Once she was standing upright, Grace pushed her right up against the quarter horse's side. The animal flinched with the contact but remained standing in place. Grace, almost a full half foot taller than Anna, bent and put her arms around the smaller woman's waist. She then lifted her enough to get her upper body across the horse's back. She grabbed Anna's leg and draped it over the horse's other side.

Anna tried to sit up, but Grace pulled her right arm down.

"Stay down, bitch," she hissed.

She then grabbed the straps that had held the two women in place, looped them around Anna's feet and used the rest to wrap around Anna and the horse's chest. She secured the other end of the strap by tying it to the loop around Anna's feet. She then grabbed the brown and gold scarf from the bag hanging from the saddle on the Appaloosa, looped it between Anna's tied hands, wrapped it around the horse's neck and tied it. She tested it to make sure it wasn't so tight as to choke or irritate the horse but tight enough to keep Anna from moving her hands more than an inch or two to either side or backward and forward. Satisfied, she went to the Appaloosa and retrieved the Colt Python. She stood over Kathleen again.

But just as she started to aim the pistol at the prone woman's face, the helicopter banked toward her. She jerked the rifle up and, steadying it with her right hand still holding the Python, aimed at the craft's nose and fired three quick shots. She saw the first strike the small right-hand window on the bottom of the nose. Whether the other two struck the aircraft, she did not see as it banked away to her left, circled around and took up its previous station.

The bullet had shattered the window, struck the peddle just under the pilot's right foot, went through the thin metal of the control peddle, through his boot just missing the little toe, continued on a slightly altered upward trajectory and lodged in the roof just behind the overhead control panel.

The pilot instinctively pushed down on the right peddle, and the helo banked to the right. He continued the turn through three-hundred sixty degrees to end up right back where it started when he saw the suspect head with a gun in her hand to the woman lying on the ground.

Grace stared at the aircraft for a few seconds. Then she went back to the horses, grabbed the lead rope for the quarter horse, mounted the Appaloosa, turned the horse west again and began moving toward the peak.

Up in the helicopter, the pilot and co-pilot tried to determine what direction she was heading. But the smoke from the grenade was still pouring out, and a slight breeze was blowing to the west, obscuring their line of sight.

⊶⊷

The small trail Fred had been following downhill narrowed a bit. His vision had started to blur several steps earlier. He suddenly felt his right shoulder smack into a solid object. The unexpected jolt made him lose his grip on the belt, and it fell loose and began to slide through the U-shaped buckle.

The deputy had the presence of mind to plant his left foot firmly on the ground to keep himself from falling after the impact of the tree. He jerked his right hand up to the top of his shoulder and felt the leather of his belt. Turning his head to the left, he saw the fuzzy outline of the buckle. The end of the belt was sticking up, still threaded through it. He put his hand over it and discovered the buckle's small retraining arm had slipped into one of the holes on the end of the belt, keeping it from falling to the ground.

Fred gripped the end of the belt and, with a finger, flipped the arm out of the hole. He then yanked the belt downward, tightening it around his wound again. He felt blood on his side and back again. It was thicker and flowing slower than before, so he knew the wounds had started to clot. The escape of the blood made him more lightheaded than he had been, and he could feel his knees going weak. He had the sensation of

180

downward motion. But it suddenly stopped, and he felt himself supported under his armpits. Shooting pains on his left side cleared his head a little, and he found himself staring at Daniel Reilly.

"Take it easy, deputy," he heard Daniel say.

Fred tried to speak, but words were not coming out of his mouth.

"Where are my sister and brother?" Daniel asked.

The deputy bent his right arm at the elbow and, using his thumb like a hitchhiker, pointed it up the hill. Then Fred was conscious of other people around him on the small trail and in the trees on either side of it. He glanced around and saw blurry shapes, but he could not make out details in the areas where their faces should be. Daniel was almost nose to nose with him, and he saw the man motion with his head. Then Fred felt other hands support him, one under his right armpit and the other on his left with his arm around his waist. That person had also taken hold of the loose belt, dropped when the deputy thumbed uphill, and pulled it tight again. Daniel's face disappeared and Fred felt himself in motion again.

Daniel headed up the hill at a dead sprint with a dozen others following him. They had all seen and heard the helicopter as they drove up to the point on Horse Creek Road where Sam, Craig, Fred and Grace had left their vehicles. They followed the noise and, not long after encountering Fred on the trail, saw the yellow smoke rising above the treetops. Within fifteen minutes they broke out of the dense trees and were in the rougher rocky terrain. Just ahead, they could see the wispy remains of the smoke. Ten more yards ahead, they found Kathleen lying on the ground.

Daniel knelt by his sister's side. Her eyes were closed, but he could tell she was breathing.

"Kathleen, I'm here," Daniel said as the twelve other men circled around her. The woman's eyes fluttered open, and she whispered his name.

"Are you shot?" he asked, looking her over head to toe for signs of blood.

"No," she said, gasping from the effort. She took a deep breath of air, grimacing in pain as she did.

"My side and my back hurt real bad," she said, then took another painful breath.

"Don't talk. Can you move your arms and legs?" he asked.

Kathleen raised each leg in turn about four inches, then raised both arms at once. That movement had her crying out in pain.

"We've got to get her down to the road," Daniel said and stood up. "But if she's got a back injury, we can't just flop her over a shoulder and go."

Several of the men fanned out and began looking for something flat. Two men came back with a tree trunk about six feet long and eighteen inches wide. It was not a complete trunk, just roughly one-third of its original circumference. The interior had been mostly scooped out, most likely from being pushed over jagged rocks by a recent landslide from higher up the hill. One end still had wood across the width. The damage to the trunk was recent enough that rot had not set in, and it was fairly sturdy.

The men laid it next to Kathleen, but one of the other men instructed it to be repositioned so the scraped-out end was where her head was. Her legs would ride higher, but that would help keep her from going into shock, he explained. Three men on each side slowly and carefully lifted her over the log and gently laid her upon it. The same six men began to lift the load, but Daniel pulled one away and took his place.

"I'm going down the hill with her," he said as he handed Fred's radio, which he took from him earlier, to one of the remaining six men. "Craig and the sheriff are up here. Call the sheriff and see how you can help them."

The six "stretcher bearers" then began their slow and careful trek down the mountain.

⚬⚬⚬

Craig and Sam heard the click and short burst of static that indicated an incoming call on the radio. They both thought each other was calling.

"Sheriff, how can we help?"

The voice was unfamiliar. Since it was addressing the sheriff, Craig stayed silent and focused on his track. Every few steps he glanced to his right to try and catch sight of Grace and the horses. A quick look at his watch told him it was just after six-thirty. That gave them about ninety minutes of good daylight left. The sun was low in the sky and throwing harsh light onto the hillside.

"Who is this?" he heard Sam say over the radio.

On Craig's next glance to his right, he caught sight of something white. It was a brighter white than was natural for the terrain. He stopped and stared at the color. It was moving!

"We're friends of Daniel's from town. We heard you were up here searching for someone," the radio voice answered.

Just when he was about to grab his radio and answer the call when, he heard his brother's name, Craig realized what he was seeing. He remembered Helen Metcalf saying Grace had taken two horses, a quarter horse and an Appaloosa. The white he had seen must be the latter. But it was farther away than it should have been if she had turned south.

Craig cursed and changed his direction, aiming for a point ahead of where he projected she was going if she had continued due west.

"How many is we?" Craig heard the sheriff ask.

Trying to watch the ground to find the best footing and looking ahead to keep the white object in sight as best he could, Craig ran as fast as possible.

"There are seven of us back here where we found Kathleen," the voice answered. "Six others, including Daniel, took her back down the hill."

Craig was confused by that response. Kathleen had been left behind? Was it because she was dead and of no use to Grace any longer? Why did it take six people to take her down? He continued to run toward his target.

"Are you armed?" the sheriff asked. Craig could hear heavy breathing each time the sheriff spoke into the radio. The voice responded in the affirmative.

"Spread out, but keep each other in sight," Sam instructed the newcomers. "Walk uphill due west. You will be our rearguard. And call 9-1-1 and tell them there is another casualty and we need another ambulance."

Through gaps in the trees Craig could see he was closing the gap on the white object. But he was still slightly behind. He tried to pick up the pace, but it was difficult. Not only was the ground still rocky but he was feeling the energy slowing draining from him. He needed to slow her advance somehow.

"Grace, you need to stop and give up," he yelled as loud as he could.

It seemed to work as the white object stopped. It was hard to tell how far away it was from him, but he guessed about fifty yards, and he was about ten yards behind her on a north-south line. He kept running, dodging left and right to avoid trees.

Suddenly, a tree trunk to his right exploded, showering his right shoulder and arm with bark and splinters. He ducked behind the next tree. He reached down and pulled the Glock 17 from its holster. He very slowly peeked around the tree. He was close enough now to see details in the bright sunshine about thirty minutes before it started to slowly fade. What he saw chilled the blood in his veins.

The Appaloosa was nowhere to be seen. Most likely, Grace had not tied the reins to a tree, and it had been spooked by the rifle shot and taken off. The quarter horse was standing broadside to him, and Anna was half sitting, half lying on its back. He could see the strap that was holding her there securely.

Grace was standing on the other side. He could see her legs under the horse's belly. The only other thing he saw was her arm extended across Anna's back. In her hand was a Colt Python with the barrel pressed against the base of Anna's skull.

Chapter 22

"Get on your radio and tell that helicopter pilot and the other cops you have up here to get the hell out of here," Grace yelled. "Or I'll blow her head off."

Craig heard Anna whimper.

"I don't have any way to contact the helicopter," Craig said. "I don't know what frequency they are on even if I had a radio."

"Don't you bullshit me," Grace said. "You were a cop once. Figure it out."

Craig glanced up and saw the JetRanger hovering about twenty yards north. But he could tell the pilot was inching the craft closer. He knew the pilot was receiving instructions from Sam to continue to provide reports of the suspect's position and actions. He could hear his voice through the radio, although the volume was down low enough that he was certain Grace could not hear it because of the distance between them.

He reached down and found the volume knob on the radio clipped to his belt. He turned the dial down to the bare minimum. He did not want anything to come through the speaker to alert Grace to anything Sam might broadcast.

Stepping back from the tree but keeping it between himself and Grace, Craig raised his arms above his head and waved them inward and outward to get the Pilot's attention. He did that for several seconds to make sure those in the aircraft saw him. Then he waved both raised arms forward several times with his finger spread wide as if he were pushing the helicopter back. After a few seconds of this, the aircraft backed off about twenty yards and then resumed hovering.

Craig stepped back against the tree trunk.

"That's not good enough. It needs to be gone," Grace yelled, then clubbed Anna in the middle of her back with the butt of the pistol. She then returned the gun to Anna's head.

Anna cried out in pain, then said, "Shit, that hurt."

"I'll do worse than that if your boyfriend doesn't do what I tell him to do," Grace hissed into her ear.

"Grace, I'm not in control of the state police or the county sheriff's office. They're not going to listen to me," Craig hollered.

It was taking all the willpower he had to keep himself from charging toward them in hopes of catching Grace off guard and subduing her before she could pull the trigger. He knew he could not cover the twenty yards over rocky ground and dodging trees in time. She would pull her trigger the moment she saw him coming, but the gun would not be aimed at him. It would blow Anna's hair, skin, bones, and brain matter all over the horse's head and neck. She would still have time to turn the gun onto him while he was still about ten yards from her.

"They better, or this bitch is dead," Grace said.

"You won't do that, Grace. She is the only thing keeping you alive," Craig said.

"You think I give a shit about staying alive?' Grace hollered. "Your sister is already dead, and once I kill this one, you'll spend the rest of your life suffering the fact that you couldn't save them or those others."

Hearing Grace say that Kathleen was dead almost pushed him over the edge to take rash action. But because of his years of police experience, he knew his best bet was to keep her talking, keep her focus on him. While it had not entered his mind when he and Sam decided to try and flank Grace on both sides, the strategy was working out to their advantage with every second that passed. But he had to keep her occupied and focused on him so she wouldn't figure it out or hear Sam coming from the other side. Craig had not seen the sheriff to the north, but he was certain he was coming.

"Why do you want to make me suffer, Grace? What did I ever do to you?" he asked after pushing the transmit button on the radio and locking it open.

As soon as he heard Craig's voice come over his portable radio, Sam grabbed it and, turned the volume down and held it to his left ear, hooking the Remington under his arm as he continued to quickly but quietly walk toward where he had heard their first exchange. Because of the distance between them, Craig and Grace were shouting loud enough to be picked up on Craig's radio mic enough so Sam could hear every word.

"You ruined it, that's why," Grace said.

"Ruined what?" Craig asked.

"What I was doing in Kansas City," she screamed.

There it was. He was right about him being the connection between the Kansas City and Dubois killings. Now he knew exactly what had happened and why. But he needed her to explain it, both to keep her attention focused on him and to have her confess it in front of at least one witness, hopefully, two if Sam was listening. But there were more. In addition to Sam, the helicopter crew was tuned in to the same frequency and, with any luck, would hear every word as well.

But for Craig's hope that Grace's confession would be heard to work, he needed Anna to survive in case no one else could hear the conversation clearly.

And there was more to her survival than playing the part of a witness to a confession. So he had to tread lightly. He had to keep her talking, but his prodding had to be subtle so as not to set her off.

"I didn't ruin it. You stopped on your own," he said. "Besides, the Kansas City police closed the case after that guy was arrested in Kansas."

"But you were helping them," she yelled.

"But they weren't listening to me. They closed the case," Craig said.

She chuckled, then went dead serious again.

"Yeah, I'll bet they really pissed you off," she said.

He didn't answer. He was scanning the forest to the northeast, looking for any sign that Sam was on his way. He saw nothing.

"With the case closed, you could have continued what you were doing in Kansas City," Craig said.

"No, I couldn't," Grace screamed. "They would have seen that you were right and opened the case again. If I didn't stop, I would have been caught."

"So why did you start again, here and now?" Craig asked.

"I wanted you to suffer," Grace hollered, then her tone changed to her normal speech patterns. "I thought about it for a few years -- how could I get back at you? What would make you suffer."

There was a short silence. Craig's scan of the forest finally brought results. He saw Sam about thirty yards to the northeast of where Grace stood beside the quarter horse with the Python pointed at the back of Anna's head. He began searching his mind for a plausible plan of attack. But even if he came up with one, how could he clue Sam in on it?

"And then I got a letter about this reunion," Grace said.

"So you decided to come here and kill our classmates to get back at me?" Craig asked. "How is killing innocent people making me suffer?"

He tried to couch the latter question in a tone of indifference.

"You care about those people," she said. "Sooner or later, I would have gotten someone you really care about. And I did, but not in the way I planned."

"Why didn't you go after my sister right away?" Craig asked, the emotion of not knowing whether Kathleen was alive or dead, as Grace claimed, rolling up his throat. He put his right hand on the butt of the Glock in the holster.

"Oh no, that would have been one and done," she said. "That wouldn't have been as much fun for me."

That remark made his blood start boiling, and he tightened the grip on the Glock.

"And then after I killed the fourth one, it became harder to get close enough to others so I could lure them away," Grace said. "Then I found out you had been hanging around with and fucking this one."

Craig had lost sight of Sam, but he knew he was out there somewhere. The sun was at the point in the sky where the light was minutes away from starting its thirty-minute fade. Something was going to have to happen soon, or they would lose the light and give Grace a chance to escape, maybe even kill Anna soon afterward.

"Maybe I should just plug her right now," Grace sneered.

Craig drew the Glock from its holster, pointed it straight up and slowly stepped out from behind the tree.

"Don't do it, Grace. Shoot me instead," he said.

Grace pointed the Colt at him as soon as he was clear of the tree.

"Oh God no, don't do it," Anna wailed.

Suddenly, Grace whirled so her back was to the quarter horse and pointed the gun with her left arm back in Anna's direction.

The end of the pistol spits smoke and flame. Craig saw it as if it were moving in super slow motion. The sound of the shot was like a clap of thunder going off right above them, and it echoed off the granite walls of Cathedral Peak, making it sound like there were multiple shots.

Craig lowered the Glock and began sprinting toward the quarter horse with Anna on its back, her head glowing red.

For several minutes Sam had been running as fast as he could up the hill west toward Cathedral Peak. He was slowed only by the brief radio exchange with the civilians who had taken Fred's radio. He had finally gotten clear of the drifting yellow smoke from the grenade, which had finally regurgitated all that it had. He caught a glimpse of a horse silhouetted by the setting sun. It was about thirty yards south and a few yards uphill from him. He continued to run uphill.

The helicopter was about five hundred feet above him. Its engine whine and rotors beating the air were loud, and the echo off the peak made it even louder. The sheriff knew the racket would mask any noise he would make this far away from the horse. But he had not seen any humans or a second horse, so he slowed his advance and cautiously swept the area ahead and to his sides. After a few strides, he saw a second horse with someone on its back.

He heard a voice, but the noise from the helicopter was too loud for him to make out the words clearly. Before he could replay the voice back in his mind to try and make out the words, he heard the sound of one gunshot. Even over the noise of the helicopter, his trained ear told him it was from a rifle. He then saw a flash of movement, and something came barreling through the trees and passed right in front of him. It was an Appaloosa, saddle on its back and bridle on its head with the reins flapping at its sides, galloping straight toward him, then diverting to a northeasterly direction.

Sam slowed down to a careful walk. It was not to avoid making noise, as the chopper noise still masked his approach. Now, he was considering options. He continued to move closer to the area where he had seen the horses, although now he caught sight of it through the trees, and there was just one horse with someone on its back and another standing next to it with their back to him.

Now, the sheriff could catch two voices conversing. He paid no attention to the words used, just the sound to try and detect where the other voice was coming from. He heard the helicopter engine fade a bit. He glanced in its direction and saw that it had moved back. Now just forty yards from the horse and people, Sam was concerned any noise he might make would give him away to the person standing by the horse, who he assumed was Grace and now pointing a handgun at the head of the person on the horse.

He stopped for a couple of seconds and listened to the voice coming from the other side of the horse. It seemed to be coming from a point in a direct north-south line with Grace and her captive. At that point he heard Craig's voice over the radio and turned down the volume and put it to his ear.

The sheriff realized that he was in a bad position. If he had to fire his weapon at Grace, he risked having Anna and the person talking to Grace, who Sam knew was Craig, in the line of fire. So he started moving slowly sideways up the hill. He got twenty yards uphill from Grace, then moved south the same distance. He was now looking at the horse head on, and Grace was broadside to him. He had a clear view through a break in the trees. He lay the rifle gently on the ground and, drew his pistol and clipped the radio back on his belt.

Now, he was far enough away from the helo that he could hear both sides of the conversation that was going on between Craig and Grace. He concentrated on the words as he pointed his pistol at Grace's mid-section.

"Why didn't you go after my sister right away?" Craig asked.

"Oh no, that would have been one and done," she said. "That wouldn't have been as much fun for me."

The sheriff put his finger through the trigger guard and started to put pressure on the trigger.

"And then after I killed the fourth one, it became harder to get close enough to others so I could lure them away," Grace said. "Then I found out you had been hanging around with and fucking this one."

Sam saw the long shadows cast by the horse, Anna and Grace and thought exactly what Craig was thinking at that very moment.

"Maybe I should just plug her right now," Grace sneered.

"Don't do it, Grace. Shoot me instead," Craig said.

Sam glanced to his right for a split second and saw Craig thirty yards away step out from behind a tree with his hands raised high in the air, his gun in his right hand. His vision went back to Grace, and he saw her swivel the gun in Craig's direction.

"Oh God no, don't do it," Anna wailed.

"Shit!" Sam said aloud.

Suddenly, Grace whirled so her back was to the quarter horse, and the Colt Python swung back and burst to life just as Sam pulled his own trigger as hard as he could.

Chapter 23

The two men escorting Fred down the mountain got him to the area just off Horse Creek Road. With the van and horse trailer, Sam's borrowed fire department pickup, Craig's Ram, Fred's sheriff-marked Tahoe and the various vehicles the fifteen men had used to get to the location, it looked like a small used car lot.

Fred was barely conscious when they arrived. The two men took him to the back of a Ford pickup and opened the tailgate. They laid him on it. One of them went to the front of the truck and retrieved a first aid kit and two sixteen-ounce plastic bottles of Powerade. The label said it provided fifty percent more electrolytes. They were able to get him to gulp down three mouthfuls.

The first aid kit was a step above basic, and the men removed the belt, his shirt and bandanna from his wound, balling the latter two up and putting one under his head and the other under the exit wound on his back. Both wounds were clotted but not completely as thick, dark red blood still oozed out. They took two heavy cotton bandages from the kit and placed them over each hole, then used a wrapping bandage and a lot of medical tape to secure them.

They were just finishing up when several people walked up to the truck. It was a small group of campers who had walked over from the campground. The helicopter was beating a steady drone in the near distance.

"What's going on?" one man asked.

"There's an incident up on the mountain," one of Fred's escorts said. "You need to go back to the campground. And tell anyone who tried to go up the mountain to stay away from there."

A woman stepped forward and looked down at Fred's bandaged shoulder.

"We heard some gunfire," she said. "Was this man shot?"

"Yes, but we have it covered," the other escort said. "Now go back to the campground."

"I'm a nurse," the woman said, examining the dressing very closely. "Did you use cotton bandages under all this tape?"

"Yes, and a wrapping bandage," an escort said.

"Well, a little overdone on the tape, but otherwise, you did pretty good," she said. "Now we need to get him to a hospital." She pulled a cell phone out of her pocket.

"I think there's an ambulance already on its way," one of the escorts said.

At that moment, they heard a vehicle coming up the road from the south at what sounded like a high speed. They looked toward the road and saw Travis pull off in his sheriff's Tahoe with the light bar flashing. The vehicle skidded to a stop, and he jumped out.

"Who has been shot?" he asked as he trotted toward the pickup.

"It's the sheriff's deputy, Fred," one of the escorts told him.

"OK, there's an ambulance five minutes behind me," he said.

By the time it arrived, they had gotten one bottle of the Powerade into Fred. The paramedics got him on a stretcher and into the ambulance. Once they got him hooked up to IVs, one jumped out of the back.

"We heard a call from dispatch on the way up here that there is another casualty," he told the two men who brought Fred down and the nurse. "Getting another ambulance up here will take several hours because it has to come from Riverton. But they have a Life Flight helicopter heading in from Jackson. They're going to need a landing zone lit up. Can some of you park your cars on this side of the road and shine your headlights onto that area? It will likely be close to dark when it arrives." He pointed to the meadow on the east side of the road.

He then jumped in the ambulance and roared down the road. One of the escorts got in the Ford, and the other jumped in a brown Dodge Ram and pulled to the side of the road as instructed. Travis drove his Tahoe and parked beside them and then did the same with the fire department pickup. The Tahoe and fire department trucks were on the ends.

Then, they stood next to the vehicles and waited.

Craig was at the horse's side within three seconds, helped by the fact that Grace's shot so close frightened it, and it sidestepped away from the noise. Thankfully, Craig was able to grab the lead rope and calm the horse before it bolted like the Appaloosa had, taking Anna with it. He wrapped his left arm, with the lead rope in his hand, around Anna's head and reached over the horse's back with his right arm, the Glock clutched in his hand and his finger through the trigger guard. He saw Grace standing about three feet away from the horse with a dazed look on her face, staring straight ahead. He began to raise the pistol to shoot her. Then, without looking in Craig's direction, she darted to her right. Craig squeezed off a shot, but sawdust and bark jumped from a tree trunk. Grace was out of sight among the pines.

Craig holstered his weapon and, still hugging Anna's head, reached under the horse and untied the strap. He put his arm around her waist and, dragged her off the animal and tried to lay her on the ground, but her hands slid around the horse's neck and stopped at its front haunches.

"Untie my hands."

The voice startled him, and he almost dropped her. And then he suddenly realized the back of her head was intact.

"Holy shit, you're alive," he whispered into her right ear.

"Untie me and let me stand up," Anna said.

He quickly undid the brown and gold scarf, then took out his pocket knife and cut through the zip ties that bound her hands. He took her into both arms and hugged her tighter than he ever had before.

"I thought you were dead," he said, tears pouring out of his eyes.

He then felt moisture on his hands. Kind of sticky moisture. Still hugging her, he raised his hands behind her head and saw in the fading sunlight his fingers were red. He released the hug and inspected her head. He found a thin trickle of blood coming out of her right ear and smudgy red under it where his hands, first his left, then his right, had been. He moved her hair aside and found no blood anywhere on the outside of her ear except where it ran down onto the earlobe and dripped on her neck.

"What's wrong?" she asked. "Did I get hit?"

"No, I think the concussion of her shot damaged your ear," he said.

"Are you going to answer me or not?" she asked.

He gently turned her head so they were facing each other.

"No, your ear was damaged by the concussion of her shot," he said.

His suspicion was confirmed with her next words.

"That bitch," Anna said. And Craig pulled her in for another bear hug and they both giggled nervously.

Then, they heard a groan from up the hill.

As Sam pulled his trigger, the notch sight at the end of his pistol barrel was right on Grace's upper chest. But anticipating that Grace would fire, he instinctively crouched down. But he had not had time to set his feet, and they were side by side and only a few inches apart. The recoil of his Glock 19 sent him sprawling backward. He hit the ground square on his back, and the air rushed out of his lungs.

As he lay on the forest floor fighting to regain his breath, his only thought was, *"Oh crap, she's going to come over here and finish me off."*

He was staring straight up and saw the darkening blue sky with some scattered white clouds framed by tall pine trees. He felt some regret that he was not going to be able to bring this case, one of the worst in the county's history, to a successful close. He also felt some guilt that his mistake in not being prepared in a shooter's stance as he advanced on Grace was going to cost Craig and Anna their lives as well.

Staring up at the sky and trees, he wondered when the movie in his head would start. That movie where your whole life flashes before your eyes before you die. The trees and sky grew darker by the second, and the movie didn't start. He was disappointed because there was a lot in his life he would have liked to review.

He also wondered where the bright light was. The light that so many people who came back from near-death experiences described. All he saw was a view that quickly faded to black.

And suddenly, the view had returned. He could see the sky again, a tad lighter than he remembered. And the framing trees were green, with a touch of another color like the white on a Christmas tree, only this was orange.

He heard the snapping of twigs underfoot. It was Grace coming to put an end to his life. He groped around with his right hand, looking for his weapon, but his hand only found rocks, grass and small pieces of wood. Resigned to his fate, he closed his eyes and was a little startled to see Grace standing over him, pointing the Colt Python at his face.

"Did you decide it was nap time?" he heard a male voice say.

He opened his eyes and saw Craig standing on his right and Anna standing on his left, staring down at him.

Five minutes later, the trio was standing by the quarter horse with the lead rope tied to a tree. Sam had his tan cowboy hat in his hands. Or what was left of it. There was a large, ragged hole in the center of the front and a larger hole in the back. When he had found it, after being helped up about twenty yards from the spot where he fell he had rubbed his hands through the hair at the top of his head. He felt some surface pain as his hand swept backward, and when he lowered the hand in front of his face, he saw it was covered in blood.

Head wounds, even very minor ones, tend to bleed a lot. He went to one knee, and Anna examined his head. Touching gingerly around the crown of his head, she found a small scratch, blood still trickling out of it. Sam fished a handkerchief out of his back pocket and pressed it to the scratched area. It stung a bit, but he kept it there under the pressure of his left hand.

Now gathered near the horse, the three were piecing together the events of the last few minutes.

"When she fired, I saw Anna's head turn red," Craig said. "It must have been the muzzle flash combined with the sun on her hair."

By this time, the sun was within a minute of slipping behind the southwestern mountains. Anna had assured them she was only injured in the elbow, and she could not hear through her right ear.

"She and I must have fired simultaneously," Sam said.

"I thought I heard a second shot, but it could have been the echo off the peak," Craig said.

"I was a little off balance, and the recoil knocked me down," the sheriff said, then looked down at the hat in his right hand. "That saved my life."

Sam took down the handkerchief and held one end. He draped it over his head from ear to ear, covering the scratch and letting the ends hang down either side of his head. Then he jammed the hat onto his head. That kept the handkerchief in place fairly tight over the wound.

"What happened to Grace?" he asked.

"After she fired she stood there for a couple of seconds, staring straight ahead, then turned and took off into the woods," Craig said, pointing in a general northeasterly direction.

"Where was the other horse?" Craig asked.

"As I was coming up the hill it was spooked by gunfire and went running past in front of me heading down the hill," Sam said, pointing to the northwest.

"Well, chances are she's not going to find that horse, and she's now on foot," Craig said.

He looked toward the sun and watched it sink below the mountainous horizon. He then looked around the area.

"We're not going to find her in the dark, and we need to get moving in case she's doubled back to take us out," Sam said.

Craig offered to help Anna get back on the horse, but she refused.

"I'm not getting back on that damned thing," she said.

Sam took the heavy-duty flashlight from his utility belt and turned it on, holding it in his left hand. With his right, he drew his Glock. The three began slowly walking, Craig leading the horse with the rope in one hand and Anna's hand in the other as the flashlight marked the way. After they had gone ten yards, Sam handed the flashlight to Craig and pulled out his radio, set it to a different frequency and instructed the helicopter to return to the clearing next to Horse Creek Road, where they had left the vehicles.

The rest of their trek down the hill was slow and careful. Craig kept the flashlight aimed at the ground, illuminating the area a few feet in front of their steps. His intent was to make sure they knew what was in front of them. He also did not want to risk sweeping it side to side in a search for Grace. That would have acted like a lighthouse on a rocky coastline. If she was in the area trying to find them, pointing it at the ground was a smaller risk.

No words were spoken for the rest of the journey. When they reached the clearing where Fred had been shot, they picked up the pace, now having small, defined paths devoid of large rocks.

As they descended, they heard the state police chopper heading back to the clearing next to Horse Creek Road. Shortly after the engine and rotor noise had died out, they heard a similar noise, first barely audible and growing in volume, coming toward them. As it got closer, they could tell the engine and rotor sound was a bit different than the JetRanger. Thirty yards past the clearing where Fred was shot, they saw over the treetop the flashing navigation lights of another helicopter.

Chapter 24

The second chopper, an EC-145 twin-engine aircraft, was on the ground in the meadow east of the road with its engine and rotors idling when Craig, Anna and Sam came out of the trees amid the collection of vehicles that had gathered on the west side of Horse Creek Road. The JetRanger was on the west side of the road on the north end of the clearing.

After putting the quarter horse in the trailer, the trio wound their way through the vehicles and people that had gathered there, including some of the visitors from the campground. Travis, near the second helicopter, saw them and ran to them.

"Anna and Sam need some medical attention," Craig said as Travis arrived.

"Where is Fred?" Sam asked. "He wasn't where I told him to stay."

"He came down the mountain mostly by himself," the deputy answered. "The ambulance took him about a half hour ago. He had lost a lot of blood and was unconscious when they left."

"So, who is the Life Flight chopper for?" Sam asked.

"Kathleen," Travis answered. Craig's head snapped up.

"I want to see her before they take the body away," he said, heading toward the chopper.

"What do you mean, the body?" Travis asked, trailing along behind him.

Craig stopped and stood dumbfounded for a couple of seconds. He had taken Grace at her word when she said Kathleen had been killed.

"She's alive?" Craig stammered. "Grace said she killed her."

"She was going to, twice," Anna explained. "But the helicopter up there distracted her both times. I'm sorry, Craig, I should have said something."

He looked into her eyes for a second. She did not see reproach. She saw relief and love. Craig gave her a warm hug and then ran over to the helicopter. A medic was getting ready to climb aboard. Craig grabbed his arm.

"How is my sister?" he asked.

"She's in bad shape, and we need to get her to Lander as fast as possible," the medic said.

"We've got two other people that need treatment," Craig said, motioning for Sam and Anna to join him.

"Don't be silly, I'll be fine. They need to get your sister to a hospital," Sam said, having overheard the conversation between Craig and the medic.

"I'm not leaving you," Anna said firmly.

The medic could see by the light from the chopper's cabin that Anna's elbow was crimson red and swollen. He reached out and felt around the joint. She winced in pain at the first touch but silently endured it the more he probed. He then put one hand on her upper arm and the other on her forearm and gently bent. Anna did her best not to react to the pain, but the medic was well-trained and picked up on the subtlest of signs.

"It could be broken," he said. "You'll have to get X-rays to make sure."

He reached into his medical kit and, shook out two half-inch capsules and handed them to her, along with a bottle of water.

"These will help with the pain and to keep the swelling down," he said, then pressed the bottle into her good hand. "Take one every eight hours." He then grabbed an arm sling, hung it from her neck, and gingerly slipped her arm into it. "Keep your arm as immobile as you can until you can see a doctor."

She nodded her head in acknowledgment.

"Don't wait too long," he said as he climbed into the chopper's main cabin.

Craig had used the medic's attention on Anna to clamber into the helicopter and beside the bench where Kathleen lay in a rescue basket. Another medic sat on the bench on the opposite side of the aircraft. Craig looked down at his sister, who appeared to be unconscious. He looked over at the medic.

"We gave her something for the pain. She is deeply sedated," he said. "She has a couple of ribs, possibly broken, and some type of back injury. We won't know for sure until we get her to the hospital."

Craig nodded and scrambled out of the helo as the other medic was finishing with Anna. Craig guided her back away from the aircraft and joined Sam near the road. The side door of the helicopter banged shut, and the engine immediately began to rev up. The trio stood at the edge of the road and watched the bird rise into the air. They watched it until it was lost in the black sky, its navigation lights quickly fading away.

⊶⊷

The morning sun began to filter through the trees as it rose above the eastern mountains of the Absaroka Range. A particular gap in the trees at the edge of the clearing next to Horse Creek Road allowed the morning light to shine into the cab of a copper Dodge Ram. It began to warm the occupant in the driver's seat, particularly the thin strip of exposed skin between his shirt collar and the thinning hair on the back of his neck.

The warmth of the sun slowly raised Craig from his slumber. He opened his eyes and slowly blinked several times to moisten his eyeballs. He found himself sitting behind the steering wheel with his head drooping down, his chin nearly resting on his upper chest where the collar bones came together. That position gave him a rather large double chin that acted as a cushion.

He raised his head slowly and heard and felt several moderate pops as the crick in his neck worked itself out. He rolled his head side to side and then up and down. His left arm lay along the armrest built into the door. His right arm was extended out about thirty degrees, and was lying on something soft.

Craig looked straight down to find Anna's head resting in his lap, face up. He turned his head to the right and saw that the center console had been pushed up and back. Anna was lying on her back the length of the center seat that was normally under the console and the passenger bucket seat. Her right leg was slightly bent upward and resting against the seat back, and her left leg was draped over the edge of the seat and dangling into the foot space in front of the passenger seat. His right arm was across her belly underneath his black leather jacket. Her left arm was still in the sling and tucked tightly below her breasts.

Anna seemed to be resting peacefully, although Craig could see the tension still written on her face from the previous day's activities.

Craig looked out the window to his right. Through the morning dew he could see Sam walking slowly, but purposely, toward the truck. He watched him circle in front of it and head for the driver's side window. Craig carefully took his right arm out from under his jacket, turned the truck's power on without turning over the engine and with his left hand pressed the power window button. The glass buzzed down, and he felt the coolness of the air flood in. It was in stark contrast to the rising sun still beating down on his neck.

"Good morning," Sam said. Craig put his index finger to his lips. Sam looked down to see Anna sleeping soundly.

"Did you get any sleep?" Sam whispered.

"Some," Craig replied quietly. "Did Grace turn up?"

"We didn't want to go searching in the dark," Sam explained. "Travis and I are going to head out now."

The sheriff looked down at Anna again. Her eyes were still closed, and she had not moved an inch.

"When she wakes up, you should take her back to town," Sam said.

"Nope. We're staying here until you find that bitch," they heard Anna say. Her eyes remained closed.

"We really should get your elbow looked at," Craig said in his normal volume voice.

"It's fine," Anna said, still with her eyes closed. "You can go if you want to, but I'm staying."

"Well, there you have it," Craig said with a shrug.

"Alright, suit yourself," Sam said. "We've got some hot coffee and some breakfast over there. We'll head out in about a half hour."

⊶

During the night, while Craig and Anna slept, Sam and Travis were engaged in a running argument with Daniel and the fourteen men who had come to the meadow from town with him. They all wanted to start searching the woods for Grace. Most of them were armed.

The campers were not involved in the heated discussions. Eleven of the 14 sites at the campground had been occupied. But once word spread of what had happened in town and on the mountain, there was a steady caravan of vehicles heading south on Horse Creek Road until the Double Cabins Campground was as deserted as the mining ghost towns on South Pass.

But Daniel was intent on avenging his sister. That was the only reason he had not accompanied her to the hospital. The other men were just as fixated on capturing or killing the woman who had murdered three of their friends and left a fourth for dead.

Sam was able to talk them out of heading up the hill during the night. He impressed upon them the fact that the darkness of night gave Grace another layer of cover and the advantage in any chance encounter.

"But the longer we wait to start searching, the farther away she will get," Daniel argued.

"The darkness also works in our favor," Sam explained. "If she is able to move at all in the dark, it will be extremely slow going. Plus, by moving fast in the dark, she runs the risk of stumbling up on a bear or moose or some other wildlife that could see her as a threat."

He did not need to explain searchers ran the same risk from wildlife. They were all well aware.

By the time this discussion took place, the Life Flight helicopter had long since departed, and the vehicles parked alongside the road flooding the clearing opposite for a landing zone were now shut down. With the campers also long gone, there was no light or much noise to help orient Grace as she blundered through the forest.

Sam was confident a delay until morning would not allow Grace to get very far in her attempt to escape. He had finally convinced them all just after midnight to stay put until daylight. But just in case, he and Travis stood alternating two-hour watches to make sure no one left the clearing.

⦿⸻⦿

As they hightailed it out of the area the night before, the campers had left a variety of food with those who remained in the clearing. As the sun peeked through the trees that morning, the nineteen people dined on bread, lunch meat, cold fried chicken, fruit and a number of other items while gulping down coffee brewed over an open fire.

With their bellies full, Sam laid out a search pattern with fourteen of the group spread out over an area from the clearing to past the campground. They were to slowly walk up the hill toward Cathedral Peak. Craig had seen Grace head north after the shooting the afternoon before. Sam speculated that she planned to circle around the campground at a safe distance and then make her way south following Wiggins Fork. The sound of the river would have been her guide in the dark.

As slow as he expected her to move through the night, Sam thought Grace would not have gotten around the campground until the sun was up. She needed the light to find her way along the river bank. His search pattern was spread from the clearing northward to allow for the possibility that she doubled back to go straight to the river south of the campground rather than north of it. Five members of the party were left behind in the clearing in case she had been waiting in the woods for the people to clear out, and she would either cross to the river there or try to follow the road back to town.

Sam knew there were gaps in the plan, but it was the best he could do until he got reinforcements. He had radioed the state police about four o'clock that morning and requested the helicopter's return and some additional officers for a more thorough search. But he did not expect them to arrive for several hours. He did not want to waste time sitting around waiting for them, nor did he believe he could contain the men much longer after the sun came up.

Anna would not leave Craig's side, so he volunteered the two of them to take the southernmost part of the search line. He figured that would be the least likely place they would encounter Grace. He was just as keen as Daniel to find her and do what needed to be done. But having Anna along might have restrained him from giving Grace the justice he believed she deserved. Had he asked her, Craig would have found that Anna was just as much in favor of his kind of justice.

He gave her his Sig P365 from the ankle holster, and he clutched his Glock. They advanced up the hill about ten yards apart, her keeping to the paths between the trees and he inside the timber but keeping her in sight. The other searchers were about twenty yards apart. Craig, Sam and Travis had their radios and checked in frequently.

Craig and Anna had just passed the point where Fred had been shot when they heard the single crack of a rifle to their right. He judged it to be about fifty yards away.

"Got her," a voice hollered as the rifle shot echoed off the peak. All the searchers on the hillside began converging on the location where they heard the shot and the yell.

Craig and Anna came out of the trees into a fair-sized clearing after working through some thick trees and then finding a path. Occasional yells of "Follow my voice" led them to it. Almost dead center in the middle of the clearing, they saw four men kneeling and standing around something on the ground. When they arrived at the knot of men, several others emerged from the trees and headed toward them.

Craig and Anna moved to the edge of the growing circle of men. Sprawled on the ground was Grace on her back. He recognized her from the clothes she had been wearing the previous day. It would have been difficult to recognize her any other way as half her face was missing, appearing to have been chewed. Her shirt and bra had been ripped open, and her left breast was a bloody pulp. Craig also noticed a blood stain on the right side of her shirt just above her waist and to the right of where her navel was. He pulled up the shirt tail and exposed a mass of blood on her belly with a neat hole in the middle of it.

Lying on the ground just out of reach of what remained of her left hand was the Colt Python. All four fingers were missing. In her right hand, tightly gripped, was a can of bear spray. Not a word was spoken by the group as the rest of the hillside searchers, including Sam and Travis, arrived. Craig showed Sam the bullet wound to her abdomen.

"I hit her with my shot," he muttered.

"She probably was going to do what you thought, but once she realized she was shot, she probably headed straight for the campground, hoping to get help."

"I wonder how long it was until the bear caught the scent of blood and tracked her down," Sam said, looking down at the bear spray in her hand. "She was obviously still alive when it found her."

Sam pulled out his radio and told the state police dispatch to cancel the request for the searchers but to let the helicopter come ahead. An hour later, when it arrived, they had the crew lower a line, and they put a loop across the dead woman's chest and under her arms and the lifeless body was hoisted up to the chopper hovering just above treetop level.

He instructed the pilot to take the corpse to the Dubois airport and wait for someone to pick it up.

The adrenaline the thirteen men and one woman built up heading up the mountain was burned off as they silently trudged back down to the clearing. Like spectators at the end of a ball game, they all piled into their vehicles and started the drive back to town. One of the men took the horse trailer, with the quarter horse inside in tow and dropped it off at the Metcalfs' small ranch, saying nothing about what took place on the mountain. The minivan was left as a silent monument to the violence that had gripped the small mountain town and the high country over the last six days.

Chapter 25

It was raining lightly when Craig and Anna climbed into the back bench seat of Daniel's Ford F-250 crew cab for the early morning drive to Lander. Daniel's wife, Beverly, was in the passenger seat. They were heading down below for a follow-up on Anna's elbow and to visit Kathleen and DeAnn.

Three days previously, after they found Grace's body, Craig took Anna to the emergency room in Lander to have her elbow checked. They found that it was dislocated. Thankfully, it was a simple dislocation.

"You are a very lucky lady," the doctor said. "If you had waited any longer to have this checked out, you could have lost motion in that elbow."

"Well, it would have been a little difficult for me to see a doctor before now," Anna said. "What with being kidnapped and hauled into the wilderness and all."

The sarcasm was not lost on the doctor, who blushed a little.

"So you must be the other one," he said sheepishly. "My apologies."

"The other one what?" Craig asked.

"They brought a woman in last night with some serious injuries, and between her and the medics, the night shift got the gist of what was going on up there," he explained as he wrapped Anna's elbow and put her arm in a fresh arm sling.

"That woman is my sister," Craig said.

The doctor told him she was in the intensive care unit and gave him directions on how to get there. He then wrote a prescription for Ibuprofen. Craig waited until the doctor was done with Anna.

"If this doesn't take care of the pain, call me, and I'll write you a script for something stronger," the doctor said. "Get some rest for a few days before you return to your normal activities, and don't use that arm."

"I've got a motel to run," Anna said defiantly.

The doctor started to protest, and Craig, standing behind Anna, mouthed that he would take care of her.

Their next stop was the ICU, but they were not allowed to visit Kathleen. Craig told the nurse at the station he was her brother and wanted to get some information on her condition. The nurse called for a doctor, who came to the station five minutes later. He explained that she had two broken ribs and another that was cracked. He also told them she had a fractured vertebra in the mid-thoracic area.

"Do you have any idea how these injuries happened?" the doctor asked. "She is still sedated and can't really recall."

"She was slammed in the side with the butt of a rifle, then she fell about three feet, landing on her back," Anna said.

"That distance shouldn't have been enough to fracture a vertebra," the doctor said.

"Well, I was on top of her, and there were jagged rocks underneath her," Anna explained.

"Okay, that makes sense," the doctor said. The quizzical look on his face drew an explanation of the circumstances from Anna.

"What's the treatment plan," Craig asked when she was through with the Reader's Digest version of the story.

The doctor asked the nurse for Kathleen's chart. He studied it for a minute or two.

"The ribs will likely heal on their own. We'll wrap her chest and do some pain management," the doctor said. "She'll have to get a lot of rest."

He looked at the chart again.

"Unless there is pressure on the spinal cord, the vertebra fracture will heal itself with pain management and rest, specifically bed rest. The ribs could be healed as quickly as three weeks, but the back will take up to six months."

"All of that in bed?" Craig asked.

"Oh no, just a month of bed rest as long as we see improvement," the doctor said.

⊶

Anna's checkup three days later went well. The doctor could see the swelling had gone down considerably. But he suggested keeping the arm in the sling for at least another week. He also said her further checkups could be done by Dr. Hall at the Dubois clinic.

"I'll forward all your records up there," he said. "Making trips down here every week will get old after a while, and that's how often you should see Dr. Hall for the next couple of months."

"But you said it should heal in weeks, not months," Anna said. "I've got a business to run."

"It should be back to normal in about a month," the doctor said. "But you should continue following up for at least another month after that just to make sure."

"I'll be there to help her with the business," Craig said. Anna shot him a questioning look.

"If Dr. Hall sees enough progress by next week, he'll probably get you out of the sling," the doctor said.

They left the doctor's exam room and went straight to Kathleen's room, where Daniel and Beverly were already chatting with her. Kathleen was still on pain-killing medication, so she was a little slow and slurred with her speech, but she was actively participating in the conversation. Craig and Anna gave her a light hug when they came into the room.

"How are you feeling?" Craig asked.

"Not feeling a lot of pain," she answered, spitting the words out past a thick tongue. Beverly gave her a spoonful of ice.

"Has the doctor explained to you what your injuries are?" Craig asked. Kathleen nodded her head.

"Please thank those guys for bringing me down the mountain," she said to Daniel.

"You remember that? You were pretty out of it," he said.

"Just barely," she responded. "I think I passed out while they were carrying me. I don't remember how I got here."

"Life Flight flew you off the mountain," Daniel told her.

He looked over at his brother and saw that he was struggling with his emotions. Daniel got up and motioned for Craig to follow him out of the room.

"Let's let the girls talk," he said as they exited.

He led his brother past the nurses' station to the end of the corridor, where several chairs were lined up against the wall. They sat down and were quiet for a few minutes, Craig bent forward with his head in his hands.

"Jesus, Daniel, if it hadn't been for me, those people would still be alive, and DeAnn, Anna and Kathleen would not have gotten hurt," Craig finally whispered.

Daniel slapped him on the back of his head, making him sit bolt upright.

"God dammit, you knock that shit off," Daniel hissed. "You had nothing to do with killing those women or hurting the others. That was all Grace Metcalf."

"But if I hadn't been involved in that first investigation, she wouldn't have hatched this insane revenge plot," Craig argued.

Daniel had seen reports on the Internet about the Kansas City killings and his brother's assistance to that police department at the time it was happening. He did not know the full details, but enough to know the basics of the case. The fact that it was Grace who had been doing the killings he learned in the previous three days through town gossip and his brother's explanation.

"And if you hadn't been involved, who knows how many more she would have killed," Daniel said.

"But it wouldn't have been people I know and care about," Craig countered.

"You don't know that," Daniel said. "Stop beating yourself up over this."

"I can't help it," Craig whimpered.

Daniel grabbed the front of his brother's shirt and shook him. Craig was surprised at the move but offered no resistance.

"Grow some balls and come to your senses," Daniel said loudly. A couple of nurses peeked their heads down the corridor from the nurses' station. "If you don't, I'll kick your ass until you do."

The intensity in his voice and his look told Craig that Daniel meant what he said. He stared at Daniel for a few seconds, then the older brother pulled him close and took him into a tight, warm bear hug.

"You're a good, decent man, Craig," he whispered into his brother's ear. "Don't let any of this change you into something you are not."

❍◦◦❍

During the ride home from Lander, the quartet was talkative, sharing their thoughts on a variety of subjects. But throughout the ninety-minute drive, Anna did not broach the subject she most wanted to talk about. That was because it was something only between her and Craig.

When they returned to Dubois, they stopped at the motel. Anna told Carlotta, who had been filling in for her since she had gone missing, that she could go home.

"Not on your life, missy," she said. "You need to rest that arm. I'm staying here until you're healed."

"No, you need a break," Anna said. "I can handle it for the rest of the day."

"You git, girl," Carlotta said, shooing her out of the back door. Then she looked at Craig. "You, boy, get her home. Make her comfortable. Wait on her hand and foot."

"That's easier said than done," he answered.

"Grow some cojones, boy, and get the job done," Carlotta said with an impish grin and a wink of her eye. It was the second time in one day someone had told him to grow a pair. Therefore, he figured he better do as he was told by both people.

"You heard the woman," he said to Anna as he turned her around and steered her to his truck.

Once back at her house, Craig sat her on the sofa, propped her arm up with a throw pillow and went into the kitchen to make coffee. When it was done, he poured two steaming mugs and took them out to the living room. He sat next to Anna on her right side so as not to bump her arm.

"What did you mean you would be there to help me with my business?" she asked after a sip of the hot coffee.

"When did I say that?" Craig asked, looking innocently off into the room.

"When the doctor was examining my arm, you turd. You know what I'm talking about," she said, nudging him with her right elbow.

"Oh, that," he said with a shrug. He stalled a bit by taking a long pull on his coffee. "I meant that I'm going to hang around here until you are fully healed," he finally said.

"Don't you have to get back to Salina?" she asked.

"What for?" he said. "I don't have a job and no other ties there. I don't have a plane to catch since I drove here."

"But I don't need any help. I can handle it on my own," Anna said stubbornly. "Carlotta will be happy to help when I need it."

It wasn't that she did not want Craig to stay on a little longer, far from it. He had committed to stay through the weekend for the reunion activities but planned to leave Monday for the long drive home. The closer that day came, the more inwardly despondent Anna became. She dreaded the thought of him leaving now that they had confessed their deep feelings for each other.

"So, if you'd rather have Carlotta hanging around and not me, I guess I should just pack up and go now," he said, feigning offense.

"That's not what I'm saying, dammit," Anna said, tears beginning to form in her eyes. The sight melted Craig's pretense, and he put his arm around her shoulder and pulled in close to her. He gently wiped the tears starting to stream down her cheeks.

"I would love having you around for a few weeks, a few months…" she stopped herself before she got to what she really wanted. "But I don't want to put a burden on you by putting you to work. You just retired for crying out loud."

"It would be no burden," he said. "I want to do what I can to help you."

He gave her a kiss, then another.

"Besides, I want to be here for Kathleen, too," he said.

Anna pulled away and put a pouty look on her face. It was her turn to put on a show.

"So, it wasn't really me you were going to stay for," she said, turning her head away from him. She could feel the smile starting to form on her lips and she wanted to keep him from seeing it as long as she could.

She heard no response from him for a few seconds. For an instant, she thought maybe she had hit a nerve and made him angry. Then she suddenly felt the slightest touches on her hip moving upward like a spider was crawling up her side. Being the ticklish type, she fought to control herself. But the sensation continued until it reached the area just under her armpit. It suddenly changed direction and started to crawl across the side of her breast. At that point, she lost it.

Anna turned her head to face him and saw a mischievous smile lighting up his face.

"You shit," she said and wrapped her right arm around his neck and pulled him toward her. The kiss they shared was long and sensuous.

Chapter 26

Slowly, life began to return to normal for Craig Reilly, Anna Welch and all the others who had gone through the ordeal in the mountains.

As predicted, Dr. Hall allowed Anna to shed the sling following her first follow-up with him. He instructed her to use her left arm sparingly, something she did for the first two days after the appointment. But on the third day, she tried to lift with her left arm only the corner of a mattress while trying to change bedding at the motel and felt sharp pain shoot from her elbow up and down her arm.

With a few days before the next appointment with Dr. Hall, Anna put the arm back in the sling, hoping that would make the pain go away.

"I thought Doc Hall said you could be out of the sling?" Craig asked when she came into the motel office.

"Oh, it was aching a little bit. I might have overdone it today," she half-lied. "It will be okay tomorrow, I'm sure."

But it wasn't. The joint had ballooned up and was as red as it had been before. She kept it in the sling constantly, except when she showered and fibbed to Craig each time he asked how it was doing. At the next appointment with Dr. Hall, Anna spilled her guts, even with Craig in the exam room with her and the doctor.

This time, Dr. Hall ordered the arm be kept in the sling for two more weeks, and she used the arm for only those things that required little or no movement of the arm. This time, she complied with all his demands. By the second week, the elbow looked and felt normal, except for a slight ache at the end of each day. Her flexibility with the joint was good and she had regained most of the strength in it.

"Okay, you can leave the sling off, but only if you do not use that arm except for the lightest things for another week," Dr. Hall told her at the end of the exam. He looked to Craig.

"Count on it," he said.

He was as good as his word. Any time Anna tried to use her left arm for just about anything, Craig scolded her and undertook the task that she was attempting. As he had done since the first doctor in Lander had treated her injury, he did the cooking and cleaning at her house and pitched in at the motel when needed. That left Anna to manage the front desk at the motel and sit around at home watching television, reading and spending time with him when his chores were done.

"You are getting quite domesticated and trained," she said one night while they sat on the couch watching John Wayne, Dean Martin and Ricky Nelson in "Rio Bravo."

"You'll make someone a fine wife," she added, poking him lovingly in the side.

"Is that a proposal?" he asked with a smile.

"Well, maybe after I've used up all the hunky guys that are always chasing me," she said deadpan.

Kathleen remained in the hospital in Lander for two weeks to allow the doctors to observe her progress.

"They just need to suck as much as they can out of the town's insurance to keep their Porches gassed up," Daniel joked during one visit. The remark drew sour looks from the doctor and nurse in the room.

At the end of the two weeks, they released her from the hospital. Her husband, Charlie, a career U.S. Marine officer stationed in Hawaii, had gotten emergency leave after hearing of her injuries and was there to take her home. He got her settled into the house on the bank of the Wind River and spent two days caring for her before his leave was up, and he had to fly back to Oahu.

Except for one quick visit the first day she was home, Craig and Daniel left the married couple to spend time together. But once he was gone, one of them was there every day to make sure she was fed and to take care of any other needs as she continued to be in bed or lying on the sofa most of the time. At first, Daniel was there most of the time as Craig continued to nursemaid Anna. But eventually, their time there was nearly equal.

⊃o⊂

Jerome and Helen Metcalf were devastated when Sheriff Sharbono broke the news to them of their daughter's death. So much so that Jerome had a mild stroke when he heard the news. Although it was not any more debilitating than his health was anyway, it sent him into a deep depression. He died within weeks.

Helen was heartbroken but carried on as best she could. With the burden of caring for her invalid husband lifted after his death, Helen's health improved somewhat.

Four days after the incidents on the mountain, Helen called the sheriff's office and asked to have a deputy sent out. With Fred still recovering from his gunshot wound, Travis drove out to the Metcalf ranch. Upon arrival, Helen led him out to the barn. In one of the stalls stood an Appaloosa. The horse had a saddle and all the trappings on its back, including a bed roll and a scabbard containing a Remington Browning automatic rifle.

But strangely, there was no bridle secured to the horse's head.

"This is the other horse Grace took that day," Helen said, tears filling her eyes as she said her daughter's name. "Look at the right side of his head."

Travis entered the stall and walked up to the horse, taking a penlight from his breast pocket. He shined the light on the upper part of the horse's head. He could see scratches in the hide and the outside of the ear. Travis reached up to feel them to determine how fresh they were and the horse pulled its head away. Helen moved into the stall and gently placed her hands on each side of the animal's snout and whispered to it. Travis tried again, running his index finger gently down the largest of the scratches on the horse's head. After a single stroke, he guessed the scratches were two days old, three at the most.

"He wandered in her this morning," Helen said. Travis could tell she was fighting to hold back sobs. "I put him in here and left all the stuff on him in case you needed to see it."

"Did you take the bridle off?" Travis asked.

"Oh no, it was gone when he came in," Helen said. "He probably stepped on the reins enough to annoy him, and my guess is he swiped his head against a tree until he worked one ear out, then spit out the bit and let the bridle fall to the ground."

The explanation seemed reasonable to Travis, who grew up around horses. He took a few notes, then used his cell phone to snap a few photos of the entire animal and then some closeups of the saddle and gear. He noticed a leather bag hanging from the saddle horn, went around the horse and took a couple of photos of the full bag. He grabbed one of the bag handles and, with the other still looped around the horn, looked inside. He quickly glanced at Helen and then back into the bag. There, staring him right in the face, was the dildo and harness.

"I'll need to take this with me," he said as he took the bag off the saddle horn.

"What is it?" Helen asked.

"It's just something we'll need for evidence," he said.

Helen remained curious about the bag's contents but decided not to pursue it. Travis hung the bag by its handles on the butt of his weapon.

"I've got pictures of all of this, so I'll unsaddle the horse for you. Where would you like it?" he asked. Helen pointed to a spot along the opposite wall. Once he had placed it there, he pulled the Remington out of the scabbard.

"I'll need to take this, too," he said. Helen nodded blankly. "We'll get it back to you as soon as we can."

"What about that bag and what's in it?" she asked.

"Yeah, probably," he lied.

Sam Sharbobo left Dubois the day after the shootings on the mountain. He had a lot of paperwork to complete and review. The first thing he did was visit Fred in the Riverton hospital to check on his condition and get his statement of events. The latter turned out to be an easy task. Fred had spent his time in the hospital so far preparing a report. Because he was left-handed, he talked the hospital staff into getting him a digital recorder.

It was quite a task as he was in and out of consciousness throughout that first day in bed, and he was straining to remember every detail through the pain medication that was being pumped into him. But he wanted to get as much recorded as he could while it was still fresh in his mind. In the days to come, he added to his statement as he remembered more and more.

Sam wanted the reports as soon as possible. Not so much to further the investigation along, because Grace's death and her confession to Craig solved the case of the multiple murders. But he wanted them because the FBI sent word they would have a man in Lander the Monday following the events. Since Grace had abducted her victims, that made it a federal crime, and FBI officials wanted all the details to dot all their Is and cross all their Ts.

Fred spent three days in the hospital but did not return to duty for another three weeks.

It took a little longer to get what Sam considered the final statement. Since Grace's fourth victim had survived, he wanted to hear from DeAnn Paxton. But it took a month before she was ready to share her story.

The blood and oxygen deprivation to her brain had nearly killed her. It had also left major gaps in her memory. For two weeks, she did not speak a word as she teetered between life and death. In the third week, she began to talk, but she could not remember anything but one- to two-second fragments of the night she was abducted. But by the end of the fourth week she was able to piece together most of what happened.

When he got the word from the hospital in Riverton that DeAnn was willing to speak to him, Sam called Craig and asked him to hightail it down below to be in on the interview.

"I remember walking out of the tavern and to my car," she said shakily, with Sam and Craig sitting side-by-side next to the bed, a doctor standing behind them in case DeAnn's condition necessitated stopping the conversation. "Then something got shoved over my mouth and nose by someone from behind me."

She paused for a moment, then went on.

"The next thing I remember is opening my eyes and seeing someone standing over me," she said.

"Could you tell who it was? Do you know where you were?" Sam asked.

"The background was really blurry, but I could tell I was in some kind of room," she said. "I could see bare walls going up to a ceiling. It looked white."

"Do you know who was standing over you?" Craig asked.

"That was blurry too, but not as much," DeAnn responded. "It looked like Grace Metcalf."

Craig and Sam looked at each other.

"I tried to sit up, but I could barely get anything to move," DeAnn said. "Then I saw this person was naked."

"Naked?" Craig asked, a little surprised.

"At least from the waist up. I saw a woman's boobs," she said.

They heard the female doctor behind them take a breath, but they ignored it.

"Then the person straddled me, and I felt something between my legs," DeAnn related.

"What was it?" Sam asked.

"I might be remembering this part wrong. But it felt like a man's....." she hesitated for a moment, appearing to be searching for the right word. "A cock," she finally blurted.

"Oh my God," the doctor said. Craig and Sam glanced around and saw she had her hand over her mouth and her skin had gone pale.

"And then that thing was inside me," DeAnn said.

"Jesus," they heard the doctor say, and she suddenly turned and dashed to the bathroom. They heard vomit come shooting out of her mouth and into the toilet. But Craig's and Sam's attention was locked on DeAnn.

"I tried to roll over, and the thing came out for a second. But it was pushed back in," she said. Her voice was starting to rattle with fear. Another rush of puke was heard from the bathroom.

"The person put a hand on one of my tits, and that's when I realized I was naked, too," DeAnn said, a couple of sobs escaping her lips. "I lifted my arms and tried to knock the hand away, but my arms felt rubbery."

"Maybe we should let her rest," Craig said.

But DeAnn raised her right hand and shook her head. She whimpered a little.

"No, I've got to get this out," she said.

"Okay, but you stop if it gets to be too much," Sam said.

DeAnn took a deep breath and continued.

"The person let go of my tit and punched me in the side of the head, then kept punching me in the belly, on my chest, in the face," she said, then paused again.

"I don't know how long that went on and things were starting to get more out of focus," she said. "Then there was something around my neck, and it was being tightened while that thing was pushed deeper inside me. It wasn't long before I must have blacked out because the next thing I remember was waking up in the hospital."

Craig and Sam were excited and sickened at the same time. Excited because now they knew what had happened to each of the victims. Sickened for the same reason.

⊶⊷

The final activity for the reunion was a memorial service for Grace's three victims. It was put together in a day and conducted Saturday night, the final night of the reunion. All other planned events for the week-long gathering had been canceled by mid-week.

The service was conducted on the high school football field to allow for as many attendees as possible three hours before sunset. Perhaps as a gesture to the dead, Mother Nature held off the rain that had been forecast for that day.

It was a somber service, with a few short prayers, some music and a long line of people who shared memories of the three women.

Their bodies would be released to the families the following day. Their husbands arranged to have the remains shipped back to their respective home communities for preparation and later burial there. Janine had wanted to be buried in the Dubois cemetery, but her husband would have none of it.

"I will not have my wife's final resting place be in the same place where she was murdered," he had told Craig following the memorial service.

Chapter 27

Craig woke from a very restful night's sleep to find he was alone in the queen bed. He lay there for a few moments, listening for any sound in the house. It was so quiet inside he could hear big fluffy snowflakes splatter against the window, blown there by the moderate breeze outside.

He glanced over at the nightstand and saw the digital lights on the alarm clock read four thirty-six in the morning. It was nearly pitch black in the bedroom. But he threw back the heavy comforter and climbed out of bed anyway. The cold air made him shiver as he groped for his jeans and shirt. As he threw his T-shirt over his head and pulled up his pants, he felt a little warm air from a nearby vent on the floor. He stopped to listen again. There it was, the very faint purr of the furnace. He had not noticed it before.

It felt colder in the room than it should have since the heater was operating. But, then again, he had been under the heavy comforter while in bed, and it kept him toasty hot. His body was just getting used to the slightly different temperature out of the bed.

He shuffled toward the half-open door that led to the living room. The hardwood floors were chilly on his bare feet, especially the further away from the heating vent he went. As he entered the living room, he felt for the switch on a standing lamp next to the doorway. When he flipped it on, the room was bathed in a soft, yellowish light, muted by the lampshade.

He looked around the room and saw Anna lying on the sofa, covered from her toes to her neck with an oversized, thick brown and gold Wyoming Cowboys blanket. She was lying on her right side, facing away from him. He could now hear her rhythmic breathing. He took a few steps toward the kitchen but was stopped dead in his tracks by her voice.

"Come over here if you want to stay warm."

He padded over to the couch and planted himself next to her as she sat up and slid her legs onto the floor. She arranged the blanket, so it covered them both from the neck down and tucked it around their legs. It was open a crack behind their calves, but warm air from the vent behind and slightly under the couch found its way through the crack and added its warmth to that of the blanket.

Craig snuggled up to her as close as he could. She was also wearing jeans and a long-sleeved sweatshirt. Her feet were also covered with thick socks.

"Are you sure about this?" she asked.

He looked into her face. The soft light from the lamp across the room made her skin seem darker than it was. The light also cast deep shadows on the left side of her face, from her cute little button nose to those sexy pouty lips. Craig cocked his head a bit and leaned in and planted his lips on hers, and held them there for several seconds.

"I think this is the best decision I could make right now," he said.

"I'll miss you," she said and kissed him.

In the weeks and months after the reunion killings, the small mountain town of Dubois, Wyoming, began to return to normal. It would be years before the stain of that horrible week would fade into distant memories, but the healing began almost immediately.

Children from kindergarten to twelfth grade filed into the one-campus school at the beginning of September. There was a moment of silence at the start of the Rams' first home high school volleyball and football games for those killed and injured during the August reunion. Counselors were on hand for any student who needed them to share their feelings, sorrows and concerns about the incidents. Some took advantage of the opportunity, as did some adults from the school staff and the community at large.

But those sessions died out by the end of September. Small-town people are made of firm stuff, and they find ways to endure hardships. Better than most in larger communities.

The first snow fell in late September. It stayed on the ground for a few days, then melted away, as it is known to do, only to be replaced days later by a new white blanket. They would be just the first of many such coverings. The snow's appearance in September was not unusual for a town that had seen snowfall on July Fourth one year.

Hunting season came and went. That gave the town's economy its usual boost as out-of-staters came in search of their trophies. Like most locals, Craig and Anna were in the mountains tracking the big game, but not for heads to hang on the wall. Local hunters were more interested in the meat the animals provided. Anna shot a big three-point bull elk, and Craig got a two-point buck deer. They took the animals to the local cold storage to have them slaughtered and packaged. They and Daniel, who bagged a three-point bull himself, shared their meat with Kathleen.

She continued to heal and was able to return to work in January for light duty. Her doctor had wanted one more month of inactivity, but cabin fever was driving her crazy, and she was tired of being waited on. Active, independent people, especially women, can only take that so long.

Once his sister returned to work, Craig decided it was time to start thinking about his future and what he wanted to do with it.

"Now that Kathleen is back to work and insisting she can take care of herself, I think it's time I went back to Kansas," he told Anna one late January evening as they shared dinner at her home.

It was not a total surprise to hear him say it, but Anna was disappointed all the same.

"You've been a big help to me at the motel," she said. "I'd hate to see you go."

"Ah, you are a strong, independent woman. You'll do just fine on your own," he said. "Besides, I can tell Carlotta's a little pissed at me because she's not there as much," he added with a half-smile.

Anna wasn't amused by the little joke.

"It's not just the motel," she said. "Having you here has been wonderful, more than I could have dreamed of."

She let her words drift through the air at him, hoping he would take the meaning. He did not respond right away, just sat seemingly emotionless as he chewed his bite of fried chicken. The longer he went without saying anything, the more nervous she became.

"What if he doesn't feel that way about me?" she thought.

Just when she was about to say the three words she had been so afraid to since he arrived in Dubois in August -- even years before that, in fact -- he heaved a heavy sigh.

"God, Anna, I have so enjoyed the time we have had together all these months," he said.

Her heart quickened a couple of beats. However, the tone of his voice implied there was going to be a "but" in there somewhere. And then it came.

"But you and I have been single and alone for so long that we are so set in our ways," he said. "Can we really get along?"

Their time together for the last six months had not been perfect. They had each snapped at each other. And each time it was not over big things but trivial matters. They had apologized after each incident and things were smooth between them -- until the next snap.

"We don't have to live in the same house. You could get a place of your own. But we'd still be together, in the same town, and we'd see each other often," Anna said on the verge of pleading.

"I never expected to come back here to live permanently," Craig said.

The statement seemed so final that Anna broke down in tears. Craig reached out and touched her hand, but she pulled it away. She continued to sob despite her efforts to get it under control.

"Then I will go to Salina and either live with you or find my own place," she said between whimpers.

"What about the motel?" he asked.

"I'll sell it," she said, finally getting her crying to stop. But tears still ran down her face.

"That motel has been in your family for years," he said. "You can't sell it. I won't allow you to sell it on my account, no matter how much I love you and want to be with you."

Those final nine words shocked Anna. They were the words she had wanted to say but could not bring herself to. He had beaten her to it. The words knocked everything else from her mind. She jumped out of her chair and threw her arms around him and squeezed as hard as she could.

"I love you, Craig, more than I've ever loved anyone," she whispered in his ear.

Three days later, three discussion-filled days in which neither gave an inch, they stood at the door to Anna's home with the big fluffy snowflakes falling outside. They had enjoyed a big breakfast and Craig had packed up his things -- all his things -- and loaded them into his truck. They were saying their final goodbyes.

"Are you sure about this?" Anna asked.

"Yes, I think it is the best thing for both of us," he answered.

She did not agree, but what could she do? His mind was made up.

"Please keep in touch," she said. "And be careful."

They shared a long kiss, and then he was gone. She watched his truck back out of the driveway, then head east on Watson Street, leaving a trail of swirling snow in its wake. Then, the truck made a right turn onto 1st

Street. She watched it through watery eyes as it disappeared behind the buildings on the west side of the street. The falling snowflakes looked more prominent, with the rising sun blazing through them.

⊖⊷⊖

A month later, Anna stood behind the half door at the motel, completing the check-in for a couple who had come to town to look at homes for sale.

"I hope you find what you're looking for," she said as she handed them a room key.

As the couple turned to head for their room upstairs, the main entrance door to the motel lobby opened and a tall man in jeans and a Wyoming Cowboys T-shirt and ball cap walked in. He strode to the counter and looked Anna in the eye.

"I'd like to book a room," he said.

"Will this be a short or long stay," she said, punching a few keys on the computer in front of her.

"That will depend on what kind of accommodations I can get," he answered.

"Well, we are booked up. Just gave the keys to the last room," she said, glancing at the couple topping the stairs. "There's a big wrestling tournament up at the high school, and we've got two teams staying here."

"Can you recommend some other place?" he asked.

"They are probably all booked, too," she said, not looking up at him. "I did say it was a big tournament."

"Well," he said, starting to turn to leave. "I guess I'll just have to sleep in my truck. Can I park it out front here?"

"It might get towed," she said.

"I'll take my chances," he said.

She glanced out the small window at the vehicle parked at the curb. It had a U-Haul trailer hitched to the back.

"I'd hate to see a great rig like that go to the impound yard," she said. "Tell you what, I know of a place you could stay, but I'll have to tell all my boyfriends they can't come over until you leave."

"Slut," he said.

"Jackass," she countered.

He walked back to the counter with a stern look on his face. She rolled her eyes upward as he reached the half door.

"What the hell took you so long, ya rat bastard?" she asked.

Craig's face broke into a wide grin.

"Oh, I poked around for a few days looking for jobs an old retired cop could do. Couldn't find any that I liked. Then it took three weeks to tie up all the loose ends down there," he said. "Boy, was it hard to convince all those women to leave me alone."

She reached up and grabbed each of his ears and pulled his face down to within a millimeter of hers.

"You turd blossom," she said, then jammed her lips to his.

Acknowledgments

When I decided to base this story in my hometown of Dubois, Wyoming I found that I had been away so long that I needed a little help to jog my memory, mostly regarding the geographic area and names of certain locations. I also needed a little memory push on the history of the area.

The Internet was a large help in the latter respect. The Dubois Chamber of Commerce website and another called Destination Dubois were a big help with history and some of the geography. Google Maps also helped me identify the road names, some of which were not named when I was growing up there, in the outlying areas. I also utilized a couple of weather websites to pin down typical sunrise and sunset times, and specific weather patterns.

Most of all, though, I need to recognize and thank my surviving siblings -- sisters Linda and Michelle and brother Steve -- for jogging my memory of places we used to go, separately and together, during our years growing up in this wonderful mountain town.

But most of all, I want to thank my lovely, wonderful wife, Jeanne. Not so much for any help with Dubois because she has only been there one time. However, as she always has been with my writing, she was a constant source of motivation and inspiration. Thank you, Baby Doll.

About the Author

Rusty Bradshaw is no stranger to writing, having gotten the bug while in junior high school and never gotten over it. Born in California, he grew up in Wyoming and spent 26 years in Oregon before moving to Arizona. He graduated from Dubois High School, attended Northwest Community College and earned a Bachelor of Science degree from Eastern Oregon State College. He then began what would be a 42-year journalism career that would see him write and photograph for several newspapers in Oregon and more in Arizona. While in Oregon, Rusty won several writing awards from the Oregon Newspaper Publishers Association. He was also named Junior Citizen of the Year in Milton-Freewater, Oregon, where he was active in United Way, was president of a local food bank and coached youth football.

Rusty retired from journalism in 2023 but continues freelance video reporting on YouTube and other social media, particularly for his home community of Sun City, Arizona. He has two grown children -- Sara in Washington and Evan in Idaho -- and lives in Sun City with his wife, Jeanne, who has a grown son -- Billy, in North Carolina. Rusty and his wife enjoy football, bingo, occasional road trips, jigsaw puzzles and any other activities they can do together.

Rusty also has a large portfolio of scenic photos available for sale. *Visit www.rustythewriter.org for information about Rusty Bradshaw's books and photography.*

Other Books by Rusty Bradshaw

The Rehabilitation of Miss Little
Moist on the Mountain
Gorge Justice
Battle for Stephanie
Death in Hazard